HOPE
CREEK

Don't miss any of Janet Dailey's bestsellers

The Calder Brand Series
Calder Brand
Calder Grit

The New Americana Series
Paradise Peak
Sunrise Canyon
Refuge Cove
Letters from Peaceful Lane
Hart's Hollow Farm

The Champions
Whirlwind
Whiplash

The Tylers of Texas
Texas Forever
Texas Free
Texas Fierce
Texas Tall
Texas Tough
Texas True

Bannon Brothers: Triumph
Bannon Brothers: Honor
Bannon Brothers: Trust
American Destiny
American Dreams

JANET DAILEY

HOPE CREEK

KENSINGTON
PUBLISHING CORP.

www.kensingtonbooks.com

KENSINGTON BOOKS are published by

Kensington Publishing Corp.
119 West 40th Street
New York, NY 10018

Copyright © 2022 by Revocable Trust Created by Jimmy Dean Dailey and Mary Sue Dailey Dated December 22, 2016

After the passing of Janet Dailey, the Dailey family worked with a close associate of Janet's to continue her literary legacy, using her notes, ideas and favorite themes to complete her novels and create new ones, inspired by the American men and women she loved to portray.

Library of Congress Card Catalogue Number: 2021951538

ISBN: 978-1-4967-3502-7
First Kensington Hardcover Edition: May 2022

10 9 8 7 6 5 4 3 2 1

Printed in the United States of America

CHAPTER 1

Kit Teague preferred the company of strangers. Impersonal greetings and casual farewells kept smiles rising easily to her lips during the day and lulled her racing thoughts at night. Working in a mountain town, amid the cheerful buoyancy of tourists and high panoramic views, had loosened the cold fear that had gripped her heart for the past fifteen years.

But there were no strangers or mountains on the island of Hope Creek, South Carolina. Just the prying eyes of locals, flat ground steeped in salt water, and the pungent scent of decay.

"Can't take it with you."

Kit glanced down at the older woman who slumped on the edge of the Hope Creek Water Taxi dock. One of her scrawny legs dangled over a wood plank, her turquoise-polished toenails skimming the water's surface. A small boat was tied up nearby.

Lou Ann Cragg . . . midfifties by now, with a penchant for bar fights, if Kit recalled correctly.

"That car o' yours," Lou Ann clarified, looking up at her. She pointed a crooked finger at Kit's white sedan, sitting sedately beneath a palmetto tree on the cracked asphalt of the small parking lot. "Can't take it to the is-land." She shook her head. "No, ma'am. No bridge, no causeway. Only way to that island from here this late in the day is on my boat, and it ain't gonna haul no car."

Kit slid her hand in her pocket and gripped her keys. Squeezed them tight until the sharp teeth bit into the soft flesh of her palm. "I know."

And it was a shame, really. Her car had always been the best place to cry.

"Wait, you one of them Teague girls, ain't you?" Lou Ann lifted a cigarette, burned almost to the butt, took a slow drag, then released a curl of smoke, which escaped on the humid late afternoon wind. "One of them twins, right?"

Kit's mouth tightened. "Yes."

Lou Ann narrowed her puffy eyes, studied Kit's face, shiny hair, unwrinkled dress suit with a two-button jacket and high-heeled shoes—then smirked. "Fancy." She took another drag. "Well, you ain't the sorry one, that's for sure. Must be the one that took off." She tipped her chin. "Where'd you land?"

Kit bit her tongue and focused on her white sedan. She didn't remember much about Lou Ann, but she did know Lou Ann had lived a harder life than anyone should have to endure, her only luxuries cold beer and recycled jokes. "Highlands."

"The who?"

"Highlands. It's a town in North Carolina, in the south-ern Appalachians."

Lou Ann grinned, glee dripping from her stained teeth. "So you done gone from up high right back down to low, huh?"

Mud caked the sedan's bumper. *No surprise*, Kit thought, considering the five-hour drive she'd undertaken down the interstate and pot-holed back roads this morning from

Highlands to Beaufort County. She'd have the car ferried to the island next week and wash it dow—

"You drag yourself back to bury your mama?"

Stiffening, Kit pinned her gaze to Lou Ann's hazel eyes. Deep crow's-feet were carved at the edges, and Lou Ann's cheeks—once high and full—had sunken in, the ruddy skin drooping toward her angled jaw. "That's none of your business. Though I will say, I didn't drive all the way back down here just to listen to you denigrate my family. My sister is a better person than most people will ever be. So was my mother."

Lou Ann's lip curled. She touched her tongue to her eye-tooth, a flash of admiration momentarily brightening her dull eyes. "Put your back down, girl. I didn't mean nothing by it. What're you now? Thirty-eight? I remember you and your sister running around in diapers, and I knew your mama well even then." She sighed, the heavy exhalation sinking beneath the waves lapping against the dock. "Nobody ought to die like Sylvie did—nobody. But at least you got out, even if you had to leave that high place of yours in order to swoop back down to the Lowcountry for her." She flicked the cigarette butt onto the dock, scattering a spray of red ash, and her gaze roved outward, over the tidal creeks, which snaked a winding trail through tall cordgrass, toward the horizon as she whispered, "Yes, ma'am. Least you got out the Low, baby girl."

Waves lapped at the dock pilings, and a blue heron, broad wings flapping against the wind, perched on top of a dock piling several feet away. The lanky bird presented its profile, one wide eye trained on Kit, and craned its neck, taking her in.

"Who found her?" Kit asked.

Lou Ann lifted a brow, expression lit with surprise. "Your people didn't tell you?"

Other than the phone call she'd received from her dad two days ago? The one lasting all of thirty seconds? Royal Teague's words, delivered in a clipped monotone, had been the only details: *She did it. Out in the creek. You can come home now.*

Eyes burning, Kit returned the heron's stare. "No."

"Your sister. She took a boat out, found your mama floating facedown—hung up on one of them cages—and hauled her in, from what I hear."

Kit flinched. The heron squawked, sprang up, and flapped its wings toward the sun lowering in the distance.

Bile rising, she swallowed hard before speaking. "A cage?"

Lou Ann frowned and looked away. She lifted one hip, dug around in her back pocket, and withdrew a crumpled cigarette pack. "You mind? Only got one left, and it tastes better out here. Last ride on a Friday—ain't no one else coming. And we got time to make it there 'fore dark." She tilted the pack toward Kit and issued a small smile. "I'll share."

Coming from Lou Ann, the offer was a fourteen-karat gold-plated truce. Her best—and only—kindness.

Kit bent, retrieved the lone cigarette, and sat beside Lou Ann. She used Lou Ann's lighter, sparking a flame with shaky, out-of-practice fingers, then closed her eyes and drew deeply, filling her nose and lungs with warm smoke, clouding her habit-free heart.

The memories came slowly. In pieces.

Her mother's hand in her hair, braiding each strand. Knuckles brushing her nape and a salty night breeze tickling her bare knees. Chirps of crickets and a chorus of tree frogs. Her mother's loose embrace, a deluge of stale smoke, the sharp scent of whiskey, and a slurred refrain: *Tomorrow I'll be better. I'm still in here. I'm still in here....*

Kit passed the cigarette to Lou Ann. "My mama loved these," she whispered after releasing her smoky breath in slow degrees.

"Been a while, huh?"

"Fifteen years." And she'd left behind so much more. . . .

They sat silently, staring as the setting sun painted the sky and sea gold, listening to the rustle of cordgrass and the rhythmic lap of the sea against the bobbing boat and still dock, the tide dragging the same waters out, then shoving them back in, constantly moving but never going anywhere.

Kit closed her eyes. A low roaring sound filled her ears, and the dock seemed to shift beneath her. She leaned forward and braced her elbows on her knees. "I loved my mother."

Lou Ann's callused fingers brushed her arm. "I never said you didn't."

The words were low and comforting, but the heavy silence that followed spoke louder. Kit opened her eyes and focused on the water rippling below, her sister's voice—along with so many others—returning, as it often had over the years: *If you loved her, you would've stayed. You got no family now.*

Lou Ann offered up the cigarette again. When Kit shook her head, Lou Ann shrugged and proceeded to finish it off, the bright golden light of the sun flooding the harsh, world-weary angles of her familiar face.

She cocked her head to the side and squinted. "You sure you wanna go back?"

"Yes." She'd thought of little else over the past fifteen years. Throat closing, Kit bit her lip. "Have you seen my sister?"

"Since it happened?"

Kit nodded.

"Nah. But me and Viv never got on too well." Lou Ann blew out a cloud of smoke, then stubbed the cigarette butt on a wood plank. "She's around, though. Usually hanging on to Beau pretty tight."

"Beau?" Kit curled her hands tight around the edge of the dock, the sun-warmed boards hot to the touch. "Beau Sutton?"

Blond, handsome heir to the Sutton family's abundant wealth and upstanding reputation. A captivating boy, two years Kit's senior, whom she and Viv had admired from their neighboring deepwater dock in Hope Creek. The few exchanges Kit had had with him over the years had been brief and stilted—their fathers' rivalry unconducive to the formation of anything more.

Last time she'd seen Beau, he'd been standing arm in arm with his new wife on the end of the Suttons' dock, their faces tipped toward the night sky, each colorful burst of fireworks highlighting their wide smiles and elegant wedding attire, as the small crowd filling the dock behind them cheered. The next morning the pair had left the island on a boat decorated with yellow jessamine.

Six months later, Kit had packed her bags and left, as well.

"Yep." Lou Ann stood and untied the dock line of her small boat from a piling. "Beau moved back into his dad's place two years ago, and your sister's been staying at that Sutton mansion for over a year now."

Kit stiffened. *Viv? Living with the Suttons? Hanging on to married Beau?* "But—"

"Look." Lou Ann held up a hand. "Lot's changed since you left. Get on the boat. You'll find out soon enough."

Kit clenched her fists around her overnight bag and lifted her face into the swift pound of wind as Lou Ann's boat sped across the water. Though years had passed since she'd last traveled these waters, the sight and feel of them remained the same: the rhythmic lift and lowering of the boat over soft waves, the pungent scent of pluff mud on the salty breeze, and the golden kiss of the setting sun against the rippling Atlantic in the distance.

Heart momentarily lightening, Kit sat up straighter and craned her neck, seeking out the familiar shape of Hope Creek Island as it emerged into view. Soft lights, each one illuminating a dock leading to a dense thicket of trees, glowed in the dusk amid tall cordgrass and sprawling live oaks hung with Spanish moss.

A bittersweet tenderness pulsed in Kit's biceps with the remembered fatigue of long, sun-soaked days of shrimping and harvesting wild oysters with Royal. The satisfaction of a hard day's work mixed with the energetic buzz of pride at having increased the profit of the family business had provided a welcome escape from troubles that plagued both of their hearts most days back then.

For a moment, she wished she could roll back time to her lithe teenage years, board Royal's shrimp trawler, return her dad's wide smile, and reclaim that faint trace of hope in the clean sea air. Hope that Sylvie would find her way back.

"Money's floating down the Ditch pretty regular now," Lou Ann called over her shoulder, her brown hair whipping in the wind. "That's what brung 'em out."

Kit frowned at Lou Ann. Money floating down the Ditch was nothing new—the Intracoastal Waterway had always been popular with wealthy home buyers seeking the enviable waterfront views and pristine beaches along the untarnished coast of Hope Creek Island. And the frequent arrival of wealthy guests vacationing at the high-priced Hope Creek Resort on the opposite end of the island was nothing new, but . . .

"Brought what out?" she asked.

Lou Ann steered the boat to the left, pointed its nose toward the mouth of Hope Creek, and slowed to a crawl through the deep water. "Them."

Them consisted of twenty or so trawl lines stretched along the deepest recess of Hope Creek, with floating cages strung at even intervals. Seagulls, perched on each buoy, cocked their heads and eyed the boat warily as it approached.

Kit leaned to the side, her stomach dipping, as water rippled around the wire frames half-submerged along the creek's surface. Dark outlines of mesh bags were just visible. "An oyster farm?"

Lou Ann nodded. "Singles. A buck each, and them oysters get eaten faster than they can grow 'em."

"Who's they?" Kit asked. As the sun lowered behind live oaks, the solid lines of the cages blurred, morphing into soggy shadows lurking in the dusk, littering the natural beauty of the tidal creek.

Lou Ann gestured toward the left side of the creek, about seventy-five feet away, where festive lights strung along the metal railings of a deepwater dock emerged, twinkling amid soft music and distant laughter. "Suttons. Beau and his dad, in particular." Lou Ann glanced over her shoulder again and cocked an eyebrow. "Your sister, too."

Kit bristled, struggling to imagine it. To even conceive of it. "Viv's been working for the Suttons? And living with them?"

Viv should be at home, working with Dad for the family business. Lord knew, Kit had sent enough money each month over the past fifteen years to keep Teague's Seafood afloat, and Viv had cashed every one of the checks. Viv's signature—scrawled in angry spikes on the endorsement line—had always been accompanied by varied phrases marked with an asterisk: *Guilt money. *Shame. *Selfish.

What had Beau said to draw Viv away? What state of mind had she been in to even contemplate going? And Mackey . . . Who was taking care of him?

"Pearl Tide Oyster Company's what they call it," Lou Ann said. "Beau's dad spearheaded it, but Beau and Viv are the muscle behind it. Viv's been helping them Suttons siphon away your daddy's business for two years now." She hesitated, glancing at the last trawl of floating cages as they passed. "That's how Viv found your mama. She was out here the other morning, tending to those cages. Your mama had killed h—" She waved a hand in the air, her cheeks reddening. "Had passed away hours earlier by your dad's dock, then had drifted, from what I hear. Her sleeve caught on one of them cages. Kept her from floating off any farther."

Stomach heaving with each roll of water beneath the boat, Kit spun away from the trawl line. She tossed her bag on the seat, shoved herself to her feet, and wrapped a shaky hand around the guardrail. Glancing up from beneath her lashes, she focused on the dark, weather-worn dock located several feet beyond the Suttons' brightly lit one. Royal's shrimp trawler and oyster boat looked forlorn.

"How much do I owe you?" Her lips felt numb. Barely moved.

"Nothing." Lou Ann's tone had turned hard. She stopped the boat, its side bumping the wooden dock.

Kit hefted her overnight bag in one hand, grabbed one of the dock pilings, and sprang out of the boat and onto the dock, breath bursting from her lips at the satisfying clack of her high heels on the wood planks.

"Baby girl," Lou Ann called.

Kit stilled.

Dusk shrouded Lou Ann's features, a spectral glint in

her eyes the only clearly visible detail. "Don't lower your eyes for no one but God. It's what your mama would've wanted."

Kit watched Lou Ann leave, listened to the slosh of water against the boat until it morphed into a dark blot in the distance, melding with the black sprawl of oak limbs and thick brush along the bank, water rippling in its wake.

The dark depths of the creek seemed to reach out, and the tang of salty air hit her tongue. A throbbing in her temple intensified. She unclenched her teeth and flexed her jaw, then walked up the long dock as night fell. Hope Creek's evening chorus rose from the murky depths below the dock, the rhythmic pulse of crickets and frogs emerging from the sticky mud and thick cordgrass, echoing against the trees, mingling with the music drifting from the Suttons' expansive property.

She barely recognized the backyard of her family home, Teague Cottage, when she reached it. Dense grass, tall enough to cling to her knees, had swallowed the stone firepit and Adirondack chairs she remembered, had choked the shrubs she'd planted, and had ensnared the picket fence she'd driven into the ground along the back deck years ago. Only a speck of yellow jessamine, her mother's favorite, managed to peek through the tangled overgrowth.

Kit gritted her teeth, flinched as the edge of a molar cut into her tongue, and trudged through the tangle of wild grass until she reached the screened-in front porch.

The outer door was locked. She pulled her keys from her pocket, sifted through them, and tried the house key she'd carried for fifteen years, but it no longer fit.

"Dad!" She pounded on the screen door with her fist, and the weak screen mesh dented beneath her assault. The inner hardwood door remained closed. "I'm home. Open up."

She glanced around. The dim front porch light struggled

to illuminate the even more overgrown front yard. A rusty truck slumped in the dirt driveway, and a metal bat had been abandoned beside a battered mailbox that barely lifted its head above the weeds, the wood post supporting it almost broken in half, graffiti emblazoned on the mailbox's metal side: *wild cat.*

Cheeks blazing, Kit pounded on the screen door again.

A soft creak broke through the vicious buzz in her ears. Her fist froze inches from the screen as the inner door swept open and a man, large spoon in one hand, wearing a collared shirt and tie, khaki shorts, and no shoes, emerged.

Kit dropped her bag on the front steps and sagged against the screen door. "Mackey."

Her brother squinted and stepped closer, a broad smile flashing across his face. It died almost instantly, and his hand, having lifted toward the screen door, dropped back to his side. "You don't live here no more."

Kit sucked in a slow breath. "I know. I haven't . . ."

She pressed her lips together and studied his face, searching for any hint of neglect but finding—thankfully—only telltale creases of age beside his mouth and below his eyes. He hadn't changed much. She'd mailed a birthday card five months ago. He'd turned thirty.

A deep ache spread through her as she pressed her palms and forehead to the screen. "It's good to see you, Mackey. I missed you."

A blush bloomed along his neck. "Missed you, too."

Kit smiled, the tight coil of her muscles easing slightly. "Are you . . . are you doing okay?"

He nodded, his gaze drifting over her hair, clothes, and shoes, then settling on the overnight bag on the step below her.

"Dad called me," she said. "So I packed a bag and came home. Where is he?"

Mackey jabbed the spoon in the air, pointing toward the

left side of the house. "Napping. He was very, very tired."
He looked away, moisture glistening along his lashes.
"That's what he said—very, very tired. I'm making him
dog cheese. For when he gets up. He'll be hungry."

Kit's smile faded. "How long has he been sleeping?"

Mackey frowned. Rubbed his forehead. "Since last
night."

"I need to talk to him. And I need to see Viv. Will you
please let me in, Mackey?"

He shook his head, his expression contorting, as he
stepped toward, then away from the screen door. "Viv said
no. She said you don't live here no more. I'm not supposed
to let you in."

Kit closed her eyes briefly. "How is Viv? Is she here?"

"No." He jabbed the spoon to the right, toward the
music and laughter echoing in the distance. "She at
Beau's."

"It's okay to let me in, Mackey. Will you please open the
door?"

"I don't want to." Accusation entered his eyes. "You
left us. You left Mama."

Kit rattled the locked doorknob once more, then sighed.
"Okay. Did Dad—did Dad talk to you? Or Viv? Have they
told you anything about Ma—"

A cry burst from Mackey's lips, and the spoon clattered
to the porch floor. "No!" He clapped his palms to his ears
and paced. "Don't say it. Don't say it!"

Kit pressed closer to the screen, and the tang of metal
hit her lips as she whispered, "Okay. I'm sorry, Mackey.
I'm so sorry." Chest burning, she forced herself to pull
away from the screen and go back down the steps. "It's
okay," she said softly, blinking hard. "You go back to
what you were doing, all right?"

He stopped pacing and looked at her, his expression
crumpling. "I didn't mean to make you cry."

Kit forced a smile. "I'm not crying. You didn't do any-thing wrong. Mackey, I'm just gonna go for a walk, okay? It's good of you to take care of Dad," she said. "I'm sorry I interrupted you. You go back to making him something to eat, okay?"

Mackey stared at her until she reached the bottom of the steps, his expression clearing as she continued smiling. Then he slowly went back inside and closed the door.

Kit walked around to the back of the house, ascended the steps, and walked along the wraparound porch. She stopped when she reached Royal's bedroom window. The white lace curtains—tinged with yellow—were pulled aside, and a lamp, turned low, cast a soft glow over Royal's tall form lying supine on the bed. One arm rested over his forehead, and his eyes were closed. A bamboo urn rested on a nightstand by the bed.

"Dad?" She rose on her toes and tapped on the window. "Dad, are you okay?"

He stirred, his arm inching higher up his brow, then slowly opened his eyes to narrow slits as he focused on the window. Stubble lined his jaw, his cheeks were pale, and his eyelids red and swollen.

Her lips trembled. "Will you let me in, please?"

A dazed look crossed his face as he focused on her fea-tures. "Go 'way, Viv."

He rolled over, presenting his back to the window, and an empty whiskey bottle rolled across the mattress, hit the scuffed hardwood floor, and shattered.

"It's Kit, Dad." Her throat ached. "The locks have been changed, and my key doesn't work. I came home as soon as I could to—" She cleared her throat and rose higher on her toes, pain pinching her calf muscles. "Please, Dad. Please let me in."

She called to him twice more, staring at his still bulk. Laughter rang out in the distance, and the throb of festive music increased. A knot of dark energy twisted tighter and tighter within her until her entire frame trembled.

Kit shoved off the window, left the porch, and stalked across the front yard onto the dirt road. She stopped once—by the vandalized mailbox—just long enough to snatch the metal bat off the ground in a white-knuckled grip.

"That girl o' yours is beating the fool out of my new gate and scaring my grandson."

Beau Sutton tossed one more handful of single-shell oysters into a metal basket, dropped the basket in a pot of water, and stepped back as a cloud of steam rose into the spring night air.

His father, Nate Sutton, leaned over an outdoor table loaded down with buckets, oyster knives, hot sauce, and melted butter in small saucers and spoke just loud enough to be heard over the throb of music and the chatter of guests several feet away.

"I know Viv's going through a hard time," Nate said, "but if she keeps that up, every guest we have is going to climb back on their golf cart, hightail it back to the resort, and we'll be hard pressed to draw the next wave down here." He gestured toward the closed wrought-iron gate at the end of the circular driveway, where a female figure, silhouetted in the soft glow of starlight, repeatedly slammed what looked like a bat against its ornate central design. "Is she drunk?"

"Probably." And understandably so. Vivid images of wide, lifeless eyes and wet hair tangled around his fingers had jerked him upright in bed, his skin slicked with sweat, two nights in a row now. He had no doubt that Viv's scars ran deeper than his own.

Wednesday morning Beau had been on one of Pearl Tide's docks, sorting oysters through the tumbler machine, when a muffled shriek had cut through the rhythmic grind of the equipment. Viv, who'd been checking oyster cages on a boat nearby, had doubled over the side of the boat and struggled to drag a limp body on board. She'd glanced up once—her panicked eyes had met his, cheeks pale and mouth open in stark terror.

He hadn't made it to her fast enough. By the time he'd plunged into the creek's depths, scrambled past the cages, and dragged himself on board the boat, she had already managed to pull Sylvie's body out of the water and was cradling her mother's wet head in both hands.

Later that afternoon, after Sylvie's body had been tugged from Viv's arms and placed on a boat bound for the mainland, Viv had boarded the boat and stood by her mother's body, staring blankly ahead, the numb look in her eyes and the hollow sound of her voice startling him. "I won't be back for a while."

Lack of cell service on Hope Creek Island had made it difficult to reach out. He'd left several messages in person with mutual acquaintances she sometimes visited, hoping to stumble upon her, but he hadn't seen or heard from her for two days. It worried him, but though they'd formed a close friendship over the past two years, Viv was a private person, and he knew when not to pry.

Beau craned his neck now, straining to make out her face. Something was different. The solid strength in her stance? The measured pace in each swing of her arms? The deliberate, intense focus of each blow?

"That's not Viv." She wouldn't have stopped at a closed gate. She'd have climbed over it or barreled Royal's old truck through it by now. Beau shook his head. "That's Kit."

Nate frowned and narrowed his gaze on the figure in the distance. "Either way, she's shaking Cal up. He can't decide whether to open the gate or run."

Sure enough, Cal, who'd been placed on gate duty for

the duration of the night's oyster roast, paced toward, then away from the gate, his muscular six-foot frame—tall for a fifteen-year-old and mistaken for that of a man on many occasions—stumbling twice as he cast worried glances over his shoulder.

Beau called to a waiter stationed nearby and motioned toward the line of steaming pots. "Will you take over, please?"

At his nod, Beau rounded the table and walked swiftly down the driveway. Nate fell in step behind him.

"Viv!" Kit struck the gate again as Beau approached, her eyes locked on Cal. "Either get my sister out here or open the gate. Those are your only two choices."

"I—" Cal's voice cracked. "I told you, she's not here."

Beau drew to a halt beside Cal and squeezed his shoulder. It trembled beneath his grip. "Viv isn't here, Kit. You want to ease up a bit and tell me what you need?"

Kit's attention landed on him, her brown eyes—exactly as he remembered, dark with equal parts passion and pain—focusing on his face, easing beneath his flesh, and looking straight through to his core.

His skin warmed. He returned her silent stare, studying her thick lashes, high cheekbones, and smooth lips. The soft, full curves of her cheeks and jaw were a bit more angled than he remembered. The quiet, intelligent girl he recalled, the shy sister who'd spoken to him only a few times, had matured and now materialized before him as an alluring flesh-and-blood woman.

"I'd appreciate it if you'd stop assaulting our gate," Nate said.

Kit blinked and refocused on Nate.

The moment was gone, but Beau's eyes followed her, his gaze clinging to the graceful curves of her profile.

"*Our* gate?" she asked softly. "Viv's, too?"

Nate remained silent.

Kit stepped closer, rested the bat against the iron rods of the gate. "She's been living here, hasn't she? Working for you?"

Nate dragged a hand through his gray hair and shifted his weight to one side. "Yes. I gave her a job two years ago."

"On that oyster farm of yours? The one that's littering up the creek, choking off the channel, and keeping my father's boats tied to the dock?" Kit gripped the gate with her free hand, her fingers curling so tight around the iron, they turned red. "Those grotesque cages my mother died on?"

Nate's face paled. He lifted both hands, palms out. "I'm sorry, Kit. Sorrier than I can say about Sylvie, but—"

"You're a leech." Her expression contorted. "An opportunist. You have everything—always have—and you take my sister, too?" She looked beyond Nate, fury lighting her eyes as laughter and music filled the air around the four-story house behind them. "And here you are, having a party when—" Her voice broke. "Where is Viv?" Her eyes, red rimmed and gleaming in the starlit night, met Beau's. "What'd you say to her? What're you using her for? An easy distraction when your wife's out of town?" She slammed the bat into the gate once more, heaving in broken breaths as she glared at Cal. "My sister's worth more than that, and I'm taking her home. You tell your sorry excuse for a security guard to open this gate and let me in."

Beau stiffened. He stepped in front of Cal, nudging him back with a hand on his shoulder. "Cal isn't security. He's my son. And just a teenager at that. His mother—my wife—passed away three years ago, and he was telling the truth when he said Viv isn't here. She took off two days ago, not long after she found your mom. Said she wouldn't be back for a while."

Kit's cheeks flushed deeper. Her breathing slowed, and she looked Cal over, regret suffusing her features as she eyed him from head to toe. "I . . . I'm sorry. I thought—"

She stumbled backward, and the bat clanged against the gate as it fell to the ground. She stared at the closed gate, a lost look appearing on her face, before she turned and trudged away.

Beau glanced at Cal. The nervous expression on his son's face had morphed into one of intense curiosity as he leaned around Beau and watched Kit leave. "Go to the house, Cal."

"But—"

"Now please."

Beau waited until he complied, then unlocked the gate and swung it open. He followed Kit, jogging a few steps until he was within earshot. "Kit."

She froze mid-step, her back to him. Her long hair spilled over her shoulders as she looked down, then turned and faced him. Tears streamed down her face and pooled in the corners of her mouth. "I'm sorry to hear about your wife," she whispered. "And I didn't realize Cal was your son. He looked so much older."

"I know." He was surprised to find his hand in midair, lifting toward her wet cheeks. He shoved both hands in his pockets and forced a wry smile instead. "Trust me, as nervous as you had him, if Viv had been here, he'd have opened that gate in five seconds and led you to her."

Kit picked at a seam in her dress pants. "How is she?"

He hesitated, his chest tightening at the flash of desperation across her expression. "I don't know. But probably not well, all things considered."

"I need her to come home. Our mom requested in her will that—" Her chest rose on a deep breath and her lips trembled. "Viv knows what we need to do, and I want to carry this out the way my mother wanted." A small sound escaped her. "I need to see Viv. I need to see her face."

He stood silently as Kit wiped her flushed cheeks, regaining her composure. Her downcast gaze was focused intently on the scuffed toes of his work boots, which contrasted sharply with the polished air of her tailored business suit and silk blouse.

"If you see her," she asked quietly, "would you please ask her to come home? Tell her the boat's setting out at dawn tomorrow?"

He nodded. "I'll do you one better. I'll find her."

"Thank you," she whispered.

Beau watched her walk away into the night, her high heels leaving indentations in the dirt, the small impressions conjuring in his mind those left behind by loggerhead hatchlings groping their way across sand toward the surf beneath the moonlight.

Footfalls sounded, and Nate's low words emerged from the darkness behind him. "Those girls are walking wounded."

CHAPTER 2

It was hard to get lost on a barrier sea island as small as Hope Creek, but Viv had done a pretty good job of it.

After Kit had rounded the bend, her shadowy figure melding with the droopy branches of oaks lining the road, Beau started out on foot. After walking two miles along dirt paths that weaved in and out of residential enclaves and live oak forests on the south side of the island, he trekked farther to a clear stretch of beach. He strolled across the cool sand beneath the starlight, lingered long enough to survey the empty beach stretching in both directions, then scoped out Viv's favorite restaurant and bar but had no luck. On his way back home, a string of golf carts, each one emblazoned with HOPE CREEK RESORT, glided by, signaling the Pearl Tide Oyster roast had ended. He knew it'd be fruitless to follow them—the upscale resort the golf carts were bound for was located on the northern half of the island, and the gates swung open only for VIP passes, big money, or good old-fashioned nepotism.

Beau possessed all these things but detested using them, and Viv, possessing none of these things, had expressed deep disdain for the prim and proper residents of Hope Creek Resort and always kept strictly to the south side of the island.

But over the past few months, he'd noticed that Viv would from time to time roam out to the public beach on her days off, sit on a sand dune with the clearest vantage point, and stare silently at the private stretch of sand reserved for use by resort guests. Her shoulders—and very spirit—would sag as smiling parents chased laughing children into the surf and happy couples, treading water, bobbed close together, sharing soft kisses and intimate whispers.

Only Viv hadn't been walking the beach or watching resort guests from a dune tonight. Instead, Beau found her two and a half hours after he'd first begun searching, at the southernmost point of the island.

She sat alone at a small table on the empty back deck of Lou's Lagoon, a dive located several miles from his father's house, nestled between a thick tangle of live oak trees and salt marsh cloaked in thin mist. Her legs sprawled out at odd angles, and one arm dangled over the back of her chair, a lit cigarette glowing between her fingers. A haze of smoke surrounded her, and a dingy outdoor light cast a dim orange glow over her relaxed form.

Hard rock thumped vigorously inside the tiny bar, each pulse of bass seeming to rattle the weathered wood walls of the structure, and the small crowd Beau glimpsed through the open windows swayed in unison with sloppy joy, bellowing a drunk chorus of familiar lyrics.

Beau made his way up the steps of the back deck, carefully stepping over planks of rotten wood, and stood by the table. "Mind if I join you?"

Viv's eyes were closed, her head tipped back against the headrest, but one corner of her mouth lifted at the sound of his voice. "Why not?" The slight smile vanished; her words slurred. "I'm not going anywhere."

He sat opposite her, the worn chair creaking beneath his six-foot-four frame, and watched her lift the cigarette to her mouth and take a drag. The smoke surrounding Viv thickened, drifting lazily on the cool night breeze.

She opened her eyes to narrow slits, then studied him. "Go ahead and say it."

A small smile rose to his lips. "Those things aren't good—"

"For me, I know." She smiled back . . . just a bit. "They're not good for my lungs, my throat, my mouth . . ." Her voice trailed off as she met his eyes. "Always the devoted friend watching out for me, huh? You're one of the last true gentlemen in the world, Beau Sutton." The teasing note in her voice disappeared. "Trust me, there are other things hurting me a lot worse than this cigarette ever will. So grant me my small mercies, will you?"

He held her gaze. Toyed with a soggy napkin that lay beneath one of four empty shot glasses on the table. "You want to talk about it?"

The salt-laden air between them grew heavy. His gut sank, swallowed up by the same wave of dread that had washed over him the past two nights. The eerie feel of the images emblazoned in his memory—and Viv's especially, he imagined—was bad enough, but putting words to them . . . ?

"No." She tipped her head farther back and stared upward.

His shoulders relaxed, and his hand grew still on the napkin.

"I hope I didn't put you and your dad out by being off the job for two days." A note of apology entered her tone. "I bet poor Cal got stuck manning the gate?"

He winced, the clang of Kit's bat against wrought iron and Cal's unsettled expression still fresh in his memory. "Yeah."

"I promise to make it up to him." She looked at him

earnestly. "You'll tell him, won't you? And I swear I'll pull my weight and then some the second I come back."

"Don't even think it," he said. "You always do more than your fair share, and you're welcome to take as much time off as you want."

Her lips twisted briefly. "Nate okay with that?"

"Of course."

"How'd the roast go tonight?" She cut her eyes his way, eagerness flickering through her expression. "Everyone show?"

"Yeah. We sold out of tickets yesterday." He winked. "The golf-cart caravan left their gated paradise on time and braved the south side of Hope just for a taste of Pearl Tide's rumored legend in the making."

"And were they impressed?"

Beau smiled, recalling the satisfied sighs and pleased expressions of the Hope Creek Resort guests who'd surrounded the outdoor table laden with raw oysters. "Suitably so. They contributed more than a promising financial start to our little company. Should be enough to impress the most reluctant when we pitch our next expansion."

She grinned slow. "Bless their sweet little wallets."

They laughed, then fell silent. Viv resumed staring at the sky, and Beau followed her gaze to the low branches that twisted together overhead. Stars peeked between the gnarled limbs, and soon the hectic beat of music inside Lou's Lagoon transitioned into a soft, steady tune.

"She came out here a lot," Viv whispered reluctantly, her words quiet. "To just"—her hand holding the cigarette tilted slightly—"float away. Be numb."

"Your mom?"

She nodded, then grew quiet again.

He tapped an empty shot glass with his knuckle. "This won't fix it, Viv."

A humorless laugh escaped her. "No. It most definitely won't."

"I'm worried about you." He pinched the rim of one shot glass and spun it slowly between his fingertips. "And I'm not the only one."

All trace of amusement drained from her face. She sat up, propped her elbows on the table, and brought her face farther into the light. Her features were identical to Kit's, her eyes the same dark shade, but rather than warm, expressive depths, they remained cool and guarded. The faint lines beside Viv's mouth had deepened with grief, and exhaustion suffused her expression. He'd bet good money she hadn't eaten anything since he last saw her. She'd been running on cigarettes and whiskey for the past couple of days, most likely.

But it was the cynicism simmering beneath the surface that concerned him most. Every day for the past few months, long before Sylvie's death, it had seemed as though her caring demeanor—and generous nature—hardened a bit more.

"I hate when you look at me like that."

Beau frowned. "Like what?"

"Like you're looking for someone else." Her mouth drew into a tight line as she examined his expression. "Kit's back, isn't she?"

He eased back in his chair. "She came to the house. Said she wants to see you."

One brow lifted. "I bet."

"Kit mentioned something about Sylvie's will," he continued. "Said the boat's setting out tomorrow at dawn and that you'd know what she meant. What the two of you needed to do?"

Her expression drew down, and a muscle ticked in her jaw. "And I bet Kit was all dolled up. Looked well. Did she impress you? Catch your eye, like always?"

"Viv—"

"Changed my mind." She stabbed the cigarette into the table, snuffing it out. "I do want to talk about it. Or, more to the point, I'd like to ask a question."

He shrugged. "Go ahead."

"If you had a choice between saving your life or Cal's, which would you choose?"

Beau spread his hands. "Cal's."

"You're sure?" She searched his expression, uncertainty in her eyes. "You wouldn't change your mind if things took a turn for the worse? If, say, you realized that Cal wouldn't make it, anyway. That no matter how hard you tried, Cal would go down, and if you held on, you'd go down with him. Would you try, anyway?"

His mouth tightened. What kind of question was this? Out of the blue? And the fact that she even had to ask . . .

He leaned forward, digging his elbows into the table. "No doubt."

Her eyes narrowed on his face. "And would he do the same for you?"

"Of course."

"Because you're his father?"

"Because he loves me." A strangled sound of frustration caught in his throat. "Where is this coming from? Don't you know me better than this by now? I don't understand what you're—"

"I loved my mother." She stabbed a finger toward the center of her chest. "*I* did. I stayed with her for years. I peeled her off Lou's barroom floor, dragged her home, and put her in bed every night. I sat beside her on the front porch at midnight, when she'd shake and scream, insisting someone was trying to kill her. I dragged her to therapy, picked up her prescriptions, made her take her meds, and stood still when she attacked me, said I was *one of them* and scratched and clawed at my face. I bailed her out of jail. Paid off her lawyers. I watched my dad wither away and my brother grow more scared and confused every day. I watched her get worse and worse and worse, until she drowned herself in that creek, and even then I still pulled her ou—"

She hit the table with her fists and closed her eyes.

"Hey." Beau reached out, covered her fists with his hands, squeezed gently until they unfurled. "Easy. You're going to hurt yourself."

She turned her hands over in his and stared down at her small dirt-stained palms as they shook in the cradle of his larger ones. "I know I'm a mess. Don't you know that I know?"

"You're not a m—"

"I am." Viv looked up; her eyes locked with his. "Because I stayed. Because her life was more important than mine, and it was worth trying to save. And as soon as she's dead, Kit breezes back in, expecting to spread our mother's ashes with me and cry her goodbyes and act like she loved her. Like she didn't make her choice fifteen years ago. Like she didn't turn her back on her own mother. Next time you look at Kit, you remember that." She trailed her hands away, then balled them back into fists in her lap. "Kit's a coward. She has no soul."

Some things you couldn't take back.

Kit slumped on the front steps of Teague Cottage, leaned back against the—still locked—screen door (she'd tried forcing it open twice after she'd trudged back from the Suttons' home) and watched as a fourth string of golf carts cruised along the dirt road toward the north side of the island. Most were quiet electric four-seaters, but a few were noisy gas-powered six-seaters equipped with underbody lights that glowed in garish pink, green, or yellow in the dark night. Occupants of the latter carts, their figures merely smudgy outlines behind the headlights, had to raise their voices above the motor's rumble to carry on a conversation. Snatches of phrases traveled across the front lawn and reached the front steps.

"Best I've ever had in my life."

"I know! So much more flavorful than . . ."

"Shame the place is stuck all the way out here. Nothing but run-down shacks and overgrown yards on this piece. Like that one. That one right there."

Kit cringed as the voice became clearer. Sharper. As though the woman who'd spoken had turned her head and focused on the neglected two-story home Kit leaned against.

"That one has charm. I'll grant it that. But it's too far gone. Someone needs to raze it, along with the rest on this block, and start over."

Kit plastered her back against the screen, her gratitude for the cover of darkness at war with the sharp sting of the affront smarting through her. Sure, even she had to admit the grounds of her family home had become an overgrown, weathered wreck. But what lay inside Teague Cottage, or rather who . . .

She rolled her head to the side, able to see Viv clearly just as she'd been twenty-one years ago—a long-legged seventeen-year-old girl with an easy grin and a sarcastic sense of humor. They'd been sitting on the same step Kit sat on now, having snuck one of their mother's cigarettes after they'd managed to get her safely into bed on the heels of a particularly painful psychotic episode.

Kit had taken only one drag and Viv had been in the middle of her second when Ty Nelson had strolled by. A scraggly man in his midtwenties who lived a stone's throw down the road and peddled dime bags on the side, he'd paused to smile in their direction.

"That's a good-looking mouth you got on you, Viv," Ty had said. "You girls as wild and friendly as your mama?"

Kit's face had flamed, the blistering profanity-laden insults that Viv had hurled at Ty making her cringe as much as Ty's lewd remarks.

"What does he know?" Out of breath, Viv had bumped Kit's shoulder with her own and made a rude gesture toward Ty's retreating back. "Boneheaded pervert is just as heartless as the rest of them. But we, dear sis"—she'd looked at Kit's face, then hugged her tight—"are above them all. Don't let anyone tell you different."

Kit rubbed her arms, the memory of Viv's protective embrace almost palpable. Viv's hugs had always been so different from her mother's: Solid and strong. Sober.

She'd missed those hugs so much over the years. She'd missed what might've been. And maybe . . . maybe things would have been different if she'd stayed. Maybe her mother would've changed her mind? Maybe . . .

No. That was the root of the problem. For years, Viv *had* been here.

The string of golf carts passed, then faded to small red taillights in the distance until the darkness swallowed them up and the air grew still again, the pulse of wildlife reviving, each chirp and cry growing louder and louder.

Kit was alone again. She stared at the trees' shadows cast by starlight along the dirt road that led to the Sutton property, until the shadows blurred and her eyes burned.

Viv wasn't going to show tonight. Kit doubted Beau had even been able to find her—fact was, she didn't blame him if he'd decided not to try after her humiliating attack on his property earlier this evening.

Oh, Lord. Kit dropped her face into her hands. She'd

lost all control and made a complete fool of herself—not just in front of Beau, but in front of his son and father, too. She'd accused Beau—a widower now?—of terrible things. Insulted his father and chastised his son. She'd never behaved more erratically in her life.

That intense scrutiny in Beau's eyes when he'd looked down at her . . . the thin lines fanning out from his eyes as he'd frowned. The cautious expression on his handsome face as he'd approached her . . . What must he think of her?

She lifted her head, and her gaze narrowed on the empty road. Exactly what everyone else on this island had always thought: The Teague girls were crazy—as wild and crazy as their mother. Nothing but trash.

Kit rubbed her eyes, shoved to her feet, then worked her way through thick weeds and grass to the back deck, climbed the stairs, and moved quietly along the wraparound porch to each window she could reach. The window to hers and Viv's childhood bedroom was shut tight and wouldn't budge; Mackey's window was locked, as well. She ventured to the opposite side of the porch and found Royal's bedroom window to be a no-go, but the battered screen hanging by one nail on the kitchen window fell off with one tug and—even better—the inner window was cracked open just enough for her fingertips to fit.

She yanked the window upward, sliding it open with a whoosh, gripped the windowsill, and heaved her upper body through the opening. A pocket on her suit jacket snagged on a nail, halting her progress. She wriggled her way out of it—bumping her forehead once on the windowsill and twice on the faucet of the kitchen sink directly below her—then kicked off her shoes and forced her hips through the aperture.

A gasp sounded as her body spilled over the sink and countertop, her limbs fumbling awkwardly for a secure grip, knocking dirty pots, bowls, and spoons to the floor in a crashing heap.

Hands and knees hitting the linoleum floor, Kit winced and looked up.

Mackey, clad in blue pajamas, stood in the kitchen doorway, one hand pressing against his open mouth and wide eyes staring at her. "You . . ." He pointed at the open window, then the pots and bowls—some broken—that littered the floor. "You're not supposed to do that."

Kit squeezed her eyes shut and pushed off the floor, flinching as muscles she didn't know she had cramped. "I know." She focused on Mackey's shocked face and gestured weakly toward the cluttered floor. "Sorry about that. I'll clean it up."

Mackey shook his head. "You don't live here no more." His attention darted from the open window to the mess on the floor, then to Kit's disheveled form, the wheels turning ninety miles a minute. "You broke in. You're a burglar."

Kit shoved her hair off her face and rubbed an ache in the back of her neck. "I'm not a burglar. I'm your sister."

"But you didn't come in through the door. You came in the window."

"Because my key didn't work."

"Because you don't live here no more."

"Because Viv," she stressed, "changed the locks to get back at me."

"Because you don't live here no more."

Kit sighed. Returned his stare.

"You broke in. You're a burglar." Mackey walked across the kitchen and picked up a cordless phone from the counter. "I have to call the cops."

"Dad invited me."

"Oh." He put the phone back on the counter and blinked. "You hungry?"

Kit rubbed her forehead. "Sure."

Mackey smiled. "I made dog cheese."

It took him five minutes to rummage around in the fridge, dump the contents of a container into a bowl, and nuke it in the microwave. He pressed the warm bowl into her hands gingerly, then cupped the back of her hands twice to ensure her grip was sound.

"You got it?"

Kit nodded, staring down at the generous heap of macaroni and cheese with bite-sized chunks of hot dog mixed in. "How do you . . . Who gets the groceries? I mean, since Viv left?"

Mackey pointed toward the front door. "The lady puts the bags on the front steps on Tuesday. Said she's beat on Mondays and won't come that day, but she always brings 'em on Tuesday." His brow furrowed. "Tuesday at five in the afternoon. Not the morning—the afternoon. At five. And I give her forty-three dollars and thirty-seven cents. 'Cept not the thirty-seven cents, cuz she don't want no pennies. She said keep the pennies and just give her one quarter and one dime. No pennies."

"What's the lady's name?"

"L.A. She said call her L.A., like the city." He looked at the ceiling, brow furrowing. "And no Miss. She said she ain't no 'Miss' nothing. Just call her L.A."

"And who cleans?" Kit glanced around the kitchen, spotless save for the clutter of pots, bowls, and spoons she'd knocked onto the floor. "Who does the laundry and—"

"I do that all." Mackey's voice rose. "I give L.A. forty-three dollars and thirty-seven cents." He whispered, "No pennies." Then nodded. "I bring the bags in. I cook the dog cheese. I clean the kitchen, wash the laundry. Wash the dishes." His chin trembled. "I don't need Viv to take care of me. I don't need you taking care of me. I don't need Mama taking c—" He pounded his fist against his chest and covered his face. "I take care of me!"

"I can see that," Kit said softly. "I can see you do, Mackey, and it was my mistake. I'm sorry. I didn't mean to offend you. It's just that . . . I guess I still think of you as my little brother, you know? No matter how old you are."

He made a face, then ran a hand through his shaggy hair. "It's okay." He glanced down at the bowl in her hands and smiled. "You want me to sit with you while you eat?"

She shook her head. "I'm going to visit with Dad. I'll eat in his room."

Mackey lingered for a moment, frowned at the mess she'd made, then smiled at the bowl in her hands again. He patted her shoulder. "Night." Then he shuffled toward the door.

"Mackey?"

He stopped on the threshold, faced her, and raised his eyebrows.

She smiled, a bittersweet ache blooming in her chest. "You've grown into quite a man."

Mackey blushed, covered his smile with both hands, then left. His bedroom shoes swooshed along the hardwood floor to his bedroom, and a door clicked shut moments later.

Kit cupped the bowl tighter in her palms, absorbing its warmth, then walked down the hallway to the last room on the right. She knocked on the closed door.

"Dad?"

No answer.

"I'm coming in, okay, Dad?"

Receiving no response, she opened the door slowly and peeked in to find Royal stretched out on the bed, exactly as she'd left him a couple of hours ago. The lamp still cast a dim glow over a portion of the room, and several bowls of Mackey's hot dog and mac and cheese mixture sat cold and untouched in a neat row on the dresser opposite the bed.

Kit entered the room quietly, stepped carefully around the broken glass littering the floor beside the bed, and placed her bowl next to the others on the dresser. She entered the small en suite bathroom and retrieved a washcloth from the scuffed cabinet below the rusty sink. After wetting the washcloth with lukewarm water, she returned to the bedroom, sat on the edge of the bed, and gently lifted Royal's arm from his forehead and replaced it with the moist washcloth.

"Dad? I need you to wake up for a minute."

His eyelids moved, opening to narrow slits. "I told you to go away."

Kit's belly tightened, the hoarse sound of his voice evoking a fresh wave of regret. "No, you didn't. You called me two days ago." She forced a smile. "So I came home."

He blinked once, then opened his eyes fully. "Kit?"

She nodded.

One hand lifted, his fingers beckoning her closer. She leaned down and brought her face farther into the lamp's dim light, sat still as his bloodshot eyes focused on her face, then roved slowly over her features.

His chin trembled. "My Kit?" He touched her face, two callused fingertips trailing over her cheek, mouth, and chin, searching for the girl he'd last seen fifteen years ago. "My baby girl?"

"Yes." She smiled wider. Her lips stiffened, and her cheeks ached. "Always."

He stared a few moments more, and a pained expression appeared, his eyes welling. "So much like your mama used to be . . ."

A tear slipped from his dark lashes, rolled down his lean cheek, and disappeared in his thick beard.

"I'm in pieces," he whispered. "Viv—my poor Viv. And Mackey. Everything . . . in pieces."

Kit wiped his wet cheek with her thumb, then wrapped her arms around his shoulders and brought her lips to his ear. "Do you remember what I promised you the day I left?"

He nodded jerkily, his coarse beard scratching her cheek.

"I promise I'll pick you up," she said, her own voice catching. She stared at the bamboo urn sitting silently on the nightstand, swallowed hard, and steadied her words. "Tomorrow morning we'll carry her away from here and set her free. Then I swear I'll pick us all up and put us back together the way we should've always been."

CHAPTER 3

B eau stood in front of Teague Cottage, palmed the card in his back pocket, and weighed his options. The first was easy: Turn around, walk back up the dirt road, and tell Viv, who trudged some distance behind him, that he was sorry, but he couldn't intrude on a private family matter. It wasn't his place, and he wasn't welcome.

He was glancing over his shoulder, contemplating doing just that, when Viv rounded the bend in the road and her unsteady frame emerged from the tree line. She winced as a ray of sunlight hit her eyes, shielded her face with her hand, and swayed on her feet.

Beau dragged a hand over his face and sighed. First hard shot of morning sunlight after an endless night of drinking? That was about right. Viv was in no shape to do this alone, and aside from that, he'd sworn last night on the back deck of Lou's run-down Lagoon to stick by her side. Had to. It'd been the only way to get her to stop drinking and consider going home.

Stopping, Viv bent over and braced her hands on her knees. "I don't feel so good."

Not surprising. After he'd managed to cajole her back to his father's house, it'd been almost three in the morning.

She'd managed to steal three hours of sleep at most before he'd woken her up, placed a hot cup of coffee in her hands, and nudged her out the door to make it to Teague Cottage by sunrise.

Beau retraced his steps until he reached her side. He cupped her elbow, his voice soft. "Nothing about this will feel good. If you want to go back, we will. But I think you made the right choice in deciding to see this through."

She looked up at him, her cheeks pale. "Why?"

"Closure." It was the only reason he could think of besides the torn expression on her face last night as she'd wavered between going home to spread her mother's ashes and refusing to give Kit the satisfaction. "If you don't follow through today, I think you may regret it later."

She stared up at him, her mouth trembling. "I'm not so sure about that."

"I am. Because I've been there." Though he hated to revisit the memory.

Helping Cal say goodbye to Evelyn three years ago had been more painful than he cared to remember. He'd walked his son past his wife's open casket in the funeral home, hugged him tight to his side, and silenced his own pain as Cal, twelve at the time, cried. Beau had known for months that day would come—had even prepared for it with Evelyn's gentle encouragement—but that day had still been the longest of his life.

"When today is over," he said, "you'll be able to move on. Not right away"—both he and Cal still struggled, even three years later—"but eventually, you'll be able to put it behind you."

Or at least . . . he hoped that would happen, not only for Viv but for him and Cal, as well.

The corners of Viv's mouth turned up, and a dry, humorless laugh escaped her. "Put it behind me?" Her eyes strayed past him toward the spray-painted mailbox at the mouth of Teague Cottage's driveway. *Wild cat.* "You know why they wrote that?"

"Yeah."

Everyone living in Hope Creek did. Although Beau had crossed paths with Sylvie only twice over the course of his life, her name had circulated the island frequently over the years. It was usually mired in a humiliating anecdote filled with enough violent or—in the most degrading retellings— sordid details to turn his stomach. The thought of anyone taking pleasure in Sylvie's pain had disgusted him. No one should be treated that way, especially not a woman as troubled and vulnerable as Sylvie.

The *what* of Sylvie Teague's struggle had been easy to pin down; Sylvie had acted out in public on a regular basis— breaking windows, shouting profane threats at strangers, in- stigating violent altercations in bars, and maintaining an almost constant state of drug- or alcohol-induced inebria- tion. The *why*, however, had been a bit harder to define, prompting neighbors to speculate. Schizophrenia? Bipolar disorder? Hard-core addiction?

But the most prevalent and offensive conjecture had rip- pled through the small community consistently after each of Sylvie's arrests: *just another trashy Teague.*

Viv had borne the brunt of repercussions arising from Sylvie's meltdowns and had defended her mother's reputa- tion on a routine basis, her balled fists and defiant glare a landmark on the tiny island, peppering locals' directions to tourists seeking scenic views: *You'll want to stick to the north side of the island. If you hit weeds and meanness, you've done gone too far south.*

"They say she had two speeds," Viv whispered, her tone hardening as she stared at the mailbox. "Wild and cata- tonic, with no in-between. A wild cat. As though she were

an animal or an object. Like she wasn't even a person."
She straightened slowly, walked to the mailbox, and
trailed her fingers over the garish paint. "She saw this.
Heard the talk swirling around her all her life. You think I
could ever put that behind me?"

Beau grimaced, the thought of what Sylvie and Viv must
have endured disconcerting. The idea that Kit had abandoned Sylvie and Viv, along with the rest of her family,
was just as troubling.

"I won't go in." Viv glared at the house. "Not while
Kit's in there. She doesn't deserve to step foot in that house,
much less live there again."

"There's no need to go in." He walked over and squeezed
her upper arm gently. "We'll just knock on the door, let her
know you're here, and she can come out to you."

"And you'll get on the boat with me?" she asked, an un-
characteristic tremor in her tone.

"That's not up to me. That'll be up to your family." He
smiled softly. "But I promise I won't leave here until you do."

Beau walked with Viv up the driveway, his step hesitat-
ing at the sight of a rusty truck.

Royal Teague might not be very accommodating. At
least, he hadn't been too friendly at the Hope Creek Community Center two years ago. A meeting had been held to
discuss Beau and Nate's proposed oyster farm and debate
its potential impact on Hope Creek and its permanent residents. Royal had been the most vocal of the small crowd,
his questions spat across the room like accusations, gar-
nering applause from several attendees and increasing the
potential for pushback regarding Beau and Viv's future
proposal for expanding the farm.

Teague's Seafood had barely broken even the year prior
to the installation of Pearl Tide Oyster Company's farm,
and now . . . well, Royal's business was on the verge of
going belly-up. Something Beau and his father hadn't set

out to do, though he knew Royal blamed them all the same. Viv, too, now that she'd become a partner in the Sutton family venture.

"They'll agree to it," Viv said. "Mama didn't leave them a choice."

They continued up the driveway, and Beau walked up the steps to the screened-in front porch. Viv stopped halfway up the steps and leaned against the rickety porch rail. Beau knocked on the frame of the screen door and shoved his hands in his pockets, listening for sounds of someone approaching, but no one stirred inside the house.

Beau tilted his wrist, glanced down at his watch, then tilted his head back and looked around. The sky blushed as the sun ascended higher above the moss-laden tree line, and a fine dew sparkled across the knee-high grass and weeds littering the front lawn of Teague Cottage. A thin ray of sunlight strolled across the driveway and up the dented porch screen before settling on the frayed armrest of a wide wicker chair by the front door.

Dawn had definitely arrived, but maybe they'd come too earl—

The front door swung open on a creak, and Kit walked onto the front porch. Her cheeks blushed the same shade as the sky when her gaze settled on him. She wore a T-shirt and jeans today instead of the polished business suit from yesterday, and she'd pulled her long brown hair back in a tight ponytail that skimmed her shoulders. Her expression was soft in the morning light, her face devoid of make-up, her thick lashes were lowered, and a hint of drowsiness was in her gaze, as though she'd just woken up recently.

Beau cleared his throat. "Good morning. I hope we're not too early."

"We?" She perked up, and her eyes focused over his right shoulder, then widened at the sight of her sister.

Beau eased out of the way.

Kit opened the screen door, walked slowly down the steps, and stood in front of Viv. Both women remained perfectly still, inches apart, each studying the other. Their gazes roved over each other's feet, legs, waist, chest, arms, shoulders, and face before locking eyes.

Kit's mouth moved soundlessly, and a look of pain and dismay passed over her face, before she lifted her arms and embraced Viv.

Beau tensed as he watched Viv stiffen when Kit pulled her close. Her hands balled into fists at her sides, and she stared straight ahead, fixing her hard glare on the tangle of live oaks on the other side of the driveway. All traces of grief and vulnerability he'd glimpsed earlier had drained from her face, and a hard, stoic look had taken their place.

After a few silent moments, Kit let go and stepped back.

Viv's glare shifted, sliding from the tree line to Kit's face. "Feel better?" she asked quietly. "Help soothe your conscience?"

Kit's chest lifted, her breath quickening between her parted lips, as she returned her sister's stare. "I missed you, Viv. More than I could ever say."

"Yeah?" Viv's lip curled. "I've been right here. Right where I've always been." One dark brow lifted. "Where've you been, huh? Where were you while Mama was dying?"

"Viv . . ." Skin prickling, Beau lifted his hand in appeal.

"What?" She cut her eyes at him briefly, then refocused on Kit. "I'm just chatting with my sister." Her lips lifted, and she bared her teeth in a slow, dead smile. "My dear, sweet, selfish sister."

Kit straightened and squared her shoulders, her dark head rising two inches above Viv's slumped form. "I don't want to fight, Viv."

Viv braced her hands on the rail at her back and pushed to her full height. The metal rail shivered beneath her forceful grip, then wobbled precariously on the edge of the steps. "No, you don't, do you? You're a coward, and cow-ards prefer to slink away and leave everyone else behind to suff—"

"That's enough." The screen door slammed, and Royal walked onto the top step. He cradled a small, cylindrical bamboo case close to his chest, his eyes bloodshot and his voice hoarse.

Viv looked up at Royal and scoffed. "Of course. Daddy to the rescue." She faced Kit again, her chin trembling, a sheen of moisture glinting in her eyes in the morning sun-light. "Always Daddy's little g—"

"I mean it, girl." Royal narrowed his eyes at Viv. "I know you're hurting, but you'll keep a civil tongue in your head for the duration. You wanna go around cracking skulls, you do it on your own time, but you ain't doing it here, and not today." His clutched the bamboo case closer, and his knuckles turned white as he repeated, "Not today."

Viv's jaw shifted as she continued glaring at Kit.

"And why in the devil are you here?"

Beau tore his attention away from Viv and glanced up at Royal, who stared down at him.

The older man had lost weight since the last time Beau had seen him, the thickly defined muscles Beau remembered having thinned out. The stern line of Royal's shoulders curved downward, sagged almost. A thick salt-and-pepper beard covered the lower half of his face, and his dark, wa-tery eyes stood out starkly against his pale, wrinkled skin.

Beau ducked his head, a sensation of shame sizzling through him, burning its way up his neck. "I'm sorry, Royal. I'm so sorry for your l—"

"He's with me." Viv moved to his side and gripped his upper arm. Her fingers trembled around his biceps. "I asked him to come."

Royal's mouth gaped, his expression twisting. "You brung a Sutton here? Today, of all days?"

"You got Kit," Viv said between gritted teeth. "I got Beau."

"You're my daughter, too—for all you like to deny it—and he ain't welcome on my boat."

"Then neither am I. I won't step foot on that boat without him."

Royal's gnarled fingers fumbled over the bamboo case. Gripped it tighter. "You'd do that? You'd do that to your own mama?"

Viv shrugged. "She wouldn't care either way."

Royal's lips thinned. "But I do."

"She can't care," Viv spat.

"But I d—"

"Because she's dead."

"Don't say it!"

The screen door slammed again, and a man, short in stature, ran out, wrapped his arms around Royal's waist, and buried his face against Royal's shoulder.

"Tell her, 'Don't say it,' " he repeated, his keening wail muffled against the sleeve of Royal's T-shirt. "Tell her, 'Don't say it no more.' "

Beau held his breath, a hard knot forming in his throat, as he watched the man—Viv's brother, Mackey?—burrow closer to Royal.

Royal tipped his head back, and his eyes glazed as he stared at the rose-colored sky. "Dear God . . . ," he whispered, his voice fading. After a moment, he blinked hard, shifted the bamboo case carefully into the crook of one arm, and lowered his other arm around his son's shoulders. "We'll head out now. Get this over with."

He moved slowly, his heavy tread pausing on each step, as Mackey's feet shuffled at a slower pace, and he brushed past Kit, then stopped beside Beau and Viv.

Beau raised his head and stilled.

Royal's eyes were on him, searing into his face, his pupils filled with anguish and fury. "You can get on the boat. But keep your mouth shut, and steer clear of me."

Viv had grown unrecognizable in almost every way. They all had.

Kit leaned forward on the stern bench of Royal's hybrid bay boat and glanced to her right. Viv, seated on the opposite end of the bench, stared straight ahead, her brown hair ruffling in the sea breeze, a muscle ticking in her jaw. She'd lost weight—way too much, her body angular and wound tight with anger.

Viv hadn't looked her way once since boarding the boat.

Closing her eyes briefly, Kit sank back against the bench and stiffened. A broad shoulder was wedged against hers, and a hard thigh pressed into her softer one. She eased an inch to the left, and her hip hung precariously off the edge of the bench.

"Sorry." Beau's deep voice rumbled against her side as he shifted to the right on the bench. "Don't mean to crowd you."

"It's okay." Kit looked down at the blond hair sprinkled along his defined forearm. It wasn't his fault that he was unfortunate enough to end up crammed on the bench seat of a boat between one sister who was dangerously close to falling apart and another who was ready to go straight for her sibling's jugular.

His tanned hand, resting on his left knee, turned palm upward, and his long fingers spread. "I'd go to the bow, but . . ."

But there was a good chance Royal might toss him overboard.

A rueful smile rose to Kit's lips. Her dad, always bullheaded, might try, but she doubted he'd be successful.

Beau had two years on her, which would make him . . . forty now? Beau was at least fourteen years younger than Royal, and she could see—had actually felt a moment ago—that Beau carried more than twice the muscle.

Her half smile fell as she studied her dad, who sat at the helm, directly in front of them. His back curved over the low steering wheel, one arm clutched the wheel, and the other curved around the bamboo case housing her mother's ashes. Apart from his warning to Beau prior to leaving the house, he hadn't said a word. He'd climbed aboard the boat, sat at the helm, and stared at the bamboo case until everyone had boarded; then he'd left the dock and headed up Hope Creek toward the Ditch.

No one had spoken as they'd passed the Suttons' empty dock, the sprawl of oyster cages floating along the upper end of Hope Creek, then traveled farther beyond Hilton Head and continued three nautical miles out into the Atlantic.

In a way, the silence had been a blessing. What was left to say after the painful—and humiliating—episode that had occurred at the house earlier?

Kit lowered her head and rearranged the towel housing a small pile of yellow jessamine in her lap. She'd untangled several lengths of the vine from the picket fence first thing this morning, the burst of honeysuckle-like scent tugging tears from her eyes as she'd unwound the flowers from the thicket of weedy overgrowth.

The vibrant vine had always been her mother's favorite.

"Gorgeous," Sylvie had told Kit once as she'd knelt by her side in the backyard of Teague Cottage years ago.

Kit flexed her fingers, still able to feel her mother's gentle touch as she'd removed one of the vibrant trumpet-shaped flowers from Kit's small seven-year-old hands. They'd spent the afternoon gardening together. That day had been a good one—quiet and peaceful. A rarity in her mother's life.

"It's beautiful," Sylvie had said, smiling down at the flower. Her black hair had spilled over her shoulder onto a delicate petal, both reminiscent of silk, making Kit's fingers itch to touch. "But poisonous." Her smile had faded, and her thick lashes had lifted as she'd met Kit's eyes, sadness pooling in the dark depths. "You should never get too close, Kit."

"Happy to stand."

Kit looked up. Beau stared down at her, his blue eyes examining her face. "I'm sorry. What did you say?"

His expression gentled. "If you need more room, I'd be happy to stand."

She shook her head. "No, thank you." There was a small cleft in his chin. . . . The curve of his jaw was strong and solid. "We're almost there."

The boat slowed. Royal cut the engine, and the boat's thrust eased to a crawl, then stopped, the craft bobbing in the waves.

After standing, Royal paused once to lean heavily on the seat with one hand, then walked onto the casting deck at the bow of the boat, the bamboo case still cradled in the crook of his arm. The sun had fully risen, and bursts of gold streaked across the blue sky in all directions, the vibrant horizon at odds with Royal's hunched, almost frail form.

Kit stood, clutching the towel filled with jessamine, and waited for Viv to join her, but Viv continued to sit and stare, the glare on her gaunt face intensifying. Beau stood instead, then rested his big palm on Viv's shoulder. Her head dipped a bit lower at his touch, but she remained otherwise unfazed.

Kit walked to the passenger seat at the helm and stood beside Mackey. "Mackey? Would you like to say goodbye?"

Sniffing, he covered his ears with his hands, curled deeper into his seat, and tucked his chin tight to his chest.

"Okay." Kit leaned down and kissed the top of his head, his soft hair tickling her nose. "It'll be over soon."

Drawing in a deep breath, she joined Royal on the casting deck. Waves lapped at the boat, and water rippled in all directions.

"This was her favorite part of the day." Royal squinted up at the sky, the crow's-feet fanning out from his eyes deepening. "She was always more like herself first thing in the morning."

The white deck below Kit's feet blurred. Blinking hard, she knelt down and placed the bundle of jessamine on the water. The thick emerald leaves and bright yellow petals spread, the vines lengthening across the undulating waters.

Royal's shoulders jerked, and he clutched the bamboo case tighter to his chest.

"Dad?" She swallowed hard and forced out the words. "Do you want me to do it?"

He jerked his head to one side, then knelt beside her, removed the top of the bamboo case with shaking fingers, and withdrew a thinner white urn from the bamboo case's interior. Leaning over the edge of the bow, he placed the biodegradable urn in the water gently and nudged it to the center of the jessamine.

The urn bobbed upright among the yellow flowers for a few minutes; then a gray cloud bloomed beneath the urn, spread throughout the water, and slowly dissipated in different directions.

A choked cry escaped Royal, and Kit reached out, covered his hands with hers, and held them tight.

The ride back to the cottage seemed longer but was just as silent, save for Mackey's soft sobs, which rose just above the burr of the boat's engine. After arriving back at the dock, Kit left the boat last, then stumbled twice on shaky legs as she followed Viv and Beau to the house.

Royal, still silent, went inside, and Mackey followed. The screen door clanged shut behind them, and Kit stood on the bottom step of the front porch, watching as Viv trudged through the high grass, her gaze pinned to the ground and Beau at her side.

"Viv?"

Her steps slowed.

"Will you stay?" Kit hesitated, unable to see her sister's face. She should leave this alone—for today, at least. But the pain within her throbbed stronger with every step Viv took. "Just for a little while?"

Viv lifted her head and turned. The circles below her eyes had darkened, and her mouth was turned down. "What for?"

"To . . ." Kit moved closer. "To talk. Or just sit."

Viv tilted her head. "Together? You and me?"

"Yes. We could—"

"Like old times?" Viv straightened. Pinned her hard gaze on Kit's face. " 'Course, I can't say that. Because we never had that, did we? Not really. Cuz you ran off and left."

"Viv . . ." Beau touched her arm.

"I'm here now," Kit said. "I'd like to be here for you now. To help in any way I c—"

"Yeah." Viv nodded. "Because it's always been about what you want. What you'd like. What you need."

Kit shook her head, her eyes burning. "No," she said softly. "I'd much rather have been here. I love you, Viv. Just as much as I always did."

"You're a liar."

Beau moved forward and placed his palm at Viv's waist. "Look, it's been a hard day for both of you. Please don't do thi—"

"Do what?" Viv bit out. "Tell the truth? Because it *is* the truth. Kit's a liar. And a coward. The only reason she's here now is that it's easy. That it's comfortable."

Kit took a step back. "That's not fair, Viv."

"Fair? You have no idea what fair is—or love, for that matter." Viv stalked closer, the disgust in her eyes slicing Kit to the core. "You shouldn't be here. You shouldn't be in that house. You shouldn't have even been on that boat."

Kit's heels hit the bottom step of the front porch. Beau had turned away, a flush spreading up his neck. He avoided her eyes.

"You sure did your part, didn't you?" Viv continued. "Keeping your head down out here—never saying a word in her defense—but giving her ultimatums left and right in that house."

"I was trying to help her. I was trying to protect her from herself and hang on to some sense of normalcy for all of us."

"She cried for days after you left." Viv stabbed a finger in the air, aimed at Kit's chest. "Asked for you every time she hit rock bottom." She shook her head slowly. "Some things you can't take back no matter how much time has passed."

"Stop it." Kit held up a trembling hand. "This won't fix anything."

"There's a word for what you did."

"I said st—"

"Abandonment." Viv's lip curled, accusation in her eyes. "You gave up on her. Abandoned her when she needed you most. You as good as pushed her in that creek."

Something snapped inside Kit, jerking her head back.

"There's a word for what you did, too." Her face flamed. "It's called enabling." She could feel the words snaking up her throat, clambering onto her tongue, hitting Viv where they'd hurt the most. But she couldn't stop them. "Who bailed her out every time she got in trouble? Who accepted her excuses and allowed her to wreak havoc in that house? Destroy her life, Dad's, and ours, too? Who gave her the money for liquor and pills to silence the voices and keep her calm? The same liquor and pills she pumped in her body three nights ago?" She snatched in a breath, a deep ache bleeding through her. "You enabled every single thing she did. Right up to the moment she drowned herself."

Viv's face blanched. Her mouth opened and closed soundlessly. She took a step back, her eyes, wide and full of pain, roaming over Kit's face. "I hate you," she whispered. "I hate setting eyes on you. I hate seeing my face in yours. Knowing you share my blood."

Some things you can't take back. . . .

Kit pressed the back of her hand to her mouth and swallowed hard, her teeth digging into her skin. She dropped her hand and reached out as Viv backed away. "No, I . . ."

Viv stumbled. Beau wrapped his arm around her shoulders, turned her around, and led her down the driveway to the road, enfolding her sagging frame against his brawny one, supporting her weight.

"Viv," Kit called out. "Please come back."

Neither of them turned around, and Kit sagged onto the bottom porch step, the late morning sun warm on her skin, but an icy pain chilling her to the bone.

CHAPTER 4

"How'd it go?"

Beau dumped the contents of a mesh cage onto a wooden culling table and flexed his gloved hands. The pile of oysters resembled a mound of muddy stones. Most were nicely rounded, with deep cups, but a few thin shells resembling fingers caught his eye. He sifted out three small oysters and returned them to the mesh-bag cage at his feet.

"That bad, huh?" Nate, who stood opposite Beau on a floating dock located behind the Sutton home, near the oyster cages, sorted through the oysters on the table, removed several with deep cups, then dropped them in a nearby bucket.

"It was . . ." Beau continued sifting as he searched for the right word to describe Sylvie's funeral and Viv and Kit's altercation. *Painful? Soul-searing?* "Nightmarish." He dug deeper into the mound of oysters, the steady clank of shells against buckets loosening the knot at the back of his neck. "You wouldn't recognize Royal if you saw him. He's lost at least ten pounds of muscle, grown a full beard, and looks like he's working hard at wasting into nothing."

Nate's hands slowed among the oysters. "Losing a woman you love will do that."

Beau met Nate's eyes, the sad half smile on his father's face having stilled his own hands as he recalled the shape he and Cal had been in when they'd returned to Hope Creek after Evelyn's death three years ago.

The details of their arrival escaped him—Beau had moved in a fog of grief and uncertainty for weeks after Evelyn had passed—but one memory still remained fresh in his mind. He had woken up late one afternoon, after another hard night of drinking and wallowing, and hadn't been able to find Cal. His son hadn't been in his room or on the Sutton grounds, and Beau had searched for almost an hour when he'd stumbled upon Cal sitting on the beach with Nate's arm around him, sobbing. Cal had looked so much younger than twelve as he'd huddled into Nate on the empty beach, a cool winter wind carrying his desperate cries.

The scene had been gut-wrenching, and Nate's question afterward, even more so.

"You love your wife more than your son?" Beau had been pouring another shot of whiskey when Nate had confronted him with a hard glare that same night. "You're not just killing yourself—you're killing that boy, too."

It had occurred to Beau then what would've happened years ago, when his own mother had packed up, left Hope Creek, and abandoned her husband and son for another man, if Nate had given up. If his father hadn't packed away his grief and anger, doubled down, and forged a path forward for himself and Beau both.

Beau had put away the shot, gotten his first night of decent sleep in months, and dragged himself out of bed early the next morning to put a plate of hot eggs and bacon in front of Cal as soon he sat at the kitchen table. They'd hit the creek an hour later and undertaken the first steps in establishing Pearl Tide Oyster Company.

He glanced to his right, where Cal stood at the edge of the dock, unloading oyster cages from a bay boat. Most days were still hard without Evelyn, but at least the pain had eased.

Cal looked over his shoulder, the small smile on his face not quite reaching his eyes, but a massive improvement over his grief-stricken demeanor three years ago. "This is the last of the first line. You want me to bring in another?"

Beau shook his head. "Nah. We've got plenty to go through for now. But how 'bout you help us out over here? Keep us company?"

Cal's smile widened. "Yes, sir."

"How's Viv holding up?" Nate asked as Cal grabbed a set of gloves and joined them at the culling table.

"Not good," Beau said. "She was asleep when I left the house."

And he felt guilty for leaving her, but there was work to be done, and Nate and Cal had shouldered the burden more often than was fair over the past few days. At least one local restaurant and Hope Creek Resort expected a delivery of singles by Monday morning. Plus, it wouldn't hurt to add another successful harvest to Pearl Tide Oyster Company's record before his presentation at the Hope Creek Community Center Monday night.

"I didn't know she had a twin," Cal said, tugging on a pair of gloves. "How come Ms. Viv doesn't talk about her?"

Beau resumed separating deep-cup oysters from the smaller ones: three inches or more in the bucket, less than three back in the cage. "They haven't seen each other in a while, and they're not getting along too well."

He winced. That was an understatement to say the least.

"How come?" Curiosity gleamed in Cal's eyes.

"Well, they . . ." Beau weighed a large oyster in his hand

and cringed as he recalled the insults both Viv and Kit had hurled at each other. "They had a falling-out a long time ago and still don't see eye to eye."

"About what?" Cal asked.

Beau grunted. Where to start? If he had to guess, he'd say the list was long. He tossed the oyster in the bucket, reached out and ruffled Cal's hair. "None of your business, that's what."

Cal smirked, a mixture of amusement and sarcasm tinging his tone, "Old folks' business, you mean?"

Nate chuckled. "You best watch that, boy. There's a difference between being old and being grown, and you ain't either yet." He shoved a stack of oysters Cal's way. "Tackle those, and before you go poking your nose in Viv's business, you remember that this ain't your problem to fix. It's a family problem—a Teague problem. Besides, getting this business off the ground is gonna take every free second we got."

Cal shrugged and started sorting through the oysters. Beau resumed the task, too, and they continued separating deep-cup singles beneath the increasing heat of the afternoon sun. But today the rhythmic clang of oysters into buckets and cages didn't clear Beau's thoughts, as it normally did. Instead, the look on Kit's face kept resurfacing in his mind . . . the deep shadows of pain and loss that had haunted her eyes when he and Viv had left.

Just the sight of that house alone would be enough to add to her troubles. Royal had become a veritable recluse over the past year, and the grounds of Teague Cottage screamed neglect. The spray-painted message on the mailbox had been enough to set Viv's nerves on edge this morning, and it had probably depressed Kit's spirits, as well.

Sweat beaded on Beau's forehead and trickled down his

back. He plucked his wet T-shirt from his chest and fanned it out, tilting his head from one shoulder to the other, stretching his neck. "You need anything from Skeeter's?" The mom-and-pop store, a catch-all of supplies, was the only one that stayed open late on the island. "When we finish for the day, I'm going to run a couple errands."

Nate shook his head. "I just picked up our order last week. What you needing?"

Beau removed his cap and rubbed his damp hair off his forehead. "A few odds and ends. Won't take me long, but I may take a walk afterward. Be back later than usual."

Nate leveled a look in his direction. "A walk where?"

"Around."

"Around where? You're not thinking of strolling past that Teague house, are you?"

"Have to. It's on the way to Skeeter's. Will you check on Viv later? Make sure she eats something and maybe coax her into sitting outside to soak up some fresh air?"

Nate narrowed his eyes. "I meant it when I said the Teagues' problems are their own. You want to be there for Viv? Great. But Royal and Kit? Neither one of them would welcome a Sutton right now—especially one who they believe enlisted Royal's daughter to help take his business."

"Probably not." Beau kneaded the knot in the back of his neck. "But Teagues aside, seeing as how I hit the age of forty several months ago, I think it's safe to say I'm in the *grown* category and therefore—"

Cal laughed. "You mean the *old* one."

"Either way," Beau stressed, squeezing Cal's shoulder and smiling, "I'm past the age of answering to my dad."

Nate grinned. "You won't ever be past that, son. Least not while I'm still breathing." His good humor faded. "It's best to steer clear of Royal and Kit—especially while Viv's still living here. Whatever the Teagues' problems are, they ain't none of ours, and the last thing you need is to find yourself stuck in the middle of 'em."

Growing up, Beau had never been very impulsive. This made him wonder why he hadn't stopped to think through the idea of setting foot on Teague property for the second time that day without being explicitly invited.

He crouched lower by the driveway, grateful for the cover of night, and eyed the front porch. A dim light barely illuminated the worn wicker chair by the front door, and only one interior light illuminated a window, the curtains drawn. If he kept quiet, he should be done in less than half an hour; then he'd slip out undetected. But if Royal came out for a smoke, well . . .

Beau glanced at the darkened road curving back toward home and almost had second thoughts. Almost.

Thing was, the act of slinging the supplies he'd purchased at Skeeter's back over his shoulder and returning home—mission unaccomplished—would be akin to admitting out loud to Nate that he'd been right.

The heck if he'd do that. Beau grinned. He'd let Royal wrap those wiry hands around his throat, choke him 'til he was blue in the face, then bury his corpse in the very dirt on which he stood before he'd let Nate say, "I told you so."

He hooked one arm over the Teague mailbox, gripped the post with his free hand, and yanked. Despite its rotten condition, the post held firm. It took three heavy kicks, a full minute of wrangling, and a smidgen of his masculine pride to pry it loose, after which, he grabbed the post hole digger he'd propped against a neighboring oak, dug the clamshell blades into the dirt, and opened up the hole more.

Attaching the new mailbox he'd bought at Skeeter's to a

fresh four-by-four post with lag screws was trickier. He'd need light for that. He grabbed a flashlight from the supplies on the ground, turned it on, and stuck the handle between his teeth, then bit down and tilted his head to direct the beam of light on the predrilled holes. The first two screws went in well, but he had trouble with the third, struggling to angle the screw just right and maintain his bite on the flashlight handle.

"Need a hand?"

He jumped, the flashlight fell from his mouth, and his teeth clamped down on his bottom lip. "Da—" Beau stifled a curse and looked up from his crouched position on the ground.

Kit knelt beside him, the fallen flashlight beaming on her regretful frown. "Oh . . . I didn't mean to . . ." She leaned closer, her dark eyes on his mouth, and the sweet scent of her shampoo—*pomegranate?*—rushed in. "Your mouth . . ." Her hand lifted; fingers brushed his lower lip. "It's bleeding."

Instinctively, he took her hand in his and tilted it into the light. A droplet of blood dotted one fingertip, and he grinned ruefully. "Bite down on it, and it'll happen every time."

He grabbed the hem of his T-shirt, searched for a clean, dry patch, and wiped the blood from her finger. "There." His hand lingered on hers, the delicate skin between her thumb and forefinger smooth and warm to the touch. "Good as new."

She smiled, just enough for the quarter-inch scar on her cheek, beside her mouth, to dimple. "Wish I could say the same for you. I'm sorry about that. I didn't mean to startle you."

"It was no more than I deserved, doing this without your or Royal's permission. I'm just lucky you caught me, instead of Royal."

Her smile dimmed. "No chance of that. I've discovered that he sleeps a lot nowadays."

He ran his tongue over the throb in his lower lip. "How long have you been out here?"

"Since you arrived." Kit gestured toward a line of oak trees on one side of the house. "There's a spot over there with a clear view of the stars. Best spot on the island for quiet contemplation." She glanced at the rotten post he'd discarded a few feet away, her grin returning. "Least it was, until you showed up and started wrestling with that pole. But you were putting on too entertaining a show for me to interrupt and interrogate."

He dragged a hand over his stubbled jaw and laughed, despite the burn in his cheeks. "No doubt. Though in my defense, it's been an exhausting day, so I wasn't at my best." He winced. "I'm sorry for intruding tonight, and this morning. Sylvie's funeral was private, and I shouldn't have been there, but Viv asked me to come."

"How is Viv?"

He hesitated. "Not well. This morning was as rough for her as I'm sure it was for you."

Kit sat back on her haunches, picked up the flashlight, and cast the beam over the new mailbox and post. "Did she ask you to do this?"

"No, but the sight of the old one upset her this morning." He picked up a lag screw he'd dropped and turned it over in his palm. "I got the new one at Skeeter's. It's plastic and rustproof. Should last quite a while. But I can put the old one back up if you want me t—"

"No." She bit her lip and frowned. "I mean, please don't. It's nice of you to do this." She glanced at the graffitied mailbox lying in the dirt and her voice softened as she said, "Even nicer to be rid of that one—though I expect you to tell me what it cost, so I can repay you."

"I didn't do this for m—"

"I know. You did it for Viv." She studied him, her expression neutral. "Are you . . . are you two dating?"

He held up a hand. "No. Never have. We're friends—that's all." The firm tone of his voice surprised him. He cleared his throat and looked away. "After Evelyn passed, I moved back here for a fresh start. Cal and I both were having a hard time, and Viv helped us through it."

"How . . . if you don't mind my asking, how did you lose Evelyn?"

"Breast cancer." He rubbed his hands over his jeans. "She fought hard for a long time, but her body just wore out." A question formed in her eyes. One he thought he recognized and had contemplated in the past. "I don't think it's any easier either way."

Her brows rose.

"Knowing whether or not it's coming," he clarified.

Silence fell between them for a moment, and he reached into his back pocket and withdrew the sympathy card he'd failed to deliver earlier that morning.

"Here," he said, nudging it toward her with an awkward hand. "I never know what to say . . ."

She set the flashlight on the ground and took the card. Smoothed her hand over her name, which he'd scrawled across the front of the envelope hours earlier. "Thank you." Her head dipped farther down, and she brushed one hand quickly across her cheek. "You and Evelyn were so happy the day you left. Of all the places you could've started over, why'd you choose to come back here?" She raised her head, and a polite mask was firmly back in place. "Was it because of your dad?"

He nodded. "And yours."

"Mine?" Her head tilted as she asked, "Because of my dad?"

He smiled. "Yeah. I remember the first day I spoke to

him—and you. I don't remember how old we were, but we were definitely young. You were still sporting a braid, and my mom had just taken off." His mouth twisted. "I was angry back then. Sat on our dock for hours on end. Saw you and your dad floating by on that boat every day. I was so jealous I could barely see straight."

She looked skeptical. "Jealous of us?"

"Jealous of how happy y'all were. How carefree. You were always smiling back then." The sad gleam in her eyes made him ache. He leaned closer. "That day I was sitting on our dock and you came prancing up yours right back there"—he pointed toward the back of Teague Cottage— "lugging a bucket almost bigger than you. It was filled to the brim with oysters. I kept thinking, How in the world did she pull all those jokers out of that creek?" Beau smiled at the memory. "And your dad had his own big bucket. He strolled off that boat, strong and tall, smiling at you like he owned every treasure in the world. I've never forgotten that. It's part of what brought me back and led us to start the oyster farm."

"Led you to steal his business, you mean?" The gentle note in her voice had changed. Grown harder. "His daughter, too?"

"No. I wanted Cal to have that. I wanted to take him out on that creek like your dad did you and bring him back with that same kind of joy." He studied her face, and the hint of distrust in her expression sent a pang of loss through him. "It inspired me to do our part to protect the oyster population in Hope Creek. To use a sustainable method of harvesting them, and boost tourism to improve the economy. I never set out to do Royal any harm. Otherwise Viv would never have taken part in it."

"Forgive me, but that's a little hard to believe. And I'm not as easily persuaded as Viv."

He sighed. "Then I guess we'll just have to agree to disagree."

Kit remained quiet and stared at the new mailbox lying on the ground next to him.

"Well," he said, moving to pick up the flashlight, "I didn't come to start an argument, and that mailbox isn't gonna put itself up."

Kit beat him to it. "I'll hold the flashlight for you." She rubbed her forearm across her brow. "I'm not up for another argument today, either."

Beau resumed working, and with Kit's help, the new mailbox was securely in place less than fifteen minutes later.

She tested the door, opening and closing it several times, and a satisfied expression appeared on her face. "Thanks again. This was a generous gesture."

"You're welcome. You want me to get the old one out of your way?"

"No. I'll take care of that tomorrow."

"Good night, then." Beau grabbed his post hole digger and flashlight, then started up the dirt road. He paused to say over his shoulder, "There's a meeting next Monday night at the community center. Viv and I are looking to expand, and I'll be pitching our plan and sharing some ways our operation is having a positive impact on the island. It's at seven, and it'd be great if you could come. I'd love the opportunity to change your mind. That is, if you'll still be around then?"

"Will Viv be there?"

Considering the state she was in this morning? He shook his head. "I don't know."

Kit watched him silently for a moment, her expression guarded, then said, "I'll think about it."

* * *

*Please don't hesitate to call if there's anything I
can do.
Beau*

Kit read the sympathy card once more and looked out
the window of her childhood bedroom. The new mailbox,
sturdy and clean, stood proud among the weeds in the
morning light, making the overgrown front lawn look
even more unruly by comparison. But the spark of anger
that had assailed her at the sight of the vandalized mailbox
had eased, and strangely, just a glimpse of the new one
Beau had installed last night had lifted a tiny bit of the
weight that had pressed on her shoulders since she'd returned to Hope Creek.

It *had* been a generous gesture . . . no matter whom
Beau had done it for. And the tender note in his voice last
night when he'd spoken of Cal and Evelyn had stirred a
familiar longing deep in her core. A bittersweet flutter
comprised of a speck of hope and a bushel of disappointment—the same emotion that had hung over her years
ago, every time she'd admired Beau from afar.

He'd changed. That clean-cut boyish face was now
lined with blond stubble; his trim, model-like frame had
filled out with hard muscle; the look in his blue eyes
seemed sharper, keener; and his smile had roughened, the
tempting curve of his mouth not bending as fully or as easily as it had in the past.

Her mouth twisted. What an aggravation her crush on
Beau Sutton had been. Back then his mere presence had
been enough to turn her head and lift her eyes his way, and
even though she'd told herself he was just a boy—and,
eventually, just a man—like any other, her heart had
fought hard against letting the dream of him go.

Viv had noticed him, too, and the same admiration had lit her eyes as she'd watched Beau walk along the neighboring Sutton dock. She'd bumped her thigh against Kit's as they'd sat on the end of their own dock, her gaze still on Beau. "Imagine that," she'd whispered. "Sturdy, gorgeous, and safe . . ." She'd looked away, frowned at the cordgrass bending with the wind in the distance. "Ain't no chance of that."

But Kit had held on, all the way up to the day Beau had married Evelyn Hampton. That had made letting go of the dream easier. No less painful, she supposed, but easier.

Only, it'd surprised her to discover that Beau had noticed her at least once. Even more so to hear him say he'd been jealous of Royal . . . and her.

You were always smiling back then.

The sad fact being that she had—at some point over the years—stopped smiling. As had Royal . . . and Viv.

She shook her head slightly, placed the sympathy card on the nightstand beside her bed, and refocused on the new mailbox. That one tiny improvement highlighted the plethora of other imperfections around Teague Cottage: the knee-high weeds, forestlike grass, and banged-up screen enclosing the front porch. Not to mention the inside . . .

Kit left the window and frowned at the twin beds occupying the room. Only one—Viv's—had been made up with sheets and a quilt, but a thin coating of dust on the headboard and quilt hinted that the bed had been left unoccupied for quite some time. The second bed had been stripped and the mattress left bare, and a pile of dirty clothes, out-of-date magazines, and old wadded-up newspapers cluttered it from one end to the other.

Clearly, at some point over the years, Viv had decided to strip Kit's bed and put it to good use.

Kit rubbed the back of her neck and made a mental note

to dig through her childhood belongings, which Viv had shoved into one of the closets. She needed to locate her pillow. Viv's bed had been good enough to crash on the past two nights, but her pillow was too firm for Kit's liking and had left her with a headache two mornings in a row now.

She left the bedroom and walked to Royal's room, resisting the urge to glance at the closed door that led to the guest bedroom. Down the hall, in the kitchen, pots and pans clanged, a sure sign Mackey was awake and tackling breakfast.

The door to Royal's bedroom was ajar, and she nudged it open. He lay on the bed amid the rumpled sheets, just as he had for most of the two days since her return. With the exception of the two hours they'd spent on the water, spreading Sylvie's ashes and saying their silent goodbyes.

"Dad." She walked over to the bed and touched his shoulder. "Wake up."

He grunted, and his heavy eyelids opened for a brief moment to glance at her face; then he rolled over and presented his back to her. "Go 'way. It's too early."

"No, it's not." She propped her foot on the edge of the bed and bounced the mattress, watching as his wiry frame was jostled. "Get up."

"Get out."

Kit crossed the room, flung the curtains open, and spun back around as morning sunlight flooded the room.

Royal threw his hand up and sucked in a strong breath, his bloodshot eyes blinking rapidly. "Didn't I tell you to get out?"

"Yep."

"Then why ain't you?"

"Because the sun's up, the air's cool, and the tide's high. I'm sick to death of dog cheese—though God love Mackey for feeding us—and I'm ready to hit the creek, reach a good spot by the time the water runs low, and hammer out some fresh nourishment." She motioned toward her high boots, ripped jeans, and worn T-shirt. "I'm dressed for the occasion and raring to go, which means all that's left is for you to do the same."

He scowled. "No chance of that. I'm tir—"

"You're not tired, Dad." She walked over and looked down at him, and his frail appearance tugged hard at her heart. "You're depressed. And you won't get any better wallowing around in this bed every day." She reached out with a tentative hand and smoothed a dingy lock of hair from his hot forehead. "You need fresh air and sunshine. You need to lift your chin, open your eyes, and breathe. It won't fix everything, but it might help you feel better for now."

His hand curled around her wrist. Tremors ran through his fingers. "I miss her so much it hurts to breathe."

"I know," she whispered. "But she's not in this house anymore." An ache bled through her as images warred in her mind: one of hard wires on floating cages and one of gray ash spreading peacefully below the water. "Closest place to her now is on the creek. Like it or not, we're going. You don't have to do a thing. You don't even have to get off the boat if you don't want."

"And Mackey?"

"He's going, too. I'm headed his way soon as I see you walk into that bathroom and turn on the shower."

One corner of his mouth hitched. "Ain't no way you'll get that boy outta that kitchen."

"Want to watch me?"

He released her wrist and dragged a hand through his hair. "No. Lord knows, I ain't up for that."

She swept her arm toward the en suite bathroom. "Whenever you're ready."

It took several minutes, but Royal slung his legs, one at a time, over the edge of the bed, put his feet on the floor, and hobbled into the bathroom. Once inside, he leaned heavily into the shower, placed one hand flat against the wall, and turned the faucet on with the other. He shivered when water shot out and splashed onto his bare shoulder.

He made a face. "You gonna stand there and watch me strip down to my unmentionables, too, girl?"

Kit smiled. A real honest-to-goodness smile that lifted her spirits. "Heck, no. I sure ain't up for that."

Reasonably assured Royal would emerge from his room clean and dressed within the hour, she made her way to the kitchen and met a more formidable opponent.

"No!" Mackey stomped his bare foot and stabbed a spatula in the air. "That ain't how we do it. I cook the breakfast, take a bowl to Dad, then sit on the porch. That's how the morning goes."

"I know, but not today," Kit said gently. "Today we're going to do something different. We're going to take Dad out on the boat, and I'm going to hammer out some oysters, then roast 'em up for lunch. And after that, I'll need help cutting the grass."

He frowned, looked at the spatula in his hand, then back at Kit. "But I make the dog cheese." He pointed toward the front door. "And then I sit in the chair."

"Yes, I know. You've made a ton of dog cheese." She gestured toward the fridge. "There's enough leftovers in there to last us a week. And you've also done plenty of sitting lately."

"I stay here, make dog cheese, and sit."

"I'd like you to go with us. It'll be good for all of us to do this together, and a dose of sunlit salt water will do you good." She smiled. "Please, Mackey."

"No."

"Please."

"Don't want to."

"But I'd like you to."

"Don't care what you like."

"Mackey." Kit firmed her voice and tugged at the spatula in his fist. "You can't live off just dog cheese. You need to eat something healthier and get some exercise for a change. You're getting on the boat, eating a nutritious lunch, then cutting the grass with me, and that's that."

An hour later, after two rounds of spatula wrestling with Mackey and one more argument with Royal, Kit boarded the boat with both men . . . though they made it clear they weren't excited about the arrangement.

Mackey sat on the bench seat beside Royal and glared at Kit as she sat at the helm. "How long you staying?"

Royal guffawed and slung an arm around Mackey's shoulders. "You tell her, son. She ought not be messing with our routine, had she?"

"Yes, I should," Kit said, glancing over her shoulder. "Especially when the routine isn't doing either of you any good."

Smile vanishing, Royal looked down as Mackey snuggled against his side, then laid his cheek on top of Mackey's head, hugged him closer, and closed his eyes.

Kit, blinking back tears, faced forward, started the engine, and eased the hybrid bay boat out into the creek. As they passed the Sutton dock, Beau, Viv, and Cal were in the process of boarding one of the Suttons' large hybrid boats.

The passage of Royal's smaller boat caught Beau's eye, and he looked up, smiled, and waved one hand in the air. Cal followed suit, though somewhat hesitantly. Viv, however, froze, one leg propped on the edge of Beau's boat and one on the dock, and stared.

Kit stared back, her breath catching at the restrained

fury in Viv's expression. It was, at least, nice to see some fire in her eyes rather than the dull numbness that had resided there when she'd first arrived home yesterday morning.

"Viv!" Mackey shouted from the bench seat. "I didn't let Kit in. She broke in. She a burglar. Make her go."

Cheeks heating, Kit tossed a stern look his way.

Mackey stuck out his tongue and burrowed deeper into Royal's side. Royal, glowering in Viv's direction, turned away from the Suttons' dock and stared straight ahead as the creek curved around a thick mound of cordgrass.

The wind picked up as the boat rounded the bend, and salty air ruffled Kit's hair, lifting it off her shoulders and slapping it against her back in a rhythmic motion. Soon, the creek widened, seagulls' cries filled the air, and floating cages emerged.

Kit swallowed hard, tightened her grip on the steering wheel until her nails bit into her palms. She glanced at Royal. His shoulders sagged and his cheeks paled as his gaze fixed on the cages.

"We'll move past them soon," Kit called over her shoulder, seeking solace in the words. Trying hard to believe them. "Then it's clear open water."

Kit drove on for several more miles, then slowed as a patch of mud emerged near the creek's shore. Dense clusters of jagged shells jutted up, their damp edges glistening amid the rippling sunlit waters. The sight of the oyster beds perked Mackey right up.

"Oysters!" Mackey sprang out of Royal's arms and off the bench seat and rubbed his hands together briskly. "I get the first one, huh, Kit? I want to get the first one."

"Oh, so you forgive me now?" She glanced over her shoulder and raised an eyebrow. "For dragging you out of the house and being a burglar and all?"

Mackey thought it over, his brow furrowing as he studied her, then the oyster bed. He bit his nail. "Yes. I for-give you."

"Then it's all yours, bud." She slowed the boat, cut the engine, and tossed Mackey a pair of gloves. "Mackey and I are gonna grab lunch. You feel like wading out with us, Dad?"

Royal didn't respond. Instead, he tried—and failed—to give them a small smile.

Kit walked to the back of the boat and knelt in front of him. "I know this is hard. But I promise, the scariest part is here"—she touched the center of Royal's chest gently—"not on this creek." She looked up and studied the sorrow-filled lines of his expression. "Do you remember the first time you brought me out here?"

His gaze fixed on Mackey, who leapt off the boat, landed on his hands and knees in the mud, and squealed with glee.

"Come on, Dad!" Mackey laughed as he sank, the sticky pluff mud oozing up over his knees and elbows. "Get the oysters."

Kit smiled. "I don't remember much about the first time you brought me out here—I was so young—but I remember everything looked so big to me," she continued. "So huge. The sky . . . the creek . . . the oyster beds. I remember leaning over the boat and asking you how deep Hope Creek was. Do you remember what you told me?" She leaned closer. Cupped his cheek. "You said Hope runs deep. Deeper than—"

"The lowest you could ever go," he finished for her softly. His dark gaze shifted, meeting hers, and his chin trembled.

Kit smiled gently, then stood and tugged on one glove after the other. "You don't have to move a finger. You can sit right here and watch me and Mackey, but I want you talking while we work. I want you to tell me every single thing you know about Pearl Tide Oyster Company and Beau Sutton. Where all he's growing, where he plans to expand, what he's shifting locally, and how much he's making. And then I want you to tell me Viv's role in it. Every detail, no matter how small."

Royal blinked and refocused on her face, confusion in his eyes. "Why?"

"Because I'm going to get your business and my sister back. And the best way to do both," Kit said, "is through Beau."

CHAPTER 5

Hope Creek Community Center had always been smaller than most. The aged structure, equipped with linoleum floors, wood paneling, and metal folding chairs, had a seating capacity of 110, but Monday night's meeting hosted by Pearl Tide Oyster Company had packed the joint, leaving standing room only.

"I can't believe you invited Kit."

Beau handed pamphlets to three stragglers, thanked them for coming, then glanced at Viv. She stood on the other side of the entrance, opposite him, pamphlets clutched tightly in one hand and an agitated expression on her face.

"Relax," he said quietly. "It's not that big a deal, and besides"—he motioned over his shoulder at the packed crowd—"unless I overlooked her, she hasn't shown."

Which, if he were being honest, disappointed him more than he'd expected.

It'd been one week and two days (not that he was counting) since Kit had returned to Hope Creek, and each time he'd passed Teague Cottage on his way to deliver bushels of oysters to restaurants or run errands, he'd hoped—fruitlessly—to stumble upon her again. Maybe enjoy another quiet exchange with those soulful eyes of hers on him.

But it hadn't happened. Instead, each time he'd passed, the yard had been empty and something had changed. The first time, it'd been the front lawn. The weeds that choked the old mailbox had vanished, and the sea of grass had been hacked back down to a respectable height and sported the fresh, clean lines left behind by a mower.

The second change had been the railing on the front porch steps. It no longer leaned to one side or dangled precariously on the edge of the steps. Someone had applied a fresh coat of paint and bolted it down. The third change had been the application of classy bronze street numbers to the new mailbox he'd installed, providing an elegant contrast to its midnight tone. And lastly—and most notably for Beau—someone had parked a muddy sedan with a North Carolina tag in the driveway, behind Royal's rusty truck.

Beau smiled. He hadn't gotten an answer from Kit regarding how long she planned to stay on the island, but having her car ferried over to Hope Creek was a promising sign that she planned to stick around for a while. So was the sight of her boating past his dock every morning for the past week, with Royal and Mackey at her side. Something that had set Viv's teeth—and temper—on edge.

"If she were here." Viv's eyes were on him, narrowed and pensive.

"I'm sorry. What'd you say?"

"I said"—a slight bite entered her tone as she leaned against the doorjamb and crossed her arms—"if Kit were here, you'd know it. She might be quiet and shy, but she's no pushover, and it'd be a mistake to underestimate her."

Beau leaned in. Was that . . . admiration in her eyes? A hint of a grin curving her lips?

"She'd have planted herself at the front of the room," Viv continued, "by the mic, prepared to verbally drag us both in front of everyone and their brother."

Beau shook his head. "I doubt that." Leaning closer, he lowered his voice. "And it would've been a mistake not to invite her. Royal has been—and still is—the most vocal opponent to our expansion." He glanced around, surprised the older man hadn't shown up himself tonight. But with the recent loss of Sylvie, he could understand the other man's absence. "Kit grew up on that creek just like you did, and for all we know, she might be inclined to hear us out. It's in our best interest to engage her in the discussion. If she's able to see the benefits in what we're doing, she may be able to sway your dad."

"Unlike me, you mean?" Viv grew quiet as she straightened and picked at the edge of a pamphlet.

"No." Wincing, he touched her arm. "I didn't mean that at all."

"It's true." She dragged her teeth over her bottom lip. "Dad always listened to her—never me. Kit's his quiet, mild-mannered, successful daughter, whereas I'm the crass, loudmouthed heathen who'll never amount to anything."

He squeezed her shoulder gently. "Viv, we've all got rough edges, and a person would be hard pressed to find someone with as big a heart or as bright a mind as yours."

"Tell that to my dad." She straightened and slapped the pamphlets against her thigh. "Doesn't matter, anyway. All three of us went our own way years ago, and what I do now is none of their business." She smiled, reached over, and placed her hand on his. "What *we* do is none of their business, and I swear I won't let you down."

"I know." He slid his hand away, his chest tightening, as her smile slipped. "After tonight, Pearl Tide Oyster Company will be well on its way to expansion. And I never would've gotten it off the ground without your guidance . . . and friendship."

Her mouth firmed, and she looked out at the empty walkway leading to the community center's entrance. "Looks like we've got all the folks we're gonna have." Her smile returned—dim but sincere—a welcome change from the sadness that had clung to her over the past week. She shut one of the wide double doors, then proceeded to close the other. "Let's get this party started."

Kit was late—just as she had been all day. She stood outside the Hope Creek Community Center, her hand on the doorknob, and listened to the low, muted tones of someone speaking inside. She glanced over her shoulder at the dirt road behind her, which was growing increasingly dark as twilight set in, and wished for the thousandth time that Royal had joined her.

He'd refused, of course, having chosen instead to ease back in one of the two recliners in the living room—Mackey had taken up residence in the other—with a beer in one hand and a plate of fresh oysters on the half shell in the other.

"I've done all the arguing with Viv that I'm gonna do," he'd said before turning on the TV and dismissing Kit.

She hadn't been completely disappointed. How could she when Royal had boarded the boat almost every morning over the past week to harvest wild oysters, had helped her and Mackey manicure the front lawn, and had offered a begrudging commentary of "It's all right, I guess," as he'd passed the new mailbox on the mower?

Heck, tonight had been a major breakthrough: Royal had actually left his bedroom to enjoy his dinner in the presence of another living, breathing human for a change. Which had been a bittersweet moment, considering the commercial season for harvesting wild oysters would officially end within the next month. There'd be little chance of fishing fresh oysters from the creek unless the season was extended, which, considering two state shellfish grounds had already been closed as a result of increased bacteria levels, was a long shot at best.

Warm sun and fresh air had done her dad a world of good, but the grief that still hung on him signaled he had a long way to go.

Kit inhaled, filling her lungs with clean salty air, opened the door, and walked inside the community center.

"Addition of acreage would allow us to expand, thereby enabling us to supply local restaurant owners"—Beau stood behind a podium at the front of the room, beside a screen on which images of oysters cages were being projected, and gestured toward a man in the front row—"like Tip Allen here, with fresh, flavorful, locally harvested oysters of consistent quality on a routine basis."

Heads nodded around the packed room, accompanied by murmurs of agreement. Only a few faces frowned, and Kit took comfort in them before refocusing on Beau.

"Consistent?" she called out.

Beau paused, his strong hands returning to the podium, long fingers gripping the sides, as he scanned the room for the source of the voice.

Kit eased around the couple standing in front of her and stood behind the last row of people seated in chairs. "As in predictable?"

Rustles and low whispers rolled around the room. She felt eyes on her from every direction but maintained her focus on the podium.

Beau found her, and his eyes locked with hers. "Yes. Consistent." He smiled. "And—if you prefer the term— predictable."

The kindness in his warm smile and blue eyes warmed her chest. She shifted her weight from one leg to the other as a movement to his right caught her eye.

Viv, seated in a folding chair to Beau's left, scooted to the edge of the chair, propped her elbows on her knees, and tilted her head as she met Kit's gaze, a warning in her eyes.

Her expression was still drawn, but her cheeks held more color than the last time Kit had seen her. More than likely gleaned from the sun during endless hours on the creek, venting her anger at Kit's return. That, at least, was a relief.

"Predictable," Kit repeated, lifting her chin at Viv. "So local restaurant owners like Tip Allen, to use your example, would be able to count on your deliveries of fresh crop with predictable regularity." She returned her attention to Beau. "Do you think of the weather as being predictable?"

Beau shook his head. "Certainly not, which is why we prepare for any eventuality."

"Like, say"—Kit shrugged—"rip currents during a hurricane or storm surge?"

"Yes. Our operation is equipped with long lines that allow us to sink the cages to the bottom to ride out storms and avoid damage."

"And the point of tonight's meeting is to convince Hope Creek residents—restaurant owners, especially—that it's in their best interests for you to expand, right? To secure a permit to add around, oh, up to seven hundred fifty more cages to the seven hundred or so you already operate?"

"Yes, that's right." Beau grinned. "Again."

Kit bristled. "How many people does Pearl Tide Oyster Company currently employ, Mr. Sutton?"

His grin faded as he studied her face. "Three."

"And those people would be . . . ?"

"Myself, Nate Sutton . . ." His hands slid over the podium. Fiddled with a stack of pamphlets on one side. "And Viv Teague."

"All of whom are already tending to the first crop."

"Yes, that—"

"Wasn't a question." Firming her tone, she asked, "How many hours do you and your coworkers spend on the water each day tending the crop you already have?"

His jaw clenched. "Assuming that was a question, the answer is that there's no fixed amount of time. We work as long as it takes."

"And, presumably, it'd take all hands on deck to lower the crop you already have to the bottom of the creek to prepare for a storm surge or an unexpected weather event. So, who would that leave to protect the new crop in a crisis?"

Viv shot to her feet, anger flashing in her eyes. "Our presentation, which you interrupted, is ongoing. A question-and-answer session follows afterward. Please reserve your questions until that time."

"Why?" Kit locked her knees and ignored the tremors running through her legs. "I don't see that my concern, or that of restaurant owners like Tip Allen, who'll be dependent upon Mr. Sutton's assurance that the production of quality crops will be consistent and predictable, will be assuaged in any way by an hour filled with slideshows and empty promises."

"Empty promises?" Viv stepped forward. "Why don't you ask Tip Allen how much he made last month off Pearl Tide's deep-cup singles?" She motioned toward the man in the front row. "Go ahead. Tell her, Tip."

Tip Allen's head moved from Viv to Kit, then back. "A-a lot."

"More than you made from other locals dealing in wild oysters?" Viv prompted.

Kit's face flamed.

" 'Bout five times more," Tip squeaked, glancing at Kit.

"Five times more than what you'd typically make off"—Viv spread her hands—"Royal Teague's clusters?"

"And what did it cost the rest of you?" Kit eyed the crowd, focusing on seated and standing members who looked skeptical. "How many of you who are traditional fishermen, like my father, have gone bankrupt or seen your business fall apart? How many acres of Hope Creek that the rest of you used to enjoy recreationally have been lost to Pearl Tide's commercial development? How many more will you lose if Mr. Sutton secures another permit to expand? Not to mention the effects of the cages on wildlife, like the dolphins that play along the creek's shores. Their effects on Hope Creek's aesthetic? Its natural, untarnished beaut—"

"Which is slowly diminishing every day, along with the wild oyster population?" Beau's voice hardened as he rounded the podium and faced her head-on. "Traditional fishermen like Royal Teague, using unsustainable harvest methods, have overharvested from Hope Creek and other tidal waters in our area and are direct contributors to the decline of our wild oyster population, as are pollution from coastal property development and wake from the heavy boat traffic of Hope Creek residents enjoying recreational pursuits. Those contributing factors, coupled with the fact that our state has a deficit in shell recycling numbering in the thousands, necessitate change to protect what's left of our local oyster population. Pearl Tide Oyster Company's harvesting methods are sustainable, economically beneficial, and environmentally safe—none of which can be said for the outdated and harmful practices of traditional fishermen."

Angry grumblings swelled around the room. The doors of the community center banged open as four men and three women standing toward the back of the room exited. Several more people seated throughout the room stood up, glared at Beau, then left, as well.

An awkward silence descended over the community center, the only sounds being the scrape of chairs across the floor, a few more heavy footsteps toward the door, and two sporadic coughs among the small group of people that still remained seated.

After glancing around the room, Beau ducked his head and dragged a hand through his thick blond hair, his handsome face flushing. "I . . . It wasn't my intention to offend anyone. I'm sorry if I . . ."

Kit tensed as his blue eyes focused on her. Regret and embarrassment darkened the blue depths, which had settled on her so warmly when she'd arrived. She looked down, her cheeks heating, as he floundered for words.

"If we could just . . ." Beau returned to the podium, straightened the stack of pamphlets, then cleared his throat. "If there are no additional questions at this time, I'd like to proceed with the presentation as planned, with a question-and-answer session to follow."

Kit couldn't look up. Couldn't face the hurt in Beau's eyes, the fury in Viv's expression, or the disgruntled glare on Tip Allen's face as he continued to stare back at her. Though she was already thoroughly ashamed of having boxed Beau into a corner, she took the easy way out and slipped through the door.

Last night had been an unmitigated disaster.

Beau loaded the last of several cages onto the hybrid bay

boat, then stepped back and dragged a hand over the back of his neck. Hours of dragging oysters out of the water and sifting through pile after pile of bivalves, collecting marketable singles, packing them in climate-controlled storage, and loading the rest back on the boat for return to the creek had strained every muscle in his body to exhaustion today. And rather than quieting his unwelcome thoughts, the day spent handling cages had only amplified them.

Viv, seated at the helm of the boat, watched as he stretched his neck from side to side. "You still doubt me?"

He raised his brows.

"About Kit." Satisfaction flashed over her expression. "I told you not to underestimate her."

He narrowed his eyes at the horizon and watched as the late afternoon sun dipped below the distant waters of Hope Creek. "I'm not in the mood for *told you so*s, Viv. I made a complete fool of not only myself last night but our fledgling business, too."

Viv made a face. "*You* didn't. Kit did. You didn't do anything wrong. All you did was tell the truth."

"Yeah." He rested one hand on his hip and fanned his T-shirt away from his chest with the other. "And I said it in a way that made half the population of Hope Creek think I look down on traditional fishermen, which, I'd like to state for the record, I *do not*."

"No one will think that."

"Oh, they already do. That's why half the people in that community center last night walked out before I even finished the presentation."

Beau stifled a curse. Of all the times to lose his temper . . . Why couldn't he have just let Kit work out whatever grudge she held against him, thanked her for sharing her concerns, then regrouped and carried on as planned without making a scene?

He knew why. Because her stubborn, righteous indignation rankled him—as did her lack of neighborly courtesy. If she disagreed that strongly with what he was doing, the least she could've done was attempt to discuss the situation like a civil adult the night he'd stopped by her dad's house a week ago. She'd had all the opportunity in the world to ask her questions while he'd unboxed, assembled, and installed a brand-new mailbox for her family's benefit. She could've voiced her misgivings and sought insight into what he was doing then.

But no. She chose to make a grand entrance into the community center, then cause a scene of reputation-crushing proportions.

"Well . . ." Viv tapped the steering wheel with the heel of her palm. "I told you not to invite h—"

"Once again"—Beau slashed a hand through the air—"I'm not interested in *told you so*s today."

Viv narrowed her eyes. "And I'm not in the mood to be snapped at. So if you want me to float this boat back out on the creek and drop these cages in the water, you'd better ask me nicely."

A stifled giggle sounded at his back.

Beau spun around and frowned at Cal, who stood farther down the dock, beside Nate, amid several buckets of deep-cup singles.

"You got a vein bulging in your neck, Dad." Cal laughed again.

Nate grinned. "And if you yell at Viv again, she'll probably shove you off that dock and into the creek to cool you off."

Viv smiled sweetly. "The thought has crossed my mind."

"Oh, y'all think this is funny?" Beau waved his hand in

the air again. "Go ahead and laugh. Get a real good giggle, because I'll expect all of you to keep on smiling when we're denied a permit to expand."

"Not gonna happen," Viv said. "We've got two years of experience under our belt, our data is great, our plan is as near perfect as you can get, and we don't need anyone's approval other than the Department of Natural Resources."

"Maybe," Beau said, "but proving your operation has adequate personnel to support it is part of the process of securing a permit. Quite frankly, Kit had a point last night when she asked about that. Plus, after last night's debacle, I'm not sure too many folks will be clamoring at the gate to apply for a position. Not if it might end up costing them their reputation as decent citizens, and certainly not if the future success of our business is in question, which—after last night's debacle—it probably is."

Viv dragged her hand through her hair. "Just try your best to wipe last night from your memory. I'll work on reserving another venue. Tip Allen's restaurant, maybe? He's definitely on our side. And we'll pitch our plan again. One good presentation is all we need."

Beau blew out a heavy breath. "All right. I'll try." He gestured toward the creek. "You best get those cages back in the water. You've had a long day, and it'll be dark soon. You need to eat dinner and get a decent night's rest if you're going to be any use to me tomorrow."

Viv pursed her lips, a teasing light shining in her eyes. "Only if I get a please."

"Please." He headed up the dock, then stopped, turned back, and summoned a half-hearted smile. "And thank you."

Viv laughed and cranked the engine. "That's the ticket."

Moments later, the steady whir of the boat's engine faded as Viv floated down the creek. Beau joined Cal and

Nate, grabbed a bucket of oysters in each hand, ignoring the dull ache in his muscles, and headed up the dock toward the small climate-controlled storage building nearby.

"Hold up there, son," Nate said. He motioned toward the front gate. "There's another Teague over there, and I'm thinking she's either here for you or Viv."

Beau glanced at the gate, and sure enough, Kit stood on the other side. As she craned her neck and stole glimpses through the gaps in the ornate bars, she caught Beau's eyes on her and lifted her hand in a weak wave.

"Good Lord above," Beau groaned, his temper sparking. "Last night wasn't enough?"

"I told you . . ." Nate lifted one shoulder as Beau glared in his direction. "Last thing you need is to get yourself stuck in the middle of Teague troubles." He pointed his left hand at the gate, his right at the creek, then both at Beau. "And look where you are."

Beau bit his lower lip and held his tongue, watching as Nate relieved him of the buckets and headed toward the storage building.

"Come on, Cal," Nate called over his shoulder. "I expect your dad will want to have this conversation in private."

Cal was craning his neck, too, straining for a clearer glimpse of Kit on the other side of the closed gate. "Why can't I meet her, too? Y'all are always shov—"

"Do what you were told, Cal," Beau said. "Grab a pair of buckets and go. Those things aren't gonna carry themselves, and you still have to tackle homework after we finish."

Cal snatched up two buckets and frowned at Beau. "I'm sick of school and work, school and work, school and work. We never do anything but work. We haven't been fishing in months or done anything else fun. I'm sick to death of work."

Beau sighed. "Cal, I mean it—"

"Yeah, yeah." Cal kicked a bucket. "I know."

Cal grumbled something else under his breath as he left. Something that included several insults regarding Beau's intelligence, but Beau didn't have the energy to reprimand him for this.

Beau waited until he and Nate were out of earshot before walking over to the gate with his hands shoved in his pockets. "What? No bat?"

Kit blushed, her dark eyes meeting his hesitantly. "I'm sorry."

"For what?" He tilted his head, eyed her face through the gaps in the iron bars and registered the rosy color darkening her cheeks, the slight tremble in her lower lip, and the slow lowering of her thick lashes. She at least had the decency to appear ashamed.

"For everything."

Beau narrowed his eyes. "Well, now, that covers a lot of ground. Doesn't narrow things down. Doesn't really tell me what you're sorry f—"

"I'm sorry for interrupting your presentation last night." She lifted her head and met his eyes. "I'm sorry for putting you on the spot, embarrassing you in front of a bunch of people, and maybe even throwing a wrench in your business plan." Her voice shook. She lowered her head again and picked at her nails. "Especially after you were so kind to me."

She'd left her hair loose today. It spilled over her shoulders, brushed her flushed cheeks, and one long strand had caught on the pink curve of her lower lip, drawing his eyes. With her downcast gaze, trembling voice, and nervous movements . . . she looked more gentle, soft, and vulnerable than ever. Reminiscent of her manner when she'd arrived over a week ago, dark eyes full of tears and hesitant voice tinged with pain as she'd asked for his help.

He jerked his head back and closed his mouth. Really? Was she serious? The woman had no right coming here after what she'd done last night. She'd humiliated him in front of an audience. Questioned his professional knowledge, preparation, and capabilities. Had as good as stabbed him in the back after he'd—as she'd so elegantly put it—been *kind* to her. Not to mention the mailbox. He hadn't had to do that. Most people wouldn't have bothered, but he'd done it. For her—no, for Viv. And despite all of that, here she was, actually thinking she could just apologize and he'd—

"Would you open the gate so I can apologize properly?" She moved closer, those big eyes gazing up at him through a gap in the iron bars. "Please?"

He flexed his jaw. Stared down at her a moment more, then opened the gate.

She hesitated on the open threshold of his property, studying his expression, then touched his bare forearm. "I *am* sorry, Beau." Her hand left him, and he missed the slight pressure and warmth of her touch. "You're a good man," she whispered. "A good man with a good heart. I shouldn't have set out to hurt you the way I did."

Pleasure whispered through him. He rolled his shoulders and looked away. Focused on the spill of golden sunlight through the low oaks lining the dirt road. "Then why did you?"

"Because you hold my father's business—and my sister—in your hands," she said quietly. "And my family is important to me. More than anything—or anyone—else."

Then why did you leave? Beau stifled the question as Viv's words returned. *Kit's a coward. She has no soul.*

He refocused on Kit's face, and the sincerity in her expression relaxed him slightly. "And I should believe what you're saying because . . . ?"

"Because I owe you the truth." She rubbed her forehead. "Because I wasn't really after you last night. I was after Viv. And I should've handled it better. I just . . . I feel like she's forgotten where she came from. Maybe even who she is, and I wanted to . . ." She spread her hands, searching for the right words.

"You wanted to remind her?" he prompted.

Kit nodded. "Yeah. That's what I wanted." She grimaced, her gaze straying beyond him toward the house at his back, resentment in her eyes. "Though I don't think it worked."

Beau blew out a heavy breath and leaned against the open gate. "Are we so different, Kit?"

She frowned up at him. "What do you mean?"

"Suttons and Teagues. I mean, forget the houses we live in. Forget the paths we've taken over the years. Forget the baggage we both carry." He motioned over his shoulder. "Years ago, I sat on my dock and you sat on yours, and we both admired the same creek. We both lost something here years ago, and we're both still trying to get it back. Is what we want so different?"

She contemplated this for a few moments, then said, "Yes. In a lot of ways."

He glanced back at the house, recalling the disappointment in Cal's expression as he'd carried buckets to the storage building. Thought of the hours he'd spent away from Cal more often than not lately, sorting singles, crunching numbers, and planning the next day's work. Remembered the bright smiles on Kit's and Royal's faces as they'd hauled buckets up their dock all those years ago.

He tipped his chin at Kit. "Then show me."

She blinked up at him, her brow furrowing. "What do you mean?"

"Take me out on that water and show me how different we are."

CHAPTER 6

Saturday morning Beau stood in front of Teague Cottage with a pair of gloves in one hand and an empty bucket in the other.

"Are we going in?" Cal asked. He stood by Beau's side, holding his own pair of gloves and an empty bucket, but rather than the disgruntled expression he'd sported earlier in the week, a smile lifted his cheeks and excitement gleamed in his eyes.

"Nah."

As pleased as he was with Cal's eagerness for the day's outing, Beau still cringed at the potential consequences of entering Royal's home. The older man might glare him down, snap a string of curses, or heave Beau through the nearest unopened window.

"No," Beau repeated firmly. "We'll wait for Kit here."

Hopefully, she'd be out soon. The idea of Royal catching him loitering on his property, with or without Kit's invitation, wasn't very appealing.

"How far out is she taking us?" Cal looked up at him, his smile wide.

Beau shrugged. "She didn't say."

As a matter of fact, Kit hadn't specified today's destination or provided details of the trip on the evening she'd stood outside Nate's gate, contemplating Beau's challenge. She'd simply stared at him for a couple of minutes, glanced once more at his house, then turned on her heel and said over her shoulder, "Be at my place at seven thirty sharp on Saturday morning."

"I'd liked to bring my son, if that's okay with you?" he'd asked.

"That's okay with me," she'd called back as she'd walked away.

And the date had been set.

Beau grinned. Not that he'd call this a date per se. It was more of a neighborly outing. One offering clean spring air, warm sun, and a lengthy opportunity to spend quality time with Cal. Kit's presence, her soft gaze, gentle voice, and pretty smile? Beau's grin grew. Well, they were just bonu—

The front door creaked open, and Royal stepped out onto the porch.

Beau's grin died. "We'll wait for Kit on the dock." He started up the driveway and motioned for Cal to follow.

"But you said—"

"Never mind what I said." Beau reached back and tugged Cal's arm, pulling him forward a few steps. "Come on. Pick up the pace."

Beau continued walking up the driveway, resisting the urge to hurry, and even found the gumption to pause, turn back and offer a friendly smile at Royal. "Morning, Royal."

The older man glared at him, a hard warning in his eyes.

Cal, oblivious to the tension and having had good manners instilled in him since birth, stopped by Beau's side, faced Royal and grinned. "Morning, sir. Thank you for inviting us."

Royal withdrew a cigar and match from his back pocket, struck the match on a rough wooden post on the porch, and lit the cigar with the match, drawing deeply on it. "I didn't."

Cal lifted his hand against the bright morning sun that peeked over the roof and squinted. "Didn't what, sir?"

"Invite you," Royal grunted. He took another deep pull on the cigar, then exhaled, blowing a thick cloud of smoke in Beau's direction.

"Either way," Beau said stiffly, "thank you all the same." He nudged Cal farther up the driveway. "Go on, son."

Once they cleared the backyard—which Beau noticed had been cut recently—the Teague's dock emerged into view, and Kit stood at the end of it, waving them over.

"Who's on the boat with her?" Cal asked, his step quickening.

Beau eyed the short man by Kit's side. He stared at them, both hands cupped above and around his eyes to block out the sun, as he leaned forward. "Her brother, most likely. Won't know 'til we get there."

Turned out the man was Kit's brother, and he was as excited for Cal to get on the boat as Cal was to be on it.

"That's Beau's son, ain't it?" Mackey shouted. He bounced in place twice as Kit confirmed it. "Hey, Cole."

"Cal," Kit corrected, smiling at Mackey. "His name is Cal."

"Hey, Cal," Mackey said. He repeated the name, rolling it over slowly on his tongue, seeming to commit it to memory, then stuck out his hand. "You shake my hand, Cal. That's so we meet."

Surprise and a tinge of confusion entered Cal's expression as he studied Mackey. He dropped his gloves in his bucket, then held out his hand. Mackey snatched it up in both of his and shook it vigorously, laughing.

"That's so we meet!" Mackey laughed. "That makes us friends."

Cal smiled, all six feet of his muscular frame jerking forward as Mackey pulled on his hand. "Yeah. What's your name?"

"Mackey." He grinned and, still gripping Cal's hand, backed toward one of the boats tied to the dock. "My name's Mackey. We met, so you can get on the boat with me now. We can hang out. Get oysters. And you can come over again one day. And I can go to your hous—"

"Slow down, Mackey." Kit halted him with a hand on his shoulder, then gently removed his grip on Cal's hand. "You always wait for an invitation to visit someone. And besides, I haven't met him yet."

Beau grinned, watching as Kit tilted her head back—Cal's head rose two inches higher than hers—and smiled.

"It's nice to meet you, Cal," she said softly. "I'm Kit." A sheepish expression crossed her face. "I'm sorry about the way we first stumbled upon each other. I didn't mean to startle you at the gate that day."

"N-no." Blushing, Cal shook his head . . . but his eyes remained glued to Kit's face. "I mean, that's no problem. No problem at all."

And just like that, his boy was gone. Kit's pretty eyes, gentle voice, and sweet smile had taken Cal in, stolen his attention, and enthralled him. Beau bit his lip as his grin widened. Man, he knew the feeling.

"I was wondering when you'd show."

Beau shifted his attention from Cal as Kit's gaze settled on him. "What do you mean?" He glanced at his wristwatch. "It's only seven thirty-eight, and we waited in the front yard for almost ten minutes. I assumed you'd be meeting us out there."

"Sorry about that. I guess eight minutes doesn't matter." Kit shrugged, dropped her head back, and glanced up at the clear blue sky. "Not today, anyway. It's a perfect morning for hitting the beds." She leaned to the side, looked past him. "Is Viv coming?"

Beau leaned into her line of sight. "What do you think?"

She straightened, a small sigh escaping her. "I think she probably gave you a hard time the moment you told her you were coming, and probably didn't let up until you were out of earshot." She scoffed. "She probably threw around a few choice words about me, too."

More than a few, Beau thought. He'd known the idea of his spending time with Kit wouldn't sit well with Viv, but she was behaving as though it was an act of outright betrayal.

Kit glanced at Cal, stepped to the side, and swept her arm in the direction of the hybrid bay boat. "Well, no need for us to wait any longer. Please come aboard and we'll head out."

Cal thanked her, then followed Mackey onto the bay boat. Mackey's voice grew louder and faster as he pointed out each seat on the boat and offered Cal first choice.

Beau glanced over his shoulder as he boarded, and noticed Royal standing on the back deck, a fresh stream of smoke drifting up above his head. Had Royal heard about his outburst at the community center? Had Kit told him the things he'd said? "Royal not coming?"

"What do you think?" Kit smirked.

"I'd say not." Beau turned away from Royal's steady perusal, his pride stinging a bit at Royal's disapproval, and faced Kit. "It's a bit early in the day to have a smoke, don't you think?"

Kit's lips twitched. "That's difference number one."

Beau frowned. "What is?"

"Smoking." Kit boarded the boat, sat at the helm, and cranked the engine. "Teagues smoke whenever they feel like it, no matter the occasion, time of day, or company."

Despite the warmth of the sun, a chill remained in the air, traveling on the swift breeze and slipping beneath the back of Beau's shirt as Kit drove the boat far out along Hope Creek. They passed the empty dock behind his house. He swiveled in the passenger seat, watched it as it faded behind them, and wondered how Nate and Viv had fared with deliveries this morning. Knowing he and Cal would take Saturday off, Beau had done his best to get a head start on deliveries throughout the week, but he hadn't made it much farther than usual. Same number of hands working the farm, same number of hours . . . His intentions didn't make much difference. Not without extra muscle behind them.

"Leave it," Kit said, her elbow nudging his.

He turned back around in his seat and glanced at her. She sat by his side, steering the boat, her long brown hair rippling in the wind. "Leave what?"

"All of it. Your business, your worries . . . There's no place for them out here." She inhaled deeply and released her breath slowly. "Just breathe and absorb."

A slow smile crossed her face as the boat gained speed, lurching rhythmically over waves and curving around deep bends in the creek. Dense cordgrass parted ahead, and the shores of the creek widened out as they reached the mouth of a neighboring river. The boat slowed to a crawl as a large oyster bed came into view, and Kit cut the engine. Low tide had arrived, and the biggest beauties of shells Beau had ever seen stood proud in tiny towers amid pluff mud, their dingy mouths raised toward the sky, a thick line of cordgrass bending in the wind at their backs.

"That's them over there," Mackey shouted from the bench seat in the back. He jogged around Beau to the bow of the boat, grabbed a pair of gloves, and tugged them on. "First one's mine. Cal, come on. And Beau, too."

"Slow down," Kit said, standing. "Let's scope it out first." She propped her hands on her hips and smiled.

"And when you have guests, the polite thing to do is offer them first choice of whatever it is you're doing. In this case, that would be harvesting the first oyster."

Mackey's exuberant smile fell. "Oh. But . . ." He patted his gloved hands together and stared longingly at the oyster bed. "I don't want to."

"I know." Kit walked over to Mackey, smoothed his bangs back, and kissed his forehead. "But when you care about someone, it's only right to be willing to sacrifice for them."

Her voice weakened, and her gaze moved outward before focusing on the horizon.

"But I want the first oyster." Mackey scowled up at her. "Can I still have the first one? Huh, Kit?"

She didn't answer, a sad—somewhat lost—look in her eyes.

Beau stood, then joined them at the bow of the boat. "Kit? You okay?"

Kit jerked her gaze away from the horizon and faced him. Her smile was forced. "Yeah. I forgot how beautiful it is out here. My mom loved it. She used to bring us here all the time."

Mackey looked down, his lips trembling. "Mama always let me have the first one."

"It's okay if Mackey gets the first oyster," Cal said, joining them at the bow and tugging on his gloves.

"See?" Mackey smiled again. "Cal said it's okay."

Kit rubbed her chin thoughtfully, a renewed smile returning to her mouth. "And what about Beau? What if he wants the first oyster?"

Mackey spun around and stared up at Beau, his eyes wide and expression solemn. "You want it?"

Beau shook his head and ruffled Mackey's windswept hair. "Nah. You take it."

Mackey released a shout of joy. "First one is mine!" He grabbed a bucket, hopped up on the gunwale, and jumped overboard.

Kit grabbed after him. "Mackey, wai—"

Too late. Beau leaned over the gunwale and chuckled. Mackey had landed feetfirst in mud up to his ankles. "How's it feel down there?"

Mackey threw his head back, his cheeks speckled with sticky mud, and squealed. "Fantastic! Come on, Beau. Cal! Kit! Come on!"

Beau bumped Cal with his hip and stepped onto the casting deck of the boat. "Beat you in, son."

"Don't do it, Beau." Kit tried for a stern look, but a smile flirted at the edge of her lips. "You're not familiar with this bed like we are. You land in the wrong spot, you'll sink up to your elbows, the creek will swallow you whole, and we'll be forced to leave you here."

Beau grinned. "I ain't ignorant, baby. I know what I'm doing."

With that, he sprang off the casting deck, felt the soles of his boots slap against soft mud, then slid down until it hugged his ankles.

Beau glanced up at Kit and Cal, who smiled down at him from the boat, and winked. "See? I know exactly what I'm doing." He pulled his right foot out of the mud and took a step toward the oyster bed. "All it takes is—"

The bottom dropped out, and his right leg sank as though a huge mouth was attempting to swallow him whole. He fell forward, sank in mud up to his butt, and scrambled for footing on more solid ground as cackles of laughter echoed around him.

"You need a hand, Dad?" Cal laughed. "Or you know what you're doing?"

Beau tried to twist around and scowl, but the suck of

the mud was too strong. He waved a hand in the air. "Much as I hate to admit it, I might need a little help." He glanced to his left. "Mackey? Want to give me a hand?"

Mackey, bent over a cluster of oysters several feet away, straightened, with a freshly culled oyster in hand. He surveyed Beau's predicament, carefully placed his oyster down, then headed over and grabbed one of Beau's hands. "Okay. Get up."

Beau tried—Lord knows, he did—but made no progress. As a matter of fact, he thought he might have sunk farther. "Not happening." He waved his hand in the air again. "Cal? Come on down here and give Mackey a hand."

Cal joined Mackey, navigating his way across the mud much more carefully than Beau had, grabbed both of Beau's hands, and pulled. It worked . . . for an inch or two. Then he sank back down three inches.

"Kit?" He made a face and waited until her full-throated laughter had subsided into soft giggles. "Much as I hate to admit that I was wrong, I need you to come down here and lend us your muscle."

"Oh?" Was that a feigned note of surprise he detected in her voice? "You need me to come down there and pull, too?"

He swallowed his pride, along with a smidge of nausea-inducing mud that had splashed onto his lower lip. "Yes."

"Down there?" she asked. "Where I told you not to jump?"

"That is correct."

There were scuffling sounds, then a plop and several sloshes. Kit walked in front of him, stepping carefully beside the tracks Cal had made, smiled down at Beau, leaned over, and held out her hand.

"Grab on, big boy."

Cal laughed.

"Mackey, when I count to three, I want you and Cal to grab Beau's other hand and pull as hard and for as long as you can, okay?" she asked.

Mackey nodded, all business. "Yeah. I'll do it. Then can I eat the first oyster?"

"Yep," Kit said, nudging her fingers closer to Beau's face. "You gotta do your part, too, you know? Can't just lie there like a slug and expect us to do all the work."

Despite his awkward position, Beau laughed as he wrapped his hand tightly around Kit's, unable to resist running his gaze over her from head to toe. Man, even while he was sloshing around in tons of sticky mud, she made his blood rush.

She smirked, a teasing light in her eyes, as she leaned closer, and then she whispered, "And stop looking at me like that, or I'll shove your head under."

He laughed harder. "Then stop teasing me. The more I laugh, the more I sink."

"All right, guys," Kit shouted, tightening her grip. "One, two . . . three!"

Kit, Cal, and Mackey heaved all at the same time, but Beau, sinking faster now, didn't budge. And on top of it all, their feet began to sink, too.

"Hold up," Beau said, the first frisson of real concern stealing up his spine. He tipped his chin at Cal and Mackey. "We keep this up and y'all are gonna get stuck, too. You two let go and let me and Kit give it a shot on our own."

"No way, Dad." Cal smiled. "She can't pull you out on her own."

Kit made a face at Cal. "Are you trying to say I'm not strong enough to—"

"Oh, no, ma'am." Cal's cheeks flushed. "I just meant that . . . well . . ."

Kit laughed. "I know what you meant." She glanced at

Beau. "And Cal has a point. It's going to take all of us to pull you out. It's just going to take one more good yank." She renewed her grip on his hand, prompting Cal and Mackey to do the same, then counted off again. "One, two, three!"

Beau slid out slowly at first, his butt, thighs, then knees emerging. Finally, the mud's vicious suck fell away, propelling him forward into all three of them.

They toppled over together and collapsed in a heap amid the sludgy mud. Kit shook with laughter beneath him, while Cal and Mackey, giggling, shoved at his chest.

Beau stayed right where he was, catching his breath and savoring the moment. Sticky grime clung to him from head to toe, he probably stank to high heaven, and he was half-afraid he'd find mud later in places he wouldn't welcome it . . . but so far, this had already been the best trip to the creek he'd ever had.

"Get off, Dad," Cal choked out through tears of laughter, shoving hard.

Mackey wriggled out from the pile and headed back to the oyster bed. Cal scrambled to his feet, grabbed his oyster hammer from the casting deck, then joined Mackey.

Beau took his time rising to his knees, his gaze roving over Kit as she lay flat on her back in the mud and laughed with unbridled joy. Mud had splashed across her chin, and her hair, now wet, clung to her neck in muddy gobs. He'd never seen a woman look more beautiful in his life . . . not even Evelyn.

The thought shocked him, guilt sweeping through him. But it occurred to him then that what precious time he'd been blessed to have with Evelyn had passed, and he found himself accepting that fact fully for the first time, longing for something different. Something more.

"That's another difference," he said softly, wiping the

mud from Kit's chin and wishing she'd open her heart and unburden herself of the sadness he'd glimpsed in her eyes earlier. Share her regrets, her fears, her wishes . . . and dreams with him.

Kit opened her eyes, and her laughter faded as she met his eyes. "What is?"

"Suttons aren't afraid to ask for help when they need it."

Kit had discovered very early in her life that an oyster harvest and roast were more fun when shared with family and friends, but in reality, Beau Sutton had never been either in her life, which made the five hours of fun she'd had on the water, harvesting oysters with him, even harder to explain.

As they'd harvested oysters, culling them in place, she'd let herself enjoy Beau's company, and despite the differences they continued to discover in each other, she'd grown more attracted to him than ever. She'd also found herself laughing and smiling throughout the day spent on the water, in her mother's favorite spot . . . something she hadn't expected to do again so soon. That had left her feeling a little guilty.

"Let's shine them up really nice." Beau, a pressure washer hose in one hand, stood by Mackey in the backyard of Teague Cottage, aiming the high-pressure stream of water at a large pile of wild oysters that were spread over a flat slab of concrete. "Especially yours," he added, focusing the stream on one large oyster resting on the outskirts of the group, "seeing as how it was the first catch of the day."

Mackey grinned. "It was the best of the day, right?"

Beau nodded. "Without a doubt." He nudged the hose toward Mackey. "Hang on to that for a sec?"

Mackey took the hose and continued spraying the oysters, his aim not quite as accurate, as Beau walked to the edge of the concrete slab and retrieved the largest oyster of the batch.

Kit bit back a smile as Beau inspected the oyster, turned it over in his big palm, and brushed a glob of mud carefully off one edge of the shell. It seemed a futile effort, considering every inch of Beau was smeared with mud—including his hands.

"You know, I think that shell would've stayed cleaner if you'd left it right where it was," Kit said.

Beau's blue eyes settled on her, a mischievous spark in their depths. "Oh, you think so?"

"I do." Kit gestured toward his tall frame, refusing to let her gaze linger on the way his damp jeans and T-shirt clung to his muscular girth.

An expression of mock affront appeared on his face as he spread his hands. "What exactly are you trying to say?" His sensual mouth turned up in a devilish grin. "Are you implying that I'm dirty and not suitable for polite society?"

Cal, carrying an armload of firewood, walked over to Kit's side and laughed. "She's saying you stink, Dad. Which you do."

"So you want in on this, too, huh?" Beau held the oyster out to Mackey with one hand and motioned with his other. "Let's swap, Mackey."

Kit held up a hand as Mackey handed the hose to Beau. "Don't you dare—"

Too late. A strong blast of water skimmed her belly and legs, sending a cold spray up to splash her face.

Squealing, Kit covered her face and doubled over, laughing. The stream of water left her and hit someone else. Cal whooped at her side, and firewood thumped to the ground by her feet. Seizing the moment, she shot forward, blinking hard through the water streaming down her face, and managed to make it to Beau and grab hold of the hose.

She wrestled with him as he chuckled, her hands slipping over his toned forearms and wet hands, until she secured a grip on the nozzle and turned it on him. Water shot everywhere—on his face, her hair, his chest, her legs—and Kit struggled to catch her breath. Her laughter and each cold burst of water against her bare skin left her breathless as Mackey and Cal cheered the water-soaked combatants.

The back door slammed. Royal walked out onto the back deck, a frown on his face.

Kit froze, her hands entwined with Beau's around the hose, the stream of water still splashing against both of their chests. It was silly, really. She was a thirty-eight-year-old woman, completely entitled to decide how and with whom she spent her time. But the displeased look on Royal's face made her feel about sixteen again.

She lowered the hose and aimed the water at the oysters piled on the concrete slab. Beau released her hands and straightened slowly, his smile fading.

"Can't no one take a decent nap around here with all that noise," Royal said.

"We got the oysters, Dad." Mackey bounced in place, smiling and pointing at the harvest. "You come down and see what we got."

Royal stomped down the steps of the back deck, walked across the backyard, and stood beside the pile of oysters.

"I got some," Mackey continued, "Kit got some, and Cal got some. Beau got some, too."

Royal propped his fists on his hips, studying Mackey's smile, then the scattered bivalves, and narrowed his eyes at Beau. "You pried these out the mud? Took the time to fish 'em out that creek, instead of dumping 'em outta one of them cages of yours?"

Beau dragged a hand over his face and returned Royal's hard stare, but his blond hair—now wet—stuck out in adorable tufts, ruining the effect. "I did, sir."

Royal glanced at Cal, who stood shivering by the pile of scattered firewood. "You too?"

Cal shoved his hands in the pockets of his jeans and nodded. "Yes, sir."

"He found one almost big as mine," Mackey shouted. He jogged over to Cal, grabbed his elbow, and tugged him across the grass toward the oyster pile. "Show my dad which one, Cal. Show him."

Cal tugged one hand from his pocket, sneaked another glance at Royal, then picked an oyster up and held it out. "This was the biggest I found, sir."

Royal took the oyster and turned it over a couple of times, weighing it in his palm. "Mighty fine," he said softly.

"This Cal," Mackey said, tugging Cal closer to Royal. "Not Cole. His name's Cal, and he's my friend. He's gonna come over again, and I'm gonna go to his house one day." He smiled at Cal, nodding eagerly. "Ain't I? Ain't we friends, Cal?"

Cal shoved his hand back in his pocket, still shivering, and smiled. "Yeah. We're friends."

Royal looked Cal over. "I expect you've caught a chill"— he glanced at Beau, his gaze hardening slightly—"seeing as how your dad hosed you down. You're about my height. I got some dry clothes and a soda inside, if you'd care to come in with Mackey and dry off?"

Cal, surprise in his eyes, smiled wider. "Yes, sir. Thank you, sir."

Royal nodded. "Take him on in, Mackey." He watched Mackey grab Cal's hand and lead him up the back steps and into the house, then turned back to Beau, a hint of grudging respect in his eyes. "Boy's got good manners."

Beau, his grin hesitant, nodded. "Yes, he d—"

"Must've got 'em from his mama." Royal headed back up the steps, opened the back door, then pointed over his shoulder at Beau as he was closing the door behind him. "You can stay out here and build the fire."

Beau shook his head, but his grin returned.

"What are you smiling about?" Kit asked.

"Your dad. He said Cal has good manners. That's about as close to a compliment as I've ever gotten from him." He raised his eyebrow, pride evident in his expression. "And," he stressed, "he said I could stay out here."

Kit laughed. "How is that a compliment?"

"He could've said I had to leave altogether, but he didn't." He grabbed the hem of his shirt and twisted it, wringing it out. "That's progress, my friend." He smiled wider and wiped the mud off his face with the damp hem of his T-shirt. "That's progress."

Pleasure tingled through Kit as one of his big hands lifted, smoothed over his stubbled jaw, then rubbed the back of his strong neck. "Are we?" she asked softly.

"Are we what?" Still smiling, he narrowed his eyes, allowed his gaze to rove over her forehead and cheeks. "I missed a spot. You still have a bit of mud on your chin." He lifted the hem of his T-shirt and motioned toward her face. "May I?"

She nodded absently. "Sure, but—" The firm but gentle rub of his cloth-covered thumb against her chin made her breath catch. She stilled, absorbing his tender touch. Admiring the strong curve of his jaw as he dipped his head closer, his wet hair brushing her temple. A pang of jealousy hit, unwanted and unwelcome.

"Are we what?" his deep voice prompted.

Kit blinked. His head had turned, and his eyes were on her, studying her expression.

"Are we . . . ?" She swallowed hard, her attention moving over his handsome face. In spite of his deep tan, the sun had burned him a little during their time on the water, leaving behind a soft rosy glow across the upper halves of his lean cheeks. She lifted her hand and traced her damp fingertips lightly over the rosy color in his right cheek, leaving two droplets of water behind. "Are we friends?" she whispered. "Like you and Viv? Is that what we are?"

He leaned closer, his smile fading, as his thumb left her chin and skimmed across her lower lip. "No."

"No?" She held her breath. Didn't move. Afraid, more than anything, that he'd draw away, removing the warmth of his wide chest and the pleasurable flutter his touch had stirred within her.

"No," he repeated firmly. "Nothing like Viv. Let's leave her out of this, okay?"

She studied the dimple in his chin. The strong column of his throat.

"Whatever this is between us . . ." He nudged the tip of her nose with his, tilting her face up, his mouth poised above hers, blue eyes dark with desire and invitation. "Whatever we have, it's different."

Relief moved through her, and she lifted to her toes, touched her mouth to his, parted his warm lips with hers. The taste of him hit her tongue, and groaning softly, he pressed closer, the rough brush of stubble on his jaw rubbing across her smooth cheek, heightening the rush of pleasure through her veins.

The door slammed open, and they sprang apart. Kit's cheeks flamed as Royal stomped down the back steps. He crossed the backyard, a glass bottle of soda in each hand, and stopped in front of Beau.

Royal shoved one of the bottles against Beau's middle. "I'll get the fire going."

Face flushing, Beau grabbed the bottle with both hands before it fell to the ground. "Thank you, R—"

"Don't care how old you are, boy," Royal bit out. "While you're on my land, you best keep your lips on that instead of my daughter."

CHAPTER 7

Though he was still thoroughly embarrassed after leaving Teague Cottage and returning home hours later, Beau couldn't stop smiling.

"And Dad got stuck in the mud." Cal, seated at the kitchen table between Nate and Viv, paused his exuberant recitation of the day's events long enough to gulp a mouthful of iced sweet tea from the glass sitting in front of him. "After we pulled him out—"

"They had to pull you out, son?" Nate eyed Beau and tried not to smile. His shoulders shook.

"Only because"—Beau held up a hand—"I happened to land in the wrong spot. It was an honest mistake that could've happened to anyone. Kit took us out to a bed I'd never been to before."

"Which bed?" Viv, seated opposite Beau, propped her elbows on the table and leaned forward.

Beau shrugged. "I don't know. It was a ways out. Almost to the opposite end of the creek. Kit said your mom used to love it there."

"It was huge, too," Cal said, thumping his glass, now empty, back onto the table. "Those oysters, Pop." He glanced at Nate. "They were at least an inch bigger than any we've ever sifted out of a bucket. And the taste . . ." He closed his eyes and shook his head. "I've never had one as good."

Beau smiled and rested his chin in his hand. His finger drifted across his lower lip at the memory of Kit's kiss. The way her soft mouth had pressed against his, her sweet taste on his tongue . . . He'd never had a better first kiss.

Well . . . He bit his nail, his neck heating. That was until Royal came stomping out of the house like a mad bull and warned him off.

"Never had one as good, huh?" Nate narrowed his eyes on Beau's face. "You either?"

Beau rubbed his chin, then took a swig of tea from his own glass. "I don't know that I'd say that, but the harvest was impressive."

"Still in clusters, though?" Nate asked.

Beau nodded. "They were flavorful, but not as briny or rich as ours, and the consistency in shape and size wasn't there, of course. I think the experience of the harvest is what made the most impression on Cal, not necessarily the oysters themselves."

"The experience, you say?" Viv's face flushed. "We work the creek and handle oysters every day."

"But not like they do." Cal grinned. A fresh set of freckles was scattered across the bridge of his nose, and a sleepy satisfaction resided in his heavy-lidded gaze. "Wasn't anybody out there where Kit took us. No one but us. No cages, no measuring, no weighing. It was muddy and stinky and messy and . . . and . . ."

"Fun." Beau reached over and ruffled Cal's hair, the sheer look of joy on his face warming Beau's chest. "It was fun, wasn't it?"

Cal smiled. "Yeah. Especially the roasting part." He smiled at Nate. "They don't use pots and propane, Pop.

They stack concrete blocks into a firepit, build a fire, and throw a piece of sheet metal on it. And they use a sh—"

"Shovel to scoop the suckers off when they're done, right?" Viv asked. "That's the old-school way of doing things. My dad's done it that way for as long as I can remember."

"I wouldn't exactly call it old school," Beau said quietly, recalling the excitement in Cal's and Mackey's eyes as Royal had tossed a batch of oysters on the hot sheet of metal, counted the minutes as they'd steamed, then shoveled them hot onto a wooden table for shucking. "It's just . . . traditional."

"And fun," Cal said before plucking an ice cube from his glass and plopping it in his mouth.

"There's something to be said for tradition," Beau continued, avoiding Nate's steady gaze. "Some things can't rival it." He glanced at Cal's sleepy, sun-kissed face and smiled. "It's been a long time since I've shoveled hot oysters fresh off a fire. Everyone had a good time."

"Even my dad?" Viv narrowed her eyes. "He didn't give you grief for stepping on his property?"

Beau hesitated, recalling the glares Royal had shot him as they'd roasted oysters over the fire. If Royal had disapproved of him before, he sure hadn't developed a newfound fondness for him after stumbling upon Beau kissing his daughter. But then again, Royal hadn't thrown him off his property, either.

"He tolerated me."

"Why?"

Beau held Viv's gaze, the suspicious gleam in her eyes making him shift uncomfortably in his chair. "For Kit's sake, I guess."

A muscle ticked in her jaw. "All this talk of tradition," she said quietly. "One morning on the creek and less than twenty-four hours, huh? That's all it took for her to suck you right on in."

Nate cleared his throat. "It's getting late. Come on, Cal. Time to call it a night."

Cal sucked his teeth. "But tomorrow's Sunday."

"Yep." Nate stood, clamped his hands on Cal's shoulders, and pulled him to his feet. "The day of rest, which means you should be in bed, resting."

Cal groaned but put his empty glass in the sink and paused to hug Beau on his way out of the kitchen. "Thanks for today, Dad."

Beau squeezed him tight before releasing him. "You're welcome."

As Cal left, he said over his shoulder, "Good night, Viv."

"Night, kid." Viv watched Cal walk down the hall and out of sight, then looked down and studied her nails. "How was Mackey doing?"

Beau smiled. "Good. Having Cal around was fun for him, I think."

A sad smile curved her lips. "Mackey doesn't get many visitors. Especially the kind that enjoy sticking around for any length of time."

"He laughed a lot today. Seemed to be doing much better than the last time we saw him." Beau's smile slipped as he thought of how devastated Mackey—all the Teagues, really—had been on the morning of Sylvie's funeral at sea. He hesitated, then said, "You should stop by the cottage sometime. Pay him a visit."

Her head shot up, a guarded look in her eyes. "Pay Kit a visit, you mean."

"Wouldn't hurt."

Viv's brows raised in a mocking expression.

"All right," Beau said, spreading his hands. "It couldn't

hurt any more than it already has. You're not the only one hurting, Viv. You cut into Kit pretty deep the last time you were over there."

"After what she did to my mother? To you?" Viv stood and left the table. "She deserved it."

Moments later cabinets opened, then shut, a bottle thumped onto a countertop, and ice clinked in a glass.

Beau stood, too, and joined Viv at the kitchen island. Her hand trembled as she poured a shot of vodka. He hooked his heel around the leg of a barstool, dragged the barstool out, then sat and watched as Viv drank the shot, her head back and eyes closed. "That's not—"

"Going to help." Viv poured another shot. "I know." She drank the second. "Nothing helps."

"Talking might."

"To you? Or to Kit?" She drummed her fingers on the island. "Did the two of you have a good conversation today? Did she apologize for what she did to you?"

"Yes, and the only reason she caused the scene she did was to get your attention—not mine."

"But she got yours, anyway, didn't she?" Viv braced her hands on the island, leaned heavily against it. "If Kit wanted my attention, all she ever had to do was show up. Just come home, or better yet, she could have stayed instead of leaving fifteen years ago," she said, her head lowered, her voice shaking. "I'm right here. I've always been here." She raised her head, met his eyes. Tears welled onto her lower lashes. "Why not me?"

He stilled as an ache spread through his chest. Lowering his head, he left the barstool and walked to the cabinets, opened one, and retrieved a shot glass.

"Beau?" Viv followed his movements with her gaze, watching as he returned to the barstool, picked up the bottle of vodka, and poured a shot. "Why not me?"

He tossed the shot back and closed his eyes as the liquor scorched a path down his throat.

"Kit and I grew up in the same house," Viv said softly. "We did the same things growing up, lived basically the same childhood . . . sometimes even finished each other's sentences." She inhaled a shaky breath, her mouth opening and closing soundlessly, before she said, "We even look the same. Exactly the same."

"But you're not the same." Beau opened his eyes, and his gut sank as a tear rolled down Viv's cheek. He balled his fists to keep from reaching out and wiping it away. "I don't want to hurt you, Viv. You're one of the best friends I've ever had, but"—he swallowed hard, his eyes burning—"I won't lie to you, either. Friendship is all you and I have ever had. It's all we'll ever have."

Her expression crumpled, and she looked down, her fingers picking at the label on the vodka bottle. "You think she was right, don't you? You think I helped my mother kill herself."

"No." He did touch her then. Unfurled his fists and cupped her chin, tipped her face up and met her gaze head-on. "God, no, Viv. I'd never think that. Not ever."

She reached up, curled her hand around his wrist, and squeezed gently. "Then you think Kit was wrong." Relief tinged her tone. "That she should never have left."

He shook his head. "I don't know. I wish I knew the answer to that, but I don't."

Viv pulled away. "Nate was right. It's getting late." She picked up her empty shot glass and placed it in the sink, then turned away. "Think I'll turn in."

"Viv." Beau hesitated, watching as she paused on the threshold of the kitchen, her back to him. "You asked me before if Cal had a choice of saving me or himself, which he would choose." He smiled slightly, recalling how strongly

Cal had pulled on his arm when he'd been buried almost waist-deep in mud. "I have no doubts that he'd choose my life over his own, but I wouldn't want him to." He bit his lip, then forced himself to ask, "Have you ever thought about what Sylvie would've wanted for you and Kit?"

Kit stood in front of the closed door to the guest bedroom on the first floor of Teague Cottage. It seemed such a simple task, really—to open the door and walk in. But habits formed over a period of almost forty years were hard to break.

"Dad said not to go in." Mackey stood by her side, wringing his hands. "He said never to go in there when Mama is in there."

Kit watched an array of emotions flicker over his face: worry, anxiety, grief, and fear. She'd grown accustomed to carrying them around herself dozens of years ago. But thankfully, Mackey had shown small signs of improvement recently.

It'd been two days since they'd taken Beau and Cal out onto the creek and harvested wild oysters. Mackey had fought off sleep for hours after the oyster roast had ended and Beau and Cal had gone home. First, he'd helped Royal put out the fire in the backyard, gathered up the discarded oyster shells, and loaded them in the back of Royal's truck. Then he'd hopped in the passenger seat, accompanied Royal to the shell recycling center drop-off, and unloaded the shells.

Kit grinned. She'd been half surprised Royal's rusty truck had started, let alone carried him and Mackey the three miles to the recycling center and back, but it'd made the round trip. When they'd returned, Mackey had followed Kit around the house as she'd cleaned each room, sorting through years of accumulated odds and ends. Over and over, he had had the same questions on his lips: "When can Cal come over again? And Beau? When can I go to Cal's?"

But she hadn't minded. Mackey's smile and renewed spirits had been a reward all their own. The oyster roast had lifted not only Mackey's spirits but Royal's, as well. Rather than retiring to his room for the night later that evening, Royal had ventured out onto the front porch, sat in one of the wicker chairs, lit a cigar, and enjoyed a leisurely smoke under the stars. When Kit had joined him, and Mackey had followed, Royal hadn't said a word. He'd simply turned his head, a slight smile on his bearded face, and leaned back in his chair to look up at the night sky.

It'd been the first time since Kit's return that the three of them had relaxed together in companionable silence. Mackey, rarely silent, had seemed to ponder Sylvie's absence a lot that night. He'd sat on the porch steps and stared at the front door of the house, as though he'd expected Sylvie to appear at any moment, and the longer the night had wore on, the more he'd sagged against the porch rail, his attention shifting up to the stars, as well.

Now Kit covered Mackey's hands with her own, stilling his nervous movements, then wove her fingers through his and squeezed. "Dad's rule for this room doesn't matter now, because Mama's not here anymore, is she?"

His eyes widened, and his gaze darted over the ceiling, wall, and floor before meeting hers. He shook his head.

"Where is she, Mackey?" Kit asked gently.

Chin trembling, he pointed toward the ceiling. "Up there. In heaven, where we can't see her. But she can see us, can't she?" His eyes widened even more, and his mouth gaped open. "What if she sees us go in? What if she gets mad?"

"She won't be mad."

"But how do you know?"

"Because Mama wouldn't mind us going in there now, Mackey. She used to love this room. She loved the view."

Kit faced the door again and rubbed her sweaty palm on her jean-clad leg. There was no other choice, no other excuse. She and Mackey had already mowed and manicured the front and back lawns, and she'd thoroughly cleaned every room in Teague Cottage from top to bottom. This room was the only one left that she hadn't overhauled, and walking past it each day only dredged up painful memories.

"She would've wanted us to use this room," Kit said. "You and Dad especially."

Mackey didn't look convinced. "How come?"

"I'll show you." Holding her breath, Kit gripped the doorknob and turned it, then swept the door open and led the way inside.

The room looked almost exactly as it had over fifteen years ago, when Kit had last stepped inside it. The double bed took center stage on the far wall, and the thin cotton sheets, imprinted with jessamine flowers, were rumpled and dangling off one side of the mattress. Empty beer bottles, pill containers, and wadded-up cigarette packs littered the dresser, above which hung a cracked mirror. And on the right side of the room, soft morning light from an overcast sky streamed in, casting a grayish haze throughout.

Kit blew out a slow breath, then led Mackey by the hand across the room, carefully stepping over the clothes and shoes strewn across the scuffed hardwood floor, and stopped in front of the window.

"There," she said. "What do you see?"

Mackey smiled. "The creek." He tugged his hand free from Kit's, placed both palms flat against the window, and pressed his nose to the cloudy glass. "That's where the oysters are. Can you see 'em out there?"

Kit's gaze traveled over the ash-laden firepit in the backyard, the low curving branches of live oaks, and the long
wooden dock toward the water rippling in the distance.
Her throat tightened and her eyes burned, the gray clouds
melting into the creek below.

She pressed her forehead to the glass beside Mackey's
hand. "No. You can't see them from here, but they're out
there."

"What's out there?"

Kit spun around. Viv stood in the center of the bedroom, staring at them as they stood in front of the window. Her hair was pulled back in a tight ponytail, and the
jeans and T-shirt she wore were baggy, accentuating her
thin frame. She looked as though she hadn't slept much
lately.

"Viv!" Mackey left the window, jogged across the
room, and hurled himself into Viv's arms.

Viv smiled as she wrapped her arms around him and
kissed his cheek. "Hey, bud." She hugged him closer.
"Have you been taking good care of the place while I've
been gone?"

Mackey smiled up at her and nodded. "I washed the
dishes and cooked dog cheese and"—he glanced over his
shoulder at Kit—"me and Kit cut the grass and went on
the creek and got oysters with Cal and Beau."

"I saw a new mailbox out front," Viv said, meeting Kit's
eyes over the top of his head. "Courtesy of Beau?"

Kit nodded slowly. "He installed it a little over a week
ago, when he stopped by to pay his condolences."

It was on the tip of her tongue to ask Viv how Beau was
doing. Kit hadn't seen or heard from him since the oyster
roast, save for a glimpse of him behind the wheel of a truck
emblazoned with PEARL TIDE OYSTER COMPANY early yesterday afternoon. The bed of the truck had been packed to

the brim with coolers, and the vehicle had slowed as it passed Teague Cottage. Beau, catching her eye as she swept the front porch with Mackey, had smiled and lifted his hand in a wave. For a moment, the truck had stopped, as though he might turn into the driveway of the cottage. Instead, Beau had lowered his hand, the engine had rumbled, and the truck had rolled on.

"I thought Dad had closed this off." Viv hugged Mackey once more, then released him, frowning as she glanced around the room.

"He did." Kit's arms ached to reach out to Viv, to hug her close the way she used to, but she folded them across her chest instead. "It's been almost two weeks since . . ." Her throat closed. She looked away for a moment, focused on the rumpled bed. "I thought it was time to clean it up a bit. To maybe sort through Mom's things. Would . . . would you like to stay for a while and help?"

Viv's lip curled. "No." She walked over to the dresser, swept her arm across the surface, knocking a pile of empty cigarette packs onto the floor, then picked up a small frame. "I can't believe she kept this."

Kit walked over to her side and glanced down at the frame in her hands. Behind the dingy glass, there was a picture of Kit and Viv. She studied it more closely, guessing they'd been around ten when it was taken. They sat side by side on the front porch steps of Teague Cottage, one arm slung around each other's shoulders, their lanky legs sprawling in different directions.

A pang stole through Kit as she studied Viv's face in the picture. Her eyes were bright—happy—with no trace of the dark circles or anger that plagued them now. Her cheeks were full, a healthy pink along the soft curves, and she smiled wide at whoever was behind the camera. Presumably, their mother.

"She said she was going to throw it away the day I moved out two years ago," Viv said. " 'Burn it to bits,' was what she told me. Said it was no more use to her than either of us."

Kit winced, her hand raised, fingers poised above Viv's shoulder. She lowered it back to her side. "She was sick, Viv. She wasn't herself. Hadn't been for a long time."

"Who would be?" Viv stared at the picture. "Pregnant at fifteen, saddled with twins eight months later, and losing your mind in between?" Her tone hardened. "We were part of what caused it. Had to have been."

"Don't say that." Royal's deep voice filled the small room. He stood in the open doorway, glaring at Viv. "I don't ever want to hear that again. Not in this house."

Viv tossed the framed photo back on the dresser and faced Royal. "Where then? The truth is the tru—"

"There ain't no truth in that," Royal bit out. "Sylvie loved you girls more than I—" Voice breaking, he dragged a hand over his beard, stared out the window for a moment, then refocused on Viv. "More than life itself."

Pain flashed across Viv's face, and a humorless smile appeared. "That's not saying much."

Royal's face reddened. "Viv—"

"I didn't come here for this," Viv said, gesturing at Royal, then Kit. "I didn't come here for some Teague reunion. I came because I finally found something that I care about and—" Her lips pressed into a tight line as she glanced at Kit. "I don't know how long you plan to stay." She turned back to Royal. "And I don't care what you think of me anymore, or how mad this makes you, but Beau and I have worked ourselves to the bone for almost three years getting our business off the ground, and the two of you have got to back off if we're going to make a go of it."

Kit clenched her jaw. "At whose expense? It's not just a matter of choice, Viv. You're talking about stripping Dad of his livelihood."

"I didn't set out to take anything, and I . . ." She looked at Royal, her gaze fixed on his chest. "I never intended to hurt you. I swear I didn't. And you know how hard it is for me to ask anything of you. I just . . . need something of my own. Something I helped build. And I got to thinking that you might be able to tolerate it if you'd just give me a chance to . . . Please, Dad. I need this."

Royal jerked away, his hand gripping the doorframe, knuckles turning white. "What're you asking of me?"

Viv released a shaky breath and stared at Royal's back. "Come to the Suttons' place tomorrow afternoon? Around four? Take a tour with me and Beau, and just let us show you what we're doing. That's all I'm asking for now."

Royal remained silent for a moment, glancing back at Kit, then Mackey, who had returned to the window and was watching them with wide eyes. "All right," he said. "We'll be there."

CHAPTER 8

"There they are!" Mackey shouted, pressing his nose between the ornate bars on the Suttons' gate and pointing at a group of people walking down the driveway that led to the large house. "Hey, Cal! Hey, Beau! And there's Viv!"

Smiling, Kit slipped her finger through the belt loop on the back of his jeans and tugged him back a few steps. "Not so fast, Mackey. When you visit someone's house, it's polite to wait to be invited in."

Mackey frowned. "But we *were* invited. That's what Viv said. She said to come today at four."

"Yes, she did say that, but it's always nice to let your host invite you in first." Kit grinned and glanced at Royal, who stood several feet behind them on the dirt road. "You coming?"

Royal looked past her toward the gate, his eyes narrowing. "Viv didn't say nothing about Nate Sutton coming out here."

"Well, Pearl Tide Oyster Company is a third his, and he does live here, too, Dad."

Royal scowled. "I know that. I just figured Viv would've had enough sense—or consideration for me—to tell him to sit this tour out and show us around herself."

"Either way, we're here now, and I don't think Mackey's going to let us back out and go home."

"Who's going home?" Mackey looked at Royal and pursed his lips. "I ain't going home. No way. I'm visiting Cal and seeing the oysters."

"Calm down, son." Royal rolled his shoulders. "No one's going home. I told your sister we'd take the tour, so we'll take the tour. You'll see Cal, and you'll see the oysters."

"You promise?" Mackey asked, his eyes skeptical.

Royal scoffed. "Yeah. I promise."

Kit stifled a smile. She didn't blame Mackey for pressing his point and securing a promise. Royal had hemmed and hawed regarding the visit ever since Viv had left Teague Cottage yesterday morning. At lunch, hours after Viv had left, he'd picked at his sandwich and pointed out the overcast sky, muttering something along the lines of it being difficult to tour anything in the rain. On his way to bed last night, he'd paused in the hallway outside the closed door to Kit and Viv's bedroom as Kit had crawled into bed, and called through the door that he thought she might be tired after cleaning the guest bedroom all afternoon, and would she like him to postpone the tour? She'd declined the offer, of course, having been too anxious to see Beau again—though she'd refused to admit as much out loud.

And this morning Royal had broken his usual routine of sleeping late and had instead smoked a cigar on the front porch before the first light of dawn, blowing smoke and frowning in the direction of the Sutton house. But to Royal's credit, he hadn't attempted to back out again. He'd shifted gears and seemed resigned to simply remain silently disgruntled about the predicament in which he'd found himself.

"I see y'all made it right on time," Beau said, striding up to the gate and sweeping it open.

Kit caught her breath, welcoming the sight of him. He looked well, if a bit tired. His tan had deepened, as though he'd spent the majority of the past several days on the water, and though he met her eyes, a pleased expression appearing on his face, his smile seemed distant.

"Viv said four." Mackey hopped from one foot to the other, an impatient look on his face, as he stared at Beau. "It's four. Can I?"

Beau's brow furrowed. "Can you what?"

"Come in." Mackey wrung his hands. "Kit said I had to wait 'til the host invited me in. You're the host, ain't you? Or Cal?"

Beau smiled wider. "Of course." He swept his arm out in invitation. "Please come in, Mackey. It's a pleasure to have you visit."

Mackey sprang forward and embraced Beau, rocking him back on his heels. "Thank you." He proceeded down the line, hugging Cal, Viv, and even Nate, who'd been a stranger to him up to this point. "I don't know you," he said, squeezing Nate's waist, "but I thank you, too."

Nate looked taken aback, his hands hovering awkwardly in the air, but he relaxed after a moment and, smiling, patted Mackey's back. "You're welcome. And I'm Nate, by the way. I'm Beau's father."

Mackey released Nate and thrust a finger in Royal's direction. "That's my dad over there. His name is Royal."

Nate's smile faded. "Yes. I know. We've met before." He eased past Beau and held out his hand. "Royal?"

Kit tensed, watching Royal's face for any hint of animosity or impending fireworks, but only a flicker of discomfort showed as he reached out and quickly shook Nate's hand.

"I appreciate your showing us around," Royal said reluctantly. His gaze moved past Nate to Viv, and his voice softening, he added, "And I thank you for taking care of my girl."

Viv, standing beside Nate, blushed. "I take care of myself, Dad."

He smiled slightly. "I know." He lifted a hand toward Nate. "But Viv told us how much she enjoys being here, working on the . . . the farm? I guess that's what you call it."

Nate's welcoming expression dimmed. "Yes. It's an oyster farm." His voice took on a mocking tone. "Though we refer to the business side of our operation as Pearl Tide Oyster Company."

"Still," Royal said, tilting his head, "it's a bit strange having a farm of oysters, ain't it? Seems wrong. Almost like a crime against nature."

Nate tensed. "A crime? How you figure?"

Beau, glancing between the two men, placed his hand on Nate's arm. "Let's just start the tour, and we can discuss things on the w—"

"Cages? And artificial tumbling?" Royal smirked. "Just don't seem right is all."

"Dad," Kit said quietly, slipping her hand around Royal's elbow. "Please d—"

"There's nothing artificial about it." Nate, mouth tightening, lifted his arm and pointed toward the creek in the distance. "Our oysters eat, tumble, and thrive in the same waters you fish yours out of. When we crack 'em open, they're bursting with the very same flavors of Hope Creek as those skinny wild ones you hack out of the mud."

Royal laughed. "You mean you dump your oysters out of cages, then crack 'em open. And your tumbling is artificial. You think I ain't seen none of them tumbling machines like what you got on that floating dock of yours?

Y'all throw em down some ol' metal chute, bang 'em around, and shape 'em all alike. There's no nature in that shaping."

"You're right," Nate snapped. "That's 'cause our oysters are floating near the surface, where the food's plentiful, and they don't have to stretch and strain to find good eatin'. Our oysters are fat and happy, and fat, happy oysters make fat, happy people!"

Beau covered his eyes with one hand and groaned.

"You ain't supposed to call people that word." Mackey leveled a stern look at Nate. "That's mean. My dad said everyone looks good in their own way, no matter how big or little they are, cuz that's how God made 'em."

"Mackey," Viv whispered loudly, her cheeks blotching. "That's not what he meant." She turned to Nate. "I'm so sorry, Nate."

Nate's brow furrowed, and his shoulders visibly relaxed as he processed Mackey's words. "No, I . . . uh, yeah, he's right. You're absolutely right there . . . Mackey. I shouldn't have said that word."

"My dad's the one who's right," Mackey stressed, pointing at Royal. "He's the one who told me."

Nate drew in a deep breath, held it, then smiled tightly at Royal. "Yes. Your dad's right, and I apologize for any offense I may have caused."

Mackey, seemingly satisfied, nodded and patted Nate's shoulder. A slow smile stretched broadly across Royal's face.

Kit rubbed a hand over her face. Clearly, Royal counted that argument as score one for the Teagues in the generation-long battle of Hope Creek against the Suttons.

Beau was the first to break the awkward silence. "Why don't we start the tour?" He motioned for Royal to proceed him. "Royal, would you and Viv like to lead the pack?"

Royal eyed Beau, a hint of suspicion in his eyes, but trudged past the gate and onto the driveway all the same. "Might as well," he grumbled. "We came to look, so we might as well start looking."

Mackey, oblivious to the tense undercurrents, grabbed Cal's hand and tugged him along behind Viv and Royal, pointing first left, then right, then left again, asking questions faster than Cal could answer them.

"Well," Kit said, lingering by the gate as the group ambled up the driveway, "I suppose we can call that a promising start."

Beau grinned, the teasing gleam in his eye renewing the flutters of pleasure he'd inspired in her the night of the oyster roast. "I'd say any sort of start between a Sutton and a Teague is a good one."

"I enjoyed our time on the water the other day," Kit said. "Mackey's been asking about seeing Cal again, so it was a godsend when Viv stopped by with her invitation." She hesitated, her stomach sinking, as his grin faded. "And I have to admit, I looked forward to seeing you again. I wondered when I didn't hear from you . . ." She shrugged, her cheeks burning. "Not that I expected you to call or anything." Oh, Lord. She was rambling like a lovestruck teenager and making it worse. "I thought about stopping by a time or two, but I knew you were working and didn't want to disturb y—"

He reached out and tucked a strand of her hair behind her ear, and his fingertip lingered against her cheek. "I missed you, too, Kit."

Her skin tingled, and she caught herself leaning into his touch, nuzzling her cheek against his palm, as her fingers curled around his wrist. Movement over Beau's left shoulder caught her eye, and she glanced ahead, her eyes meeting Viv's as she turned back and stared in Kit and Beau's direction.

"I . . . think we'd better join the rest of the group," Kit said, releasing his wrist slowly. "With our dads in each other's company, we might have to head off another squabble."

A flash of disappointment entered his expression, but he stepped back and touched the small of her back, inviting her to precede him.

The first leg of the tour started off well. After she and Beau joined the rest of the group on the dock, they all boarded one of Nate's hybrid bay boats—a model much sportier than any Royal had ever owned—and rode out onto the creek. Yesterday's overcast sky still lingered, and a brisk breeze shoved wispy clouds along and swept across Kit's bare arms.

"Weather report this morning said storms are kicking up out in the Atlantic," Nate said, tipping his face up from his seat at the helm. "Rain might hit in the next day or two. You can smell it in the air."

Royal, standing by the casting deck, nodded, his gaze drifting in the direction of the sea, eyes narrowing. "Can feel it, too. My bones started aching today."

Viv scoffed and leaned back in the passenger seat beside Nate. "Good grief, anyone listening to you two would think y'all were some ancient, world-weary seafarers. You're not old—or decrepit—Dad."

Royal glanced over his shoulder at Viv and frowned. "Most days, I certainly feel world-weary. Especially when I'm arguing with you."

Nate's head swiveled, moving from Royal to Viv, then back. Laughter burst from his lips. "Viv has a point, Royal. When I was half her age, I sat around listening to my dad spout the same lines on the water, and he wasn't near as young as you. What number you hauling around these days?"

"Fif . . ."

Nate cupped a hand around his ear. "What's that?"

"Fifty-six," Royal shouted over the whir of the boat's engine. "And I never said I was old, just weary."

Nate grinned. "It's kind of hard to tell what age you are on account of that beard. I've never seen you sport one before. Thought of growing one myself a time or two." He rubbed his own smooth-shaven chin. "But that kind of style would only make me look older than I am."

Royal's lips twitched. "And how old's that? I know you got some years on me."

"Sixty-five," Nate said proudly. "Ain't nothing but a number, Royal."

"Guess not." Royal turned back to the water and watched the wake rippling behind the boat, then looked ahead. His expression fell as floating cages, bobbing along the creek in parallel lines, emerged into view. "But sometimes my number feels like it carries the weight of a lifetime."

Breath catching, Kit stood from her seat beside Mackey on the casting deck and moved to Royal's side. She slipped one of his hands between both of hers and looked up at him. He continued to stare at the cages.

Nate slowed the boat, then cut the engine. Silence fell, and Kit leaned against Royal; the metal cages made her gut churn.

"I'm sorry about Sylvie," Nate said quietly. "She was a good woman, Royal."

A small sound escaped Royal, and he hung his head, one long arm lifting, winding around Kit's shoulders, and tugging her tight against his side. "Beautiful too. She was the most gorgeous woman that ever walked this earth. Inside and out. No matter what her troubles were." He lifted his head and cut his eyes Viv's way, his chin jutting out.

"And she loved our kids. Every single one of 'em, with all her heart."

Viv held Royal's stare, her eyes glistening. She looked down and twisted her hands in her lap.

Her own eyes welling, Kit pressed her cheek to Royal's chest and closed her eyes, the heavy beat of his heart against her skin easing the pain inside her. It had always been a sore spot with Viv that they'd been unexpected. That she and Kit had been—as she'd always seen it—a mistake, their conception merely a mishap of one careless night when neither Sylvie nor Royal were fully grown, much less capable of being stable parents.

It hadn't helped matters that the twins had carried the weight of Sylvie and Royal's mistake, as well as those of grandparents they'd never known, every time they fielded rumors, innuendos, and thinly veiled insults while they were growing up on the island. Hope Creek was small, mouths were big, and juicy gossip traveled fast. And for most people on the island, there had been nothing juicier than Teague family troubles revolving around unexpected teen pregnancies, Sylvie's increasingly odd behavior, and Royal's failure to lift them all to solid ground.

Kit opened her eyes and straightened, glancing at Viv, who still stared down at her hands. She couldn't blame Viv for being resentful. The gossip and assumptions that had swirled around them on the island for years had tarnished their reputations before they'd had a chance to establish identities of their own. Which, Kit thought, surreptitiously wiping her eyes, might very well have been part of what drove Viv away from home and drew her to the Suttons instead.

"I apologize if I upset you," Nate said, reaching over and covering Viv's hands with his own. "We can always turn around, Royal. You just say the word, and we'll head back."

Royal glanced at Viv, then looked down at Kit, studying her eyes and expression, and tipped her chin up gently with one knuckle. "No," he said softly. "Ain't no need to go back. Only thing to do now is keep moving forward."

Beau dumped a mesh bag out onto the wooden culling table housed on a dock near the floating oyster cages. "And this is where we cull 'em."

Royal rounded the table to stand opposite Beau and eyed the pile of oysters on the table. He sifted through a few, flipping a couple over with one finger, then glanced at Beau. "How often you dump 'em out?"

"Every three or four months we go through each cage and separate the market-sized ones from the babies." He pointed at a stack of buckets sitting at the other end of the table. "Mature ones with deep cups go in the bucket. Then we store them in climate-controlled packaging and deliver 'em out to Hope Creek Resort and local restaurants. The biggest deep cups go to Vernon's Raw Oyster Bar—he sells them almost faster than we can deliver them. We pull the cages out regularly and send the oysters through the tumbler to grade and shape them—give 'em a little workout, so to speak—then bag them back up and drop them back in the water to mature."

Mackey, standing beside Royal, grabbed a small oyster, held it up against the sun, which sat low on the horizon, and turned the shell one way, then the other, his smile growing. "The baby," he said. "What you do with it?"

Beau smiled, the excited gleam in Mackey's eye reminding him of the first time he'd culled one of the cages. "Those go back in the cage, then back in the water."

Nate leaned his hands on the table. "They'll float in the creek for a few more months, eating good, getting nice and fa—" He bit his lip, his cheeks flushing. "Getting nice and healthy. Then we'll pull 'em out and check 'em again. If they've matured enough, we pack 'em up and off they go."

"Off they go," Mackey repeated with a whoop, smiling wider.

Beau laughed softly and glanced at Kit. She stood at the other end of the dock with Cal, talking as she pointed at a bend in the creek several feet away, probably describing another plentiful wild oyster bed he'd overlooked on his daily ventures down Hope Creek.

Cal said something, and Kit laughed, her head tilting back, the steady breeze blowing her long brown hair over her shoulders. Despite the initial tension between Royal and Nate, she seemed to be enjoying the afternoon tour and had asked almost as many questions as Royal, then had listened intently to Beau's and Viv's answers.

Beau glanced at Viv, who stood by his side, explaining a step in the farming process to Royal. She spoke confidently but kept glancing at him, then over her shoulder at Kit, an intense look in her eyes.

He dragged a hand over the back of his neck and stifled a sigh, regretting, for the millionth time, the scene that had transpired between him and Viv. Though he'd spoken the truth regarding their current relationship and the potential for a romantic relationship—or rather, the *lack* of potential—being honest with Viv about this had left him feeling like the worst kind of friend. Not only had he struggled to find a way to reject her gently—a feat he didn't think was actually possible—but he'd also found himself avoiding any direct discussion with Viv regarding his feelings for Kit.

Beau glanced back at Kit, and his heart tripped as her dark eyes met his. His feelings . . . What exactly did he feel for Kit? Attraction, for sure. Though short-lived and embarrassingly interrupted, that kiss had stayed on his mind almost constantly over the past several days.

I looked forward to seeing you again.

He smiled at the memory of her words earlier this afternoon, wishing he were at liberty to stride over, gather her close, cover her mouth with his, and enjoy her sweet taste again. She had no idea how much he'd longed to call or stop by, but the situation had become . . . complicated.

Beau bit his lip and turned back to Viv. The hint of pain and accusation in her eyes made him feel like a bigger heel than he already did. *Complicated* . . . to say the least.

"Don't grow them ourselves. Right, Beau?"

He started and glanced around. His neck heated when he noticed Royal's narrowed eyes on him. "I'm sorry." He turned back to Viv. "What were you saying?"

She pressed her lips tightly, then together said, "My dad asked if we grow the seed ourselves. I told him we buy our seed from hatcheries."

Beau nodded. "Local hatcheries. From Tidewater Farm on Lady's Island, actually. When we first get them, they're around five to six millimeters long."

"And how much time does it take to get from that to market size?" Royal asked.

"For the fastest growers," Beau said, "eleven months on average."

Royal's brows rose. "Eleven months?" He looked pensive. "Takes about three years in the wild," he muttered.

"All year round," Nate said. "Those babies grow out there all year round. We grow and fish them out in fall, winter, spring, and summer, too. Summer's our best time of year. Owners of raw oyster bars are chomping at the bit for deliveries. Summer tourist demand and a plentiful local supply make for the perfect combination." He smiled. "No more shipments from the Chesapeake Bay for Hope Creek. Uh-uh. This island's summer harvest is local, straight from the creek to the table, regardless of wild oyster season."

Royal's expression fell. "A season that's about to be over."

Beau shifted uncomfortably from one foot to the other. Here they were, boasting of their young farm's success while Royal was staring at the end of the line for his oyster harvest. Since April had just given way to May, his harvest was about to end, while theirs was just revving up.

A fine mist dampened their faces and Royal glanced up, frowned at the clouds. "What happens when the storms come? Them waves will break those cages up as easy as they do a boat."

"We prepare as best we can for that." Beau gestured over his shoulder toward the poles at each end of the lines of floating cages. "Our system's rigged so we can lower the cages to the bottom of the creek when necessary. The crop is safer from storm surge, debris, and wind damage down there."

"But it's the time it takes," Royal said, skepticism in his eyes. "Storms don't wait on no prep. Teague Cottage has weathered more than its fair share, and almost every time, no matter how good we board the place up, we come out on the other side with a busted window or roof." He lifted his chin toward the creek. "That's what you're missing here. Them clusters out there . . ." He shrugged. "Nature has its own way of protecting at the same time it destroys."

"Not always," Beau said. "Hope Creek's wild oyster population is in decline. Has been for years. If things don't change, bountiful oyster beds like the one Kit took us to won't just be rare. They'll be nonexistent."

Royal's lips twisted. "And you'll be their savior, huh?"

Beau bit his tongue.

"Here, Royal." Nate fished an impressive deep cup out of the pile of oysters on the table and nudged it in Royal's direction. "Try one. Tasting is believing, and I'm telling you, these oysters will rival the very best you've ever pulled out of the creek."

Beau pulled his gloves from his back pocket and tugged them on, grabbed his oyster shucking knife, and took the oyster from Nate. He cracked the shell open, revealing a full, fleshy oyster on the half shell, and presented it to Royal.

Royal stared at Beau for a moment, then the oyster, but finally took it, tipped it into his mouth, and rolled it over his tongue before swallowing it whole. His eyes drifted shut, and a look of surprised pleasure appeared on his face. Then he opened his eyes and studied the empty shell in his hand.

"Viv did that," Beau said.

Royal's eyes met his. "Did what?"

"Raised that oyster." He motioned toward the pile of oysters on the table. "Those too. That entire line's worth of cages, actually. That's her crop."

Royal's attention shifted to Viv, a look of pride crossing his face. "I'm not surprised," he said softly. "My girl always did have a way with the water and everything in it." His chin trembled. "Couldn't be more proud of her if I tried."

Viv's arm brushed Beau's, and he glanced over. His smile grew as she blushed and a small grin made its way to her face at her father's praise. That smile was a welcome sight.

"Thing is, though," Royal said loudly, clearing his throat. "You can't beat the flavor of a cluster of wild oysters steamed fresh over a flaming pile of wood."

Nate scoffed. "Our deep cups roast just as well as wild ones. Taste better, too."

"Bull." Royal tossed the empty shell on the culling table. "Ain't no way these fat suckers—"

"Dad!" Mackey jabbed Royal in the arm, glaring.

Royal held up a hand and softened his voice. "Ain't no way these oysters of yours steam open as sweet as mine." He jerked his thumb toward a stack of stainless-steel pots sitting at the end of the dock. "'Specially since they're cooked in those contraptions over propane."

Nate stiffened. "Want to put it to the test? I'll feed you an oyster so fat, juicy, and perfect that it'll choke you!"

Someone snorted behind Beau, the noisy outburst a mixture of shock and humor. "Pop!"

Beau turned to find Cal and Kit standing behind him, looking over his shoulder at Nate and Royal. Cal sported an enthralled excitement in his eyes. Kit look downright horrified.

She shook her head at Royal. "Dad, what in the worl—"

"All right, then." Royal smacked the culling table with the palm of his hand. "You're on. You got enough blocks and wood hiding around this place for me to build a fire?"

Nate harrumphed. "More than enough."

Royal stuck out his hand. "You want it?"

Nate thrust his hand in Royal's and shook it vigorously. "It's on!"

Beau could think of at least three things off the top of his head that he'd rather do with his time than referee a shouting match between Nate and Royal: kissing Kit, for one. He swigged the last of the iced water from the glass he held and looked out the glass patio doors on the back side of his house.

Night had fallen, and the moon, almost full, shone

bright, glowing down on the two men below. Nate stood on one side of the patio, poised in front of a row of pots, each positioned over a propane burner, and dumped a bucket of farmed oysters into an insert basket. He turned his head and said something to Cal, who stood by his side with a bucket in his hands. Cal shook his head and handed over the bucket, then smiled as Nate dumped the oysters out into a second insert basket.

Royal, stationed on the opposite side of the patio, threw another set of logs onto a makeshift firepit, spraying hot embers and ash into the spring night air. He grabbed a large piece of sheet metal, slid it over the fire, then motioned to Mackey, who dunked a large section of burlap into a bucket of water. Royal dumped a bucket of farmed oysters onto the sheet metal, spread them out with a shovel, then took the burlap from Mackey and spread it over the oysters.

Seemingly satisfied, Royal propped his hands on his hips and shouted something in Nate's direction. Nate dropped one of the insert baskets filled with oysters into a pot, stabbed a finger in Royal's direction, and shouted back.

"What are they fussing about now?"

Beau turned away from the patio doors, looked at Viv, and shook his head. "Who knows? They've been going at it so long, I had to come in here just to get my sanity back."

Viv, standing on one side of the kitchen island, pouring water from a pitcher into glasses, smirked. "No telling what kind of smoke Dad's blowing at Nate. That resentment of his has been building for at least a decade."

Kit, standing on the opposite side of the island, sliced a lemon with more force than necessary. "Can you blame him? He's lost thousands of dollars of business to Nate, you, and Beau just over the past few months." She glanced over her shoulder at Beau and smiled, her cheeks turning a pretty pink. "Sorry. No offense."

Beau tipped his empty glass at her. "None taken."

And he had to admit, it was true. The day he'd spent with Kit on the creek, sloshing through pluff mud, prying wild oysters free of their beds for hours, his muscles aching and wind gusting in cool bursts over his sweaty skin as they'd boated back to Teague Cottage . . . Well, he'd grown to appreciate the traditional harvesting method. Though, he also had to admit, the same traditional method was unsustainable, and change unavoidable.

Pearl Tide Oyster Company, however much disdain Royal might hold for it, served a beneficial purpose not only to the economy but to the environment, as well.

"Either way," Beau said, grinning, "no one's going hungry tonight, that's for sure."

Viv laughed. "Lord knows, that's the truth. There are enough oysters out there to stuff the bellies of at least thirty people." She finished filling one glass with water, set it aside, and started filling the next. "I put the hot sauce on the patio earlier. It's on the table, by Nate's station." She smiled. "It's the spicy one, not the sweet one. That homemade stuff they sell at Vernon's bar that you like so much."

"Thanks." Beau rubbed his stomach, laughing, as it growled at the mention of a fresh, spicy feast of oysters. "No matter how much they fight, it'll be worth it when we get to dig in."

"And it's a perfect night for it." Viv finished filling the last glass and held up the pitcher. "Want some more?"

"Sure." He walked to the island and handed his glass to Viv, then glanced at Kit. Her cheeks flushed deeper under his scrutiny, and her fingers fumbled over the knife as she sliced another lemon. "Careful," he said, stilling her hand with his. "You'll cut yourself."

Kit glanced up and smiled, her thumb lifting and brushing his oh so slightly. Just her warm touch and smile were almost enough to bring him to his knees. "Here." She lifted a slice of lemon. "For your water?"

"He doesn't like lemon." Viv thrust a glass between them, sloshing water onto both their wrists.

Beau stilled.

Kit and Viv grew silent and eyed each other from opposite sides of the island, remaining motionless. Neither of them had said very much to each other during the tour. The closest Viv had come to addressing Kit directly had been when they'd entered the kitchen an hour earlier and set about making side salads and gathering condiments for the oysters. Kit had asked where the knives were, and Viv, a retort in her eyes, had tightened her lips, then said sharply, "In the drawer. Behind my back."

"I don't really need your help in here, you know?" Viv said now, still staring at Kit. "I know the kitchen, and it takes a lot less time to get things done when I don't have to point out where everything is."

"I know you don't need me, and I don't mean to make things difficult for you," Kit returned quietly. "But I'm happy to help if it allows me to spend some time with you."

A muscle in Viv's jaw ticked.

"Viv." Beau narrowed his eyes when she glanced at him. "Thank you for the water," he said, a warning in his tone. He removed the glass from her hand then turned and smiled at Kit. "And I think I will try some lemon, please." As he removed the slice of lemon from her hand, his fingers lingered on the back of hers for a moment, and then he dropped the lemon in his glass of water. "Thank you."

She smiled hesitantly. "You're welcome."

Both women returned to their tasks, casting glances at Beau, then each other. Beau backed away slowly and headed for the patio doors, grateful—for once—that Royal's and Nate's voices had risen to shouting levels again outside.

"I think I'm needed outside." Smile tight, he opened one patio door and slipped out, then breathed deeply when cool night air hit his face.

But the relief was short-lived.

"And where the devil have you been?" Royal shouted, striding away from the fire and waving a shovel in the air.

Beau set his glass on a patio table and raised his hands, palms out, in front of him. "You want to put that shovel down, Royal? It's for scooping oysters, not bashing in skulls."

"It'll do for, either." Royal glanced at the patio doors, then glared at Beau. "What is it with you and my daughters? Every time I turn around, there you are, right at their elbows."

Muffled laughter sounded, and Nate turned around, smiling. "I told you not to put yourself in the middle, son."

Beau bristled. "And I told you, I'm tired of the *told you sos*. I'm not interested in your *told you*—"

"You're not interested in anything but my daughters," Royal said, frowning. "Kit, especially. I done told you once, you better treat her with the respect she deserves."

Beau lowered his hands and straightened. "I assure you I plan to do just that, sir."

Royal sighed and rubbed his forehead.

Cal, mouth hanging open, glanced from Royal to Beau, his eyes wide.

"Aw, I didn't mean to bring that up in front of your boy." Royal gestured toward Cal. "I . . . er . . ." Royal cleared his throat. "I apologize for that, son. Your dad's a . . ." He shot Beau a look. "Well, he's a good man, so far as I can tell. Least he has been to Viv so far. Beau, I want to tell you and Nate both, while I got the gumption," he muttered, "that I appreciate all you've done for her. Viv went through a hard enough time with Sylvie before her . . . passing. And that's on top of the way we lost her."

Beau, speechless, held Royal's gaze. The older man's praise stirred pride within him in much the same way that he imagined Viv must've felt when Royal had complimented her. It was unexpected and . . . heartfelt.

He smiled at Royal, saying warmly, "Thank you, R—"

"That's enough of that." Royal waved a hand in the air and walked back to the fire. He tugged on his gloves and removed the burlap, revealing a hot batch of freshly steamed oysters. "These are ready, if y'all care to dig in?"

Mackey and Cal were first, rushing over and piling their plates high. Nate and Beau followed and cracked into their first oysters with murmurs of thanks.

Beau moaned, savoring the flavor. "You steamed that one to perfection, Royal."

Royal guffawed. "Don't I know it?" He turned to Nate, who'd just tossed one back, too. "And yours?"

Nate smiled with satisfaction. "I'm not too prideful to admit when I'm wrong. Don't know that all fire-steamed oysters are better than my pot-steamed ones, but I have to say yours are."

Royal practically beamed. He propped his hands on his hips and glanced at Cal and Mackey, who were in the midst of cracking open their third and fourth oyster. "I ain't above admitting that y'all grow dang fine oysters. And tonight's been nice." He smiled, warm and sincere. "The nicest night I've had in a long time." He tossed a wry look in Nate's direction. "Even with the arguing. Y'all have been good company, and it's only right a man repay one kindness with another." He looked at Beau, expression hesitant. "Roe season just opened up early, and I haven't broke out my shrimping boat yet this season. If a storm sets in later this week, like they forecasting, I expect this is the best time to squeeze in a run. Y'all feel like taking a day off from farming tomorrow? Maybe ride out with me?"

Spend another day on the water with Kit? Laughing and sharing time with Cal, free of the daily grind? Beau smiled. "We'd love to."

CHAPTER 9

Kit tugged a pink short-sleeved T-shirt over her head, glanced at her reflection in the mirror on the dresser, then, frowning, yanked it back off.

"Hey, you ready yet?" Royal's deep voice and heavy knock sounded on her closed bedroom door. "Mackey's 'bout to have a fit to get going, they'll be here any minute, and I need your help packing and loading the coolers on the boat. A body can't do any sort of decent shrimping without cold soda or beer."

"I'll be out in just a minute," she said, grabbing a blue T-shirt she'd discarded a half hour ago and tugging it back over her head. "I'm just brushing my hair."

"Well, brush it faster. The shrimp don't care what your hair looks like."

No . . . but Beau might notice. Kit rolled her eyes and rubbed her temples. This was ridiculous. It was absolutely ridiculous to spend this much time choosing what to wear and agonizing over her appearance just to board a stinky shrimp boat and get blown around like a rag doll in the wind. She was a thirty-eight-year-old woman and above such vanity. Beau had already noticed her and must've been attracted to her—after all, he'd kissed her, for heaven's sake—which made all this worry over an outfit even more ridiculous.

She jerked the T-shirt down over her waistband, stuffed her feet in her tennis shoes, and grabbed one of the light jackets Viv had left behind in the closet. No need to be late or keep Royal and Mackey waiting. They were going on a shrimping trip, not attending a gala.

Still, she slowed in front of the mirror once more and smoothed a hand over her ponytail before opening the door.

"Good night above, girl. You'd think I'd asked you to put on formal attire."

Kit stopped and stared.

Royal stood in front of her, dressed in jeans and a neatly pressed T-shirt. His hair had been combed down, and his face was clean-shaven, revealing his handsome features.

"Dad . . . you . . ." She shook her head. "Your beard?"

Royal smiled, flashing even white teeth. "Gone. It was itching me." He rubbed his fingers over his chin and smiled widely. "Smoother than butter. Forgot what it feels like. And I woke up refreshed this morning—first time that's happened in ages. Must've been all that fussing with Nate yesterday that wore me out."

Kit stared, taking in the strong angles of his face and the bright, rested look of his eyes. He looked at least ten years younger. "You just . . . you look so different."

"Well, hitch your jaw back together and stop your gaping." He turned and walked down the hall, then paused, glanced back at her, and winked. "I've always been a handsome man."

It took Kit and Royal ten minutes to fill three coolers with ice and pack each with soda cans, bottled water, and beer. She would've finished faster, but she couldn't stop looking at Royal. The transformation—courtesy of a shave and lifted spirits—was remarkable.

Royal, Mackey, and Kit had just started hauling the coolers down the front steps when Beau, Nate, Cal, and Viv walked up the driveway. Beau noticed them first and hustled over to relieve Kit of the cooler she held.

"I'll get that," he said, smiling.

Kit smiled back, a giddy rush she hadn't felt since her teenage years surging through her. "Thank you."

"No problem." He hitched the cooler into one hand and reached for Mackey's, too. "I'll take that for you, Mackey."

"Thank you." Mackey handed it over, then jogged down the steps to Cal's side and held up his hand for a high five from his new friend, who obliged him. "Ready to catch the shrimp?"

Cal nodded. "I've never been shrimping before."

"Then you're in for a real treat, son." Royal offered a curt nod to Beau, then ambled down the steps and halt in front of Cal. "My boat's called the *Sylvie Lee*." Sadness shadowed his smile. "After the most beautiful woman in the world." He caught sight of Viv and held out his hand. "She looked a lot like this beautiful woman right here."

Kit grinned. Viv looked as shocked as Kit had felt minutes earlier, when she'd first caught sight of Royal. "It's overwhelming, isn't it?"

Viv glanced up at her, surprised. "He looks so much younger."

Royal laughed. "Well, ain't you the one that snapped at me yesterday, telling me I wasn't old yet?" He shrugged, his voice softening. "I just figured it was a new day." He swept an arm toward the patch of blue sky that peeked between high, wispy gray clouds. "A new day with a dab of sunshine. Something we haven't had much of the past couple of days."

"And less to come," Nate said, strolling over. "Forecast shows storms kicking up stronger. Morning report said there may be one headed this way in a day or two. Supposed to be somewhat of a gully washer."

"Then that's all the more reason to head on out and net up the shrimp now." Royal gripped the cooler tighter in his hand and headed up the driveway toward the backyard, waving an arm in the air. "Y'all best come on. I'm gonna put you to work."

Forty-five minutes later, they had all boarded the *Sylvie Lee* and were well on their way out into the Atlantic. The wind picked up as Royal's shrimp boat gained momentum. Clouds floated by more swiftly overhead, leaving patches of sharp morning sunlight in their wake, the bright rays sparkling in every direction, painting the water into a vast sea of gold silk that moved and rippled. A flock of seagulls and pelicans took flight above the lowered steel outriggers, flapping and squawking, excited about the day's potential meal.

Royal stood inside the pilothouse, showing Mackey and Cal, who stood by his side, all the gizmos and gadgets he thought might interest them. Beau and Nate leaned on the gunwale on the starboard side, chatting quietly.

Kit, standing near the bow of the boat, tipped her head back and closed her eyes, soaking up the morning sun. Her cheeks warmed, and she breathed deep, filling her lungs with fresh ocean air, a hint of salt on her tongue.

"Been a while, huh?"

Kit started, then glanced to her side. Viv stood beside her, watching her face, studying her expression. It was the second time since she'd returned home that Viv had actively sought her out.

Viv frowned. "What?"

Kit shook her head. "Nothing. I just . . . Someone else asked me that same question when I first arrived."

"Who? Dad?" Viv asked, glancing at a pelican that perched on the port handrail, several feet away from the port outrigger.

"No." Kit squinted at the sunlight bouncing off the water and recalled the day she'd returned to Hope Creek. Things had seemed so dismal then, so daunting. "Lou Ann Cragg."

Viv made a small sound of irritation. "The Marshland Messiah? Last time I saw her, she was knocking some poor guy senseless at Lou's Lagoon. That woman's always in everybody's business."

"She listens to talk," Kit agreed, "like everyone else. But she doesn't always believe it." She glanced over at Viv and smiled at the healthy pink glow the sun had coaxed to the surface of her sister's pale cheeks. "She offered me a cigarette. It was the first one I'd had in years. It reminded me of Mama."

Viv turned her head away, and her long hair, whipping in the wind, obscured her face.

"She remembered Mom," Kit continued. "Said she remembered us running around as kids, too. In diapers, no less." She hesitated, then asked, "Do you remember Lou Ann being around that far back? Do you remember if—"

"What are you doing, Kit?" Viv spun back around, her eyes, full of anger and pain, seeking Kit's. "Trying to relive good memories? Reminisce about our oh so happy childhood full of laughter and fun?" She shook her head. "Cuz if you are, I'll tell you right now, there are none. The earliest memory I have of Mom is when she threw a whiskey bottle at Dad's head and accused him of trying to kill her." Voice shaking, she drew in a heavy breath. "You and I were nine, curled up tight together under the kitchen table, too scared to move. How's that for a memory?"

Kit wrapped her hands around the bow pulpit railing and squeezed. "My earliest memory is different. It was on this boat, in fact." She gestured toward one of the lowered outriggers. "Dad brought all of us out here—well, except for Mackey. He wasn't born then. We were around six or seven, and Mom was having a good day. One of the best ones she'd ever had, I think."

Viv had turned away again, but at least she hadn't left. Instead, she stared out at the water rippling in the sunlight.

"She showed us how to work the gear and set the nets." Kit grinned. "I remember her smelling like sunscreen and hair spray. She even dolled up for a day on the water, but, boy, could she haul some shrimp. When those nets came up, she yanked that line, and we plopped down right over there"— she pointed toward the aft work deck—"and sorted through shrimp and bycatch for hours. It was hot—sweltering almost—but she sang out of key the whole time we worked, made us laugh and forget we were working. That is a good memory. That's what I choose to hold on to."

Viv tucked her hair behind her ears, her fingers sweeping quickly over her cheeks.

"Can we try that?" Kit asked.

"What?"

Kit slipped her arm around Viv's and curled her hand around her sister's elbow. "Can we pretend, just for today, that you don't hate me?" She swallowed hard, past the lump forming in her throat. "Can we set everything aside for a few hours and be sisters again? Just for today? For a few hours on the water? Because that's something I need, Viv. And that's all I'm asking for now."

Viv stayed silent for a few minutes, tears flowing freely, the wind drying them on her cheeks. "I'll try," she whispered. "Just for today."

Beau hadn't quite figured out what had changed between Kit and Viv since the shrimp boat left the deepest waters of Hope Creek and reached the even deeper waters of the Atlantic, but whatever it was, he'd take it.

"You're weak!" Viv threw her head back and laughed, her arms wrapped around one end of two large, flat rectangles of wood. She watched as Kit struggled to lift her end and maintain her hold on a metal rod above her head.

Kit, cheeks red and an adorably fierce expression on her face, squatted lower by the side of the boat, renewed her grip on her end of the wide planks of wood, and heaved them upward with a groan. "There!" Her arms trembled as she held the wood up, and a bright smile wreathed her face. "See. I'm not weak. I just had to warm up is all. And besides, it's not the weight. It's Dad's jacked-up system."

Viv laughed harder and palmed her cap lower on her head. "His system is not jacked up. You've just been sitting behind a desk for too many years, that's what."

Unable to sit by and watch Kit struggle, Beau strode over, reached around Kit, and secured a firm grip on the wood, taking some of the weight off Kit and freeing up her grip. He glanced down at her flushed face and smiled. "Better?" At her relieved nod, he asked, "What exactly is it that you do, anyway?"

Kit, puffing her hair out of her eyes, blinked up at him. "Marketing." She paused, breathing hard. "I'm in marketing."

He stifled a smile and lifted more of the weight with his hands. "What do you market?"

"Lingerie, cosmetics, cars, and ceiling fans," Viv shouted over the blustery ocean breeze and the squawks of birds overhead.

Beau raised an eyebrow at Kit and grinned. "Lingerie? Really?"

If possible, Kit's face turned redder. "Once," she said. "And it was a great-paying gig. I manage campaigns for a vast"—her grip slipped as the boat bounced over a swell, and she winced, stumbling two steps to the right—"array of products."

"Y'all got them doors lowered yet?" Royal shouted from the opposite side of the boat.

Beau glanced over his shoulder and shouted back, "Not yet. Still working on it."

"Well, tell them gals to get a move on." Royal turned back to his own task, calling directions loudly over the wind and waves and pointing out equipment to Mackey and Cal, who were assisting him.

"All right," Kit said. "Let's drop 'em."

Viv nodded, and Beau followed their lead as they shifted the wood up and over the side of the boat and lowered the doors that would hold the nets open into the deep water below. Kit and Viv immediately began pulling a series of cables, dragging the doors away from the boat and lifting them up to the end of one of the outriggers.

"Done," Kit said, clapping her hands together once with satisfaction. "Nets are next."

Viv eased by him, tugging at his shirtsleeve as she passed. "Come on. If you're on the boat, you got to work."

Beau stood still for a minute, watching Kit and Viv work in tandem as they unhooked nets, carefully unfolded them, then grabbed a long thick line. It was the strangest thing, the two of them working side by side without frowns or speaking in tight-lipped monotones.

"Come on over here, Beau," Kit said, smiling up from her crouched position on the deck, beside the nets. "These knots aren't gonna tie themselves."

Cal walked over and knelt beside Kit. "Royal asked if you're done yet."

"Almost." Kit smiled at him. "Did you help launch the other line?"

Cal nodded. "Royal showed me how to tie the knots."

"Would you like to tie these?" she asked.

Beau moved closer and held out a hand. "Wait a sec. He's never been on a shrimping boat, much less set up a trawl line."

Kit shrugged and handed Cal the line. "Then this is the perfect time for him to practice."

Beau gestured toward Royal. "I don't think your dad would be too pleased if those knots didn't hold and he lost his—"

"Is this your boat?" Kit asked, her lips twitching.

Beau, smiling, shook his head. "No."

"Then you don't call the shots." Kit nudged Cal's knee. "Go ahead, Cal. Tie that bag line."

Several minutes later, the doors were in place, and the nets and trawl lines were set. Royal conducted one last check on both outriggers, then deployed the nets. Cables lowered the gear on both sides of the boat, the doors opened as they sank below the water, and the nets stretched, billowing out and down.

"How far down do they go?" Cal asked, leaning over the starboard gunwale and watching the trawl lines sink.

"All the way to the bottom." Royal joined Cal and pointed at a trawl line just before it disappeared from view. "See them doors? They open right up underwater and spread those nets out like a bag. There's a chain on the front of the nets called a tickler."

Cal laughed. "A tickler?"

"Yep." Royal made a sweeping motion with his hand. "It skims the bottom and tickles those shrimp, making 'em jump right in."

"And the dolphins," Mackey said, shaking Royal's arm. "Tell him about the dolphins."

Royal leaned his elbows on the gunwale and grinned. "Oh, I won't need to tell him, son. He's gonna see for himself soon enough."

And Cal did see—as did everyone else. Bottlenose dolphins showed up first, diving along the wake of the boat, diving deep and picking off fish caught in the nets. Brown pelicans arrived next, swooping low in flocks around the outriggers, hovering close, some perching on various areas of the boat and others diving along the trawls, picking off fish, shrimp, and anything else that caught their eye. Gulls joined the gang of scavengers, as well, flying in low circles, waiting patiently for the nets to be hauled up out of the water.

The excited flurry of wildlife captivated Cal and Mackey. They shot from one side of the boat to the other, their gazes darting up, around, and down, trying to take in all the sights and sounds. They stood with Kit and Viv for a long time, asking questions and listening intently to each answer.

Beau smiled, watching as Cal edged closer to Kit and looked over the gunwale at the dolphins diving alongside the boat.

"What if something you don't want gets caught in the net?" Cal asked.

"Unfortunately, that happens," Kit said. "That's called bycatch. But there are safeguards in place to protect vulnerable species, like sea turtles. Royal outfits the trawls with these things called TEDs. Stands for turtle excluder devices. If a turtle gets trapped, that gear provides a way out. And another safeguard is gear called a bycatch reduction device, which helps fish find their way out, too. But bycatch can't be avoided altogether, and it mostly ends up being fish and crabs."

"What does he do with the bycatch that's there when he pulls the nets up?"

"We sort it out from the shrimp," Viv said, leaning around Kit and smiling at Cal. "Then we ice and store what we think we can sell, or we deliver a high-end feast"—she gestured at the birds and dolphins—"for these guys."

"Can I help when it's time?" Cal asked.

"Sure you can," Viv said.

Kit met Beau's eyes and grinned. "Your dad, too. Sorting's the best part."

Soon Royal announced it was time to haul up the nets. Everyone pitched in: Mackey and Cal joined Royal and Nate at one outrigger, while Beau, Kit, and Viv worked the other. Nets were hauled to the surface by a winch, then hoisted onto the boat with cables. Then Royal, Kit, and Viv popped the bag lines by undoing the quick-release knots, allowing the catch to spill free of the nets and fill the aft work deck.

Beau grabbed a bucket and sat on the work deck with Kit, Viv, Cal, and Mackey. They formed a large circle around the pile of shrimp, fish, and crabs, which jumped, wriggled, and rolled in a chaotic mass. It took several hours to sort the shrimp into buckets, certain species of fish into another, and crabs into a third. The remaining bycatch, which couldn't be salvaged or sold, was shoved off the boat in small batches, drawing hordes of pelicans and gulls, which scrabbled over each other to scoop up the fresh fish.

Mackey whooped and cheered, and Cal pulled out his cell phone and took pictures, aiming in every direction, unable to keep up with the flurry of activity.

Beau sagged back against the bulkhead of the work deck, his legs, arms, and back aching, but a pleased smile had formed on his lips.

"Enjoy yourself?" Kit teased, the same tired pleasure he felt filling her expression as she sat across from him on the work deck, leaning back on her hands.

"I did." Beau lifted an exhausted hand toward Cal and Mackey, who roamed cheerfully around the boat, chatting with excitement, taking pictures of pelicans, and watching dolphins play nearby. "The boys had a fantastic time, too. I'd say we all did."

Even Royal and Nate had relaxed in the pilothouse, Nate sipping a beer and Royal enjoying a smoke as he navigated the boat back to Hope Creek.

"It was a nice day," Viv said quietly, leaning back against the same bulkhead that was supporting Beau. She tugged her cap lower on her head and looked at Kit. "Was it as good a day as you remembered?"

Kit's expression dimmed, but she smiled. "Not exactly as I remembered, but close."

Beau hesitated, glancing from Kit to Viv as they avoided each other's eyes. "Did y'all do this a lot in the past?"

They both remained silent for a moment. Then Kit said, "I did. But Viv stopped coming out with me and Dad when we hit our teens. When we were kids, our mom used to work with us when our dad took us shrimping. Viv always came then."

Viv rolled her head to the side and met Beau's eyes. "Kit

asked if we could set aside our differences and try spending a day on the water together like we used to."

Beau smiled. "It seems to have worked." He glanced at Kit. "You two worked well together."

"Just for today," Viv said softly, her gaze moving from Beau to Kit and back. "But no matter what we do, nothing will ever be the same."

CHAPTER 10

Kit hefted a large bucket filled with freshly caught shrimp off the work deck of Royal's boat, propped it on one hip, and carried it off the boat and onto the dock. "You coming or what?"

Viv, who was standing on the work deck, lifted her cap and dragged the back of her hand over her sweaty forehead. Her lips twitched. "You rushing me or what?"

Kit smiled. In spite of Viv's initially cool reception, the day on the shrimp boat had gone well. They'd worked together, dropping trawl nets, hauling them up, dumping the catch, and sorting out shrimp. The longer they'd worked, the more Viv had relaxed, the tight set of her shoulders easing and the anger in her eyes fading. She had laughed several times and had even indulged in a playful water fight with Cal and Mackey when they'd begun hosing the work deck down after returning to Teague Cottage and tying up the boat at the dock.

"All those hours hunting down and handling wild shrimp ran you down while it gave me a second wind, that's what." Kit lifted her bucket briefly in the direction of the work deck, where Cal and Mackey still tussled good-naturedly over a long hose, stealing it from each other and spraying water over each other's legs, arms, and chests.

Viv dodged the spray of water, a small grin fighting its way to her mouth. She walked onto the dock, lugging the bucket with her. "The harvesting part of oyster farming isn't all that different from shrimping. We pull our catch out of the water, dump it out, and sort it, just like Dad does his. It's just that he uses nets to chase them down, while we pull them out of cages."

Viv's step slowed as her grin faded. A haunted look entered her eyes.

Heart breaking at the pain in Viv's eyes, Kit reached for her, but the weight of the bucket in her grip halted her movements, and loud bursts of laughter from Cal and Mackey as they horse played on the work deck reminded her this wasn't an ideal time to delve into the pain Viv had experienced from discovering Sylvie on the water. And . . . the brief glimpses of joy she'd seen in Viv's expression made her long to help Viv hold on to whatever happiness remained in the day.

"You impressed him," Kit said, smiling. "He's missed you. It's the main reason he swallowed his pride and invited the Suttons over today. It was so he could spend more time with you."

Viv blinked, and her expression cleared. "Dad, you mean?"

"Yeah."

"He said that?" Viv asked. "That . . . I impressed him? And that he wanted to spend more time with me?"

"He didn't have to," Kit said softly. "It was plain on his face."

One corner of Viv's mouth lifted. "His shaved face." She laughed. "I still can't believe he shaved that forest off his chin. He's been hanging on to that beard for years."

Kit laughed with her. "I know. I couldn't help staring when I saw it. I was glad to see him finally loosen up a little bit, decide to leave the house and soak up the sun without me having to shove him out the door."

Viv nodded. "It hurt him—" Voice breaking, she looked away, and her gaze fixed on the water rippling by the dock. "*I* hurt him when I moved out a couple years ago. I didn't think he'd ever forgive me for it, but yesterday, when he said he was proud of me . . ." She met Kit's eyes and shrugged. "Well, it was nice to hear."

Kit glanced down at the bucket in her hands and eyed the shrimp, weighing her words. "You must have been relieved that he's forgiven you." She waited, feeling the weight of Viv's gaze on her, then motioned toward the small shed in the backyard that served as Royal's fish house. "We better take these in and ice them down."

The fish house, small though it was, had served Royal well over the years, and as she entered it, Kit couldn't help but smile. Everything was just as she remembered: a floor-to-ceiling storage cabinet—one her dad had constructed from scraps of driftwood they'd collected over the years—still stood against one wall, probably still stuffed to the brim with fishing tackle he'd carefully organized. Buckets, baskets, and pots of various sizes were stacked to one side of the storage cabinet; fishing rods were lined up in a neat row and leaned against the wall; and a large freezer, stocked full of ice, hummed low with electric current in its position flush against the back wall. Fluorescent lights overhead and two large, uncovered windows brightened the small workspace.

The room was immaculate, had always been so, and had served as Royal's private refuge during Sylvie's roughest spells for as long as Kit could remember. Often as a child, Kit had followed him from the house to the shed, his drawn expression and moist eyelashes urging her to comfort him. He had never spoken during those moments; he'd just paused and held the fish house door open with one hand long enough for her to catch up to him and slip inside. Then he'd open the doors of the storage cabinet and take each piece of tackle out, inspect it for damage, and reorganize it all neatly in the cabinet.

After that, he'd stared out the window and smoked his cigar, the only sign he still remembered her presence being when he curled his hand around hers as she leaned against his side.

"That the last of 'em?" Royal, standing at a large wooden table that served as a culling and deveining surface, gestured toward the buckets in Kit's and Viv's arms.

Kit nodded. "Cal and Mackey are still hosing down the work deck. They should be finished soon."

"Good." Smiling, he tapped the table in front of him. "Set those down and let's rinse, ice, and pack a few bags. I called Vernon last night, told him I'd be shrimping today, and he said he'd take an order so long as I have them to him today."

Nate and Beau, who'd preceded Kit and Viv into the fish house with buckets of shrimp, set their buckets on the floor beside the table.

"Thank you for having us on your boat, Royal," Nate said, holding out his hand. A pleased expression crossed his face. "Been a while since I've been shrimping—years, actually—and I enjoyed it."

Royal shook his hand, then rubbed his chin, studying the buckets of shrimp at his feet. "Only half this haul is headed to Vernon's." He glanced out the window. "And them clouds have cleared out. Ain't nothing better than fresh Frogmore stew by the creek. I'll set it up if you'd like to join us?"

Nate glanced over his shoulder at Beau, who'd walked to the storage cabinet to admire Royal's craftmanship. "What you think, son? Cal and I can tie up a few loose ends at the farm and come back in a couple of hours." He leaned to the side and looked out the window toward the docked boat, where Cal and Mackey stood, laughing, on the work deck. "Mackey's asked several times today when he could visit the farm again. I'd be happy to have him come along with me and Cal to help us out, if that sits well with you?"

Royal glanced at the boys through the window, his brow creasing. "Mackey ain't gone off much on his own without me, but—"

"Mackey will be fine," Kit said, setting her bucket down. "He'd jump at the chance to go and"—she smiled at Beau—"Cal's been a great friend to him."

He'd been more than that, really. He'd been patient, kind, and compassionate. Cal was very much like his father.

Beau looked up from the storage cabinet and met her eyes. His windswept hair and crooked grin of appreciation as he studied her face made her breath catch.

"Besides," Kit said, turning back to Royal, "Mackey let me know in no uncertain terms that he's capable of taking care of himself, and he would give you a very hard time if you told him no."

Royal considered this, a wry smile curving his lips. "You're right about that. I suppose it's all right if he goes, and I thank you for inviting him." His smile slipped. "We haven't had many guests over the years, so the past couple of days have been a real treat." He waved a hand in the air, his smile returning, then grabbed a bucket of shrimp and dumped it on the table. "I'll get to icing and bagging, and after I make the delivery, I'll the get the stew going."

"I'll help you." Viv eased past Kit and set her bucket of shrimp by the table. "Do you have fresh potatoes and corn in the house, or do you need me to go pick some up?"

Royal, surprise in his eyes, remained silent for a moment, his gaze lingering on Viv's small smile. "I'd love that," he said softly. "And yeah, there's plenty of potatoes and corn in the kitchen. Sausage in the fridge, too. I'll devein us some shrimp after I finish bagging Vernon's order."

"And I'll help you out there," Kit said, "by making the delivery for you." She smiled at Viv, a bittersweet ache moving through her. "That way you and Viv can build the fire and start cooking without having to rush."

"I'll go with you," Beau said, his warm gaze settling on Kit.

Royal dumped another bucket of shrimp on the table. "Then it's settled. Viv and I will ice and bag, and then you and Kit can take my truck and make the delivery. By the time all of you make it back," he said, grinning, "there'll be a feast fit for royalty waiting on you."

"By the time we make it back, huh?" Beau, seated in the passenger's seat of Royal's truck, flashed that adorable—and aggravating—crooked grin. "You sure we'll be able to make it back?"

Kit hunched farther over the steering wheel, turned the key in the ignition for the third time, and listened to the engine sputter and cough, willing it to start. "Maybe," she muttered, trying a fourth time.

The engine rumbled to life . . . thank goodness.

"Hallelujah!" Laughing, Kit shifted gears and backed slowly out of the driveway of Teague Cottage onto the dirt road. "Long as it gets us to Vernon's before the ice melts and the shrimp spoils, we'll be good to go. We can walk back if we have to."

"A walk in the moonlight, just you and me?" Beau winked. "If the truck doesn't break down, that might be enough incentive for me to tamper with the engine."

Kit stifled a smile and focused on the dirt road curving in front of them as she eased the truck toward Vernon's Raw Oyster Bar a few miles away. "I see the frisk is back in your tail."

Beau raised an eyebrow. "Excuse me?"

"I'm referring to earlier this week." She drummed her fingers on the steering wheel. "I mean, you passed the house a few times, saw me, and didn't stop—not that you had to. Or that I expected you to or anything." Great. Just great. She was rambling again. She readjusted her grip on the wheel. "You just seemed a bit cool, is all. Like you were taking a step back maybe?"

He didn't answer. Not at first. Instead, his long legs shifted restlessly, and he looked ahead, too, his blue eyes roving over the gradually descending twilight. Shades of pink and lavender glowed low on the horizon, filtering between the long branches of live oaks, and cast a rosy hue over his ruggedly handsome features.

"I did," he said quietly. "For a second. Then I changed my mind."

Kit frowned, mulling it over. "What made you change your mind?"

He moved at her side, and the weight of his direct gaze warmed her skin even more. "You."

She curled her hands tighter around the steering wheel, her head and body leaning his way before she forced her attention back to the dirt road. Oh, she wanted to look at him. To reach out, take his hand, and weave her fingers between his. To hold on to him in some tangible way.

But she couldn't ignore the look on Viv's face the past couple of days. The possessive way she'd acted in Beau's kitchen last night, during the oyster roast, and the pained expression on her face whenever Beau had sought Kit out on the boat today.

"You mentioned you were in marketing earlier," Beau said, easing back in his seat. "You enjoy it?"

Kit nodded. "I do. I help people get their businesses off the ground and present their products in the best light. It's rewarding."

A humorless laugh burst from his lips. "Really?"

She sighed. "I told you I was sorry for the way I behaved that night at the community center—and I am," she stressed. "Truly."

His hand, warm and caressing, covered hers on the steering wheel. "I know, and I accepted, so it's behind us." He squeezed the back of her hand before releasing it. "It was just that you opened the door, you know? I couldn't help but walk on in."

The teasing note in his voice made her smile.

"Is it remote?" he asked.

"Is what remote?"

"Your job. Is it one you could do from here, if you chose to?"

The low lights of Vernon's Raw Oyster Bar emerged as she drove around a curve. Hands trembling, she slowed the truck and turned into the parking lot. "I suppose that could be a possibility."

"And have you thought about it?"

The place was packed. Only one parking spot remained empty; all the others were taken up by golf carts, with the exception of four cars and two trucks.

Avoiding his eyes, she parked the truck. "Have I thought about what?"

He sighed. "If you don't want to talk about it, that's okay."

Kit cut the engine, inhaled deeply, and faced him. "It's not that I don't want to talk. It's just that I have other concerns about where this is going. One in particular."

He lifted a hand in appeal. "I'm not trying to pressure you or—"

"Viv's in love with you, isn't she?"

Beau froze, his eyes fixed on her mouth, as though he were still piecing together her words. He moved to speak, then seemed to think better of it and looked away, his gaze moving to the beach that lay beyond the parking lot.

"I'm right, aren't I?" she whispered, her throat tightening painfully. "Has she told you?"

His jaw clenched. "Kit . . ."

"Because I need to know."

His teeth dragged over his bottom lip as he continued staring out the windshield. Then he said quietly, "Viv and I are friends, and whatever she shared with me about her feelings was in confidence. So if you want to know the answer to that question, you'll need to ask her."

"But I can't, can I?" Kit turned away, too. Stared at the waves crashing onto the sand beneath the fading colors of the sunset and the rapidly emerging moon. "Viv and I are hardly sisters anymore. Haven't been in a long time. Today was the first day in over fifteen years that even remotely felt like I might have a chance at setting things right between us, and even now it's a long shot." She turned back to Beau and tried to steady her voice. "I know you asked me to keep Viv out of this. Out of whatever you and I might have. But that's not possible, is it?" she asked. "For either of us?"

"No." His eyes met hers, wounded sincerity in their depths. "You're right. But I'd rather not betray Viv's trust. Just as I wouldn't want to betray yours."

"I know," she said, smiling. "You're an honorable man. It's one of the things I l—"

She shook her head and clamped her mouth shut. *Love?* The word—and deep emotion—had swelled in her chest and settled on the tip of her tongue almost before she could keep from saying it. She'd known her attraction to Beau had resurfaced, but . . . love? Yes . . . that was exactly what it felt like. Which made the situation all the more heart wrenching.

"I appreciate your respect for both of us," she continued slowly, "but there's no way around this, is there?"

"Kit"—he spread his hands—"this is new for me. All of it. I'm not sure how to navigate it."

"No matter how we go about this, if we pursue each other, we risk losing Viv." She searched his face, the same longing she used to feel years ago returning. "This wasn't supposed to happen. I didn't plan on this. I didn't expect to see you again and fall for you all over ag—"

Kit pressed her lips together, her face heating.

Beau leaned closer, his mouth parting. "Again?" At her nod, he covered her hands with his, his thumb smoothing over the pulse in her wrist. "I noticed you, too." He smiled slightly. "As far back as I can remember. We were on different paths then. I guess it just wasn't the right time for us to meet, to understand each other. But now . . ."

She closed her eyes and turned her hands over, threaded her fingers through his. "I don't know that now is any better."

His palm cupped her cheek, and his forehead pressed against hers. "I hope it is. Because I know what I want. I loved Evelyn—was lucky to have the time I had with her for as long as I did—but I'm not the same boy I was when I met her. I'm not even the same man I was when I was still married three years ago. I'm different, and I want different things out of life. I value every minute I have now, every breath. And I want to hang on to everything—and everyone—I treasure." He brushed his mouth across hers, so lightly that she thought for a brief moment that she'd imagined it. "I'm falling for you, too. More and more every day. And no matter what happens—or what Viv thinks—I don't want to give up on this thing between us. I don't want to let you go."

She smoothed her hands over his wide chest, slid her palms up his neck, and cradled his face, the stubble lining his jaw rough against her fingertips. "I don't want to let you go, either."

His head dipped lower, his lips brushing hers again, and she met him halfway, pressing her mouth to his. His big palm slid around her waist and caressed her back, cupped her shoulder blades, and kneaded her nape. The light, rhythmic pressure of his callused fingers against her bare skin stirred delicious shivers of pleasure that coursed through her veins and coaxed her closer.

His arms tightened around her, drawing her in, his spicy masculine scent and tender touch enveloping her completely for a moment. Then, with a soft groan, his arms loosened, and he pulled away.

Kit opened her eyes and looked up at him, her breath catching at the heady longing in his blue eyes and the soft flush of heat along his chiseled cheekbones and sensual mouth.

"I don't know what the answer is here," he said softly, trailing his hands over hers again. "But I know I'm not ready to give up on what we could have."

The fire burned high, the moon hung low, and even the deepest waters of Hope Creek glowed bright beneath the starry night sky, rippling in a tidal dance to the rhythmic chorus of tree frogs and crickets populating the Teagues' backyard. Savory aromas of shrimp, sausage, and corn billowed up from the large pot hanging over the center of the fire Royal and Viv had built, and mingled with the crackle of hot embers and light smoke drifting heavenward. It was a perfect night—just as Royal had said—for fresh Frogmore stew slowly boiled to perfection over an outdoor fire.

Beau smiled. But, he conceded, the most eye-catching jewel of the night was the sight of Kit standing by the fire, laughing, soft moonlight cascading like silvery tendrils over her dark hair. She glanced up, met his eyes, and smiled. Flames flickered higher, warming her cheeks to a pretty pink and highlighting the smooth curves of her lips.

He gripped the cold bottle of beer in his hand tighter, the label, having grown soggy in the humid air, clinging to his palm. He recalled the warm, soft feel of Kit's neck, shoulders, and back beneath his palms just two hours earlier. It'd taken every ounce of self-control he had to pull away. To lift his mouth from hers, remove his hands from her, and give her the space he knew she needed to decide how—or if—she wanted to pursue the attraction between them.

No. More than that. He lifted the beer bottle and rolled it over the base of his neck, cooling his overheated skin. But the icy feel of the glass did nothing to still the longing that tugged deep within his chest. That familiar but somehow unique throb of desire, need, and tenderness. A feeling he'd never felt as strongly or as deeply before . . . not even with Evelyn. Only with Kit. An emotion he couldn't shake or deny. Quite frankly, he didn't want to.

Viv's in love with you, isn't she?

Beau stiffened at the memory of Kit's words. It must've shown in his expression, because Kit's smile dimmed, and her eyes strayed from his. He followed her line of sight to the opposite side of the fire, where Viv stood, stirring the contents of the large pot hanging over the flames.

Viv hadn't said much since his and Kit's return from their shrimp delivery run. She'd studied them closely when they'd returned, her eyes examining each of their faces as they'd walked up the dirt driveway to the backyard. Her mouth had tightened, and she'd returned to her task of cutting potatoes in halves on a long wooden table by the fire.

He had no doubt that Viv knew he was attracted to Kit—she'd implied as much before on a couple of occasions. She'd certainly made it clear the night she'd confessed her feelings for him.

He'd been honest with Viv that night. He hadn't left any doubt as to the parameters of their friendship. But a different sort of complication existed that hadn't occurred to him before.

As much as he wanted to build a relationship with Kit, she wanted to build one with Viv. She wanted . . . No, judging from the pleading tone in her voice and the desperate look in her eyes, Kit *needed* to reestablish a connection with Viv, to find a way to reconcile their past and future and put their pain behind them for good. And a potential relationship with him, maybe even his presence alone, might prevent their reconciliation.

Even though he knew that, the thought of walking away from Kit, from what they could have, was too painful to consider. But if pursuing a relationship with Kit harmed her chance at reconciliation with Viv . . . well, he didn't know if he could live with th—

"You're eyeing my girls again."

Beau started at Royal's low words, beer sloshing out of the bottle in his hand and splashing across his wrist.

"Don't think I didn't notice." Royal, having left Viv's side and rounded the fire, butted Beau's elbow with his and angled up to Beau's side. "And don't think just 'cause I have a newfound appreciation of the decent human being you are that I'm going to give you any kind of free pass to either of my daughters."

Beau closed his eyes and rubbed his eyelids briefly before facing Royal. "I don't know what you're getting at, Royal. Though"—he dipped his head—"I appreciate your recognizing and admitting that I am, as you put it, a decent human being." His mouth lifted in a crooked smile. "I'll take that as a compliment, even though I'm fairly certain you didn't mean it to be one."

"Heck, no, I ain't mean it to be," Royal scoffed. "But I ain't no liar, either, and I give credit where credit's due." He sniffed. "I just wish you'd make up your mind or leave my girls alone."

Beau shook his head, watching as Kit moved to Viv's side and motioned Nate over. "It's not like that. Not the way you think."

Royal narrowed his eyes, staring at him. "Then what way is it?"

Beau lifted the bottle of beer to his lips, tilted his head back, and took a deep swig. "I don't particularly want to have this conversation with you, Royal. I'm too old, for one, and too private for anoth—"

"Nothing's private with you, son. Every thought you think and emotion you feel gets plastered all over your face almost before it occurs to you." He smirked. "Besides, you're never too old to answer to the father of a woman you love."

Beau faced him, his mouth parting. "What . . . ? Where are you getting this from? And why do you think—"

"Oh, I know," Royal said quietly. He examined Beau's expression, then turned his attention to Kit, who smiled and stepped back as Nate lifted a big strainer pot filled with Frogmore stew from the larger one and hauled it carefully across the yard to the wooden table. "One look

at your face the day you kissed Kit. I seen it for myself."
He turned back to Beau, gave a small smile tinged with
sadness. "Way you looked at Kit, I used to look at her
mother." He grew quiet, then said, tone sobering, "I know
more than people give me credit for. You tell me if I got it
wrong."

Was he? Was Royal wrong? Of course he wanted Kit . . .
in every way possible. He wanted to know her mind, her
thoughts, her wishes and dreams. Wanted her hands on
him, his hands on her, sharing whispers and making love.
Maybe even sharing more than that. Maybe . . . sharing
his days and nights with her, and hers with him, for whatever time he had left in this life. Every precious second . . .

Heart thumping against his rib cage, Beau looked back
at Kit.

"No," he said softly. "You don't have it wrong."

Royal hesitated; then, his voice low, he sought confir-
mation. "It is Kit you're in love with?"

Beau pulled in a shaky breath, his whole body trembling, and met Royal's eyes. "Yes. I'm in love with Kit."

"And Viv?" he asked. "Where do you stand with her?"

"We're business partners," Beau said. "And friends.
That's all we've ever been."

Royal tilted his head and peered past the fire, to where
Viv stood helping Nate tilt the pot and dump its aromatic
contents on the table. "Does Viv know that?"

"How I feel about her? Yes." Beau curled his fist tighter
around the bottle in his hand. "Does she know how I feel
about Kit? No."

Nate finished spreading the Frogmore stew over the table.
Fragrant, piping hot shrimp, potatoes, corn, and sausage
rolled and settled in small piles, bathed in the flickering orange light of the fire and the cool white glow of the moon
above.

"Come on, y'all," Viv shouted, smiling at Beau and Royal. "I didn't spend the past two hours breaking my back over a hot pot just for you two to skip the best part." She waved an arm in the air. "Get over here."

Cal and Mackey, seated at the table between Nate and Kit, banged their hands on the table and howled playfully, ready to dig in.

"Let's eat!" Cal yelled. "I'm starving."

Kit, laughing, ruffled his blond hair and pointed out several plump shrimp near his end of the table. He grabbed one, popped it in his mouth, and chewed, a look of bliss spreading across his face. Kit did the same, then hummed her approval as she smiled at Viv, thanking her for cooking.

"That right there," Royal said in a low voice, "is the first time my girls have shared a table in over a decade. It's what Kit's always wanted. It's why she came back, no matter what Viv thinks." He looked at Beau, an unsettling sympathy mixing with the warning in his eyes. "For Kit, family always comes first."

CHAPTER 11

Some things you just couldn't see coming until the last minute.

"Can we paint it, Beau?"

Beau, standing halfway up a ladder that leaned against the front of Teague Cottage, braced himself against a swift gust of wind and glanced down at Mackey, who stood several feet below him in the front yard of Teague Cottage. "I don't think that'll be possible, Mackey," he called down. "The storm's coming in pretty fast now, and it'll be dark in a couple hours."

Mackey frowned. He waved the paintbrush he held in the air and squinted as the wind picked up even more, blowing his hair across his forehead and into his eyes. "But what if we don't paint but write? We could write, *Go away, Winny*! Ain't that what kind of thing they write, Beau? I saw a lady on TV write that on one of her boards. She had a lot of them."

Beau leaned against the ladder with one hand and withdrew a nail from his pocket with the other. "Yeah, some people do, and if we had more time, we might, but we're stretched as it is."

And that was an understatement.

Two days ago, after enjoying a late evening Frogmore

stew with Kit at Teague Cottage, Beau had walked home beneath the bright light of a full moon with Cal, Nate, and Viv. They'd arrived home with tired eyes and full bellies, and after turning in for the night, Beau had tossed and turned, his mind restlessly picking apart his conversations with Kit and Royal. Finally giving up on sleep, he left his bed before dawn, dressed, and paused in the kitchen long enough to pour a cup of coffee, then carried it with him to the boat, sipping the hot brew along the way.

As he set out on the water at sunrise, there was a slight change on the horizon. Rather than the clear skies of the night before, a few wispy clouds could be seen lingering high in the sky, and the normally peaceful saltwater breeze blew harder than usual. Throughout the day, as he hauled cages out of the water and lifted them onto the boat, the clouds increased in size and number.

The weather report and alerts scrolling across the bottom of the TV screen that night were just as he suspected. Hurricane Winnifred, having first appeared as a weak early season tropical storm in the central Atlantic had meandered its way north, strengthened near the Bahamas, then begun traveling northwest, evolving into a Category 3 hurricane with a trajectory that would propel it toward the southeastern coast of the United States.

The good news—if any surrounding a hurricane were possible—was that Winnifred had lost steam and weakened, and thus had been reclassified as a Category 1 hurricane. They hoped that it would weaken again before skimming along the eastern coast and avoiding a direct hit to South Carolina's barrier islands. Hope Creek should not—if all reports proved accurate—be damaged by the storm.

But Winnifred was still headed Hope Creek's way, and Beau wasn't willing to gamble against the storm.

He sat down at the kitchen table with Nate and Viv and

sketched out a list of tasks immediately. The plan was familiar—they'd hashed it out three years prior, when they'd first applied for a permit to establish Pearl Tide Oyster Company.

Beau and Viv spent most of the next day harvesting as many market-sized oysters as possible, dragging cage after cage out of the creek, hauling them to the floating dock, and sorting through them as quickly as possible. When they returned each cage to the creek, they lowered it to the bottom—a process that wasn't as easy or as fast as Beau had envisioned, especially with a major storm on the horizon.

"We can take care of this, you know," Kit said, pulling him from his reverie. Standing on the screened-in porch of the cottage, she hammered a nail into one corner of a large wooden board positioned over a window. She pulled on the board, confirming it was secure, before she turned to face Beau. "It was very considerate of you to come over and help us prepare for the storm, but I know you must have a thousand things left to do on the farm."

Beau studied her through the screen. Wind gusted, filtering through the mesh wire and scattering the long brown strands of her hair over one shoulder. Her eyes were bright, and a firm smile was in place, but the exhausted note in her soft voice belied her easy words.

"After Dad and I finish boarding the house up, we'll secure the fish house and raise the dock lifts." The same smile appeared again, tired and unsure. "He's been listening to the newscasts almost nonstop since yesterday and says he thinks there's a good chance Winnifred will turn out to be nothing more than a rough thunderstorm."

"A gully washer," Royal said, striding around the side of the house, a hammer in one hand and a bag of nails in the other. "Shouldn't be no more than some whipping wind and rain. Then she'll be outta here."

"I hope so," Beau said, retrieving another nail and rolling it between his thumb and forefinger.

Royal dragged the back of his hand over his forehead and looked up. His eyes roved slowly over the overcast sky. "Tell you what, though. One thing you ought never bet on is the weather."

Beau noted the lines of strain around Royal's mouth and the slight tremble in his hands. When Beau, ladder in hand, had arrived two hours ago, Royal had been standing on his own ladder, propped against the back side of the cottage, hammering boards into place, periodically reaching down to Kit, who passed him the boards, while Mackey passed him nails. All three of them had been at it awhile, and they had made it only halfway around the house when Beau joined them.

They'd made significant progress since—Beau and Kit had taken over boarding up the front of the house, while Royal and Mackey had finished up the back.

Royal narrowed his eyes at Beau. "Why don't you head on back? 'Specially with what you got at stake. Me and Kit can take care of the rest of this and the boats, and Mackey can batten down the fish house. Can't you, son?"

Mackey smiled and dropped the paintbrush. "Yeah, I can do it." He sauntered over to Royal's side and clamped a hand on his father's shoulder. "What should I do, Dad?"

Grinning, Royal handed him the hammer and lifted his chin toward the back of the house. "I'll show you, and you can tackle it while I help Kit finish boarding up the front of the house."

Beau smiled as Royal slung his arm around Mackey's shoulders and guided him toward the backyard. Royal stopped after a few steps and glanced over his shoulder.

"It was real decent of you to come over like this," Royal said. "'Specially seeing as how we were short a set of hands." He nodded, the small smile on his face slipping. "Real decent. And I know Kit appreciates it. We all do."

Beau smiled, the rare compliment—which, he noted, had become a more frequent occurrence lately—sitting well with him. "I was happy to do it, sir."

Royal issued another curt nod, then left, giving Mackey directions along the way.

"He misses Viv." Kit pushed her hair back over her shoulder and tucked it behind her ear as she watched Royal and Mackey walk around the house and out of view. "So does Mackey." She returned her attention to him and smiled, but sadness shadowed her eyes. "We had such a nice time the other night. All of us in one place, together . . ." Her chest rose on a strong breath. "It felt like we were a family again, even if it was just for a few hours."

Beau looked down at the nail in his hand, recalling how quiet Viv had become after the Frogmore stew dinner two nights ago. She hadn't said much at all during the walk home—Cal, still excited from the day's fun, had done most of the chatting—and she'd grown more withdrawn throughout the next day, as she'd culled oysters. Several times, her hands had paused while sifting through the crop and her attention had drifted off, her eyes focusing on the clouds building and the water rippling in the distance.

"She enjoyed the night we spent here, too," Beau said, meeting Kit's eyes. "Too much, I think, for her own comfort. It was hard for her to leave home two years ago, and I think it brought up a few regrets."

Kit moved closer and touched the screen with one hand, her dark eyes seeking his through the mesh wire. "Did she tell you why?"

"Why she left?"

Kit nodded, her expression eager.

Beau hesitated, unsure how much of what Viv had revealed to him was really his to share. "I know things had become very difficult here. She and your mom . . . Well, Sylvie wasn't doing well at all, and it was taking a toll on Viv." He glanced at the side of the house where Royal and Mackey had disappeared, and lowered his voice. "Royal had become pretty down—he rarely left the house—and he and Viv didn't talk much anymore. Viv was worried for him and your mother. Sad and confused. She felt alone."

Kit bit her lip and turned her head. Wind whistled through the screen again, spilling her hair over her shoulders. She pushed it back absently. "She told you that?"

"She didn't have to," he said, wincing as he recalled the night Viv had knocked on the front door of his and Nate's house. It'd been raining that night, she'd walked from Teague Cottage, and her hair and clothes had been drenched when she arrived. She'd stood shivering in the doorway. "I could see how alone and afraid she was."

"Did she . . . ?" Kit closed her eyes briefly, then looked up at him, a wary expression crossing her face. "Did she come back here at all after she left? To visit my mother? Or check on her?"

Beau fiddled with the nail he held. "A few times in the beginning. But after the first few months, she stopped by only occasionally to check on Mackey and deal with a few odds and ends that Royal hadn't handled. She and your mother . . . Well, she never gave me specifics, but they weren't getting along well at all." He turned his head and studied the darkening sky, then positioned the nail he held against an unsecured corner of a board. "Your dad was right. We better speed this up if we're going to have a chance of finishing before dark. If you'll keep working in there, I'll—"

"Head back to the farm while I take over."

Kit froze, her gaze moving beyond Beau. He glanced down to find Viv standing in the same spot Mackey had vacated, hands on her hips and a stoic expression on her face.

Beau winced. Had she overheard?

"We've lowered half the cages," Viv continued, eyeing him. "But Nate needs your muscle for the last few lines. I told him we'd swap jobs."

Yep. The hard note in her tone told him she'd heard every word.

Beau turned back to Kit, and the apprehension on her face made him ache. He propped the hammer he held on the top rung of the ladder and pressed his palm to hers against the mesh screen. "I guess we're swapping. I'll finish as quickly as I can, then come back and check on you. See if you or Royal still need help securing anything."

Kit shook her head, her fingertips curling against the screen, pressing against his palm. "The storm will be setting in soon. I don't want you caught in the middle of it. We'll be fine." She glanced at Viv, then met his eyes again. Her voice resigned, she added, "Teague Cottage has ridden out storms worse than this in the past."

Wind roared around Teague Cottage, a sharp crack rang out, and a loud crash reverberated outside.

"What was that?" Mackey, seated opposite Kit at the kitchen table, glanced around, his eyes wide and hands curling tight around a glass of water.

Kit smiled, hoping the nervous tremors running through her didn't show. "Probably just a branch falling off one of the oak trees by the driveway. Those oak limbs are heavy, and with the wind picking up, one may have snapped and hit the ground."

Right along with about a dozen other limbs, if the violent crashing and banging were anything to go by, Kit thought, taking a slow sip of iced water from her own glass.

"Not to worry about that," Royal said. He reached out from his seat beside Mackey at the kitchen table and patted his hand. "None of those limbs are near this room. You're safe inside the house."

Viv, who stood across the room, leaning with her back against the kitchen sink, crossed her arms. "You sure about that?" she asked quietly. "That hasn't always been the case. Least not how I remember it."

Kit stiffened. She looked over Mackey's shoulder and locked eyes with Viv. "It's safe tonight."

Viv's mouth tightened, but she remained silent.

Kit stifled a sigh of relief, returned her attention to Mackey, and smiled. "Everything's going to be fine. This will blow over, the storm will move on, and you'll wake up to a beautiful morning tomorrow."

Or at least she hoped so.

After Beau had left several hours ago, Viv had taken his place on the ladder and helped board up the rest of the front of the house. They hadn't spoken much, but the side glares Viv had cast in her direction had hinted that she was offended to hear Kit grilling Beau for information about her and their mother.

Kit had concentrated on the work at hand, boarding windows, carrying the wicker chairs from the front porch inside the house, and helping Royal and Mackey raise the boats. Upon the completion of each task, she'd tipped her head back and studied an overcast sky that grew darker and angrier with each passing hour, her thoughts continually returning to Beau. He'd lost so much time helping her board up the cottage that he might very well have risked losing additional crop.

She stood on the end of the dock and studied the Suttons' empty dock in the distance. Even now, Beau, Nate, and Cal were probably out on the rough waters of the tidal creek, racing to lower cages to Hope Creek's bottom before the approaching storm and putting themselves in the precarious position of not having enough time to seek safe shelter from the dangerous storm.

Her legs moved, carrying her several swift steps back up the dock, her gaze squinting against the increasing gusts of wind as she sought a glimpse of the dirt road that led to Beau's house.

"Kit!"

She halted at the sound of Royal's shout and looked over her shoulder.

"What are you doing?" Royal, crouched on the dock, where he'd located the bunks of the boat lift below the water, stopped waving directions to Viv, and studied Kit over his shoulder. "We still got another boat to lift, and there ain't enough time for Viv to finish this one and get the next. I need you to jump on the hybrid, crank it up, and steer it in while we finish up here."

Kit hesitated, glancing across the yard toward the dirt road curving beyond the mailbox, then turned around and walked back down the dock to the bay boat. "All right," she shouted over the brisk kick of wind. "Wave me in once I get it turned around."

By the time they finished raising the hybrid bay boat on the lift, the sudden onslaught of fierce wind and fat raindrops had made it clear that Beau wouldn't be able to make it back to check on them and that Viv wouldn't be able to return safely to the Sutton house. Rather, Viv, at Royal's insistence, trudged reluctantly behind Kit into Teague Cottage, filled a glass with ice water, and took up residence by the kitchen sink.

She'd barely moved or spoken since.

"Mackey," Royal said as he pushed his chair back and stood. "Why don't you and I go straighten up your room a bit? Change the sheets on your bed? Then you can take a shower, crawl into bed, and try to get some sleep."

Mackey made a face and shook his head. "I don't think I can sleep with all that noise."

"Well, we'll try, anyway, okay?" Royal tapped the back of Mackey's chair. "Come on. Sitting here listening to the storm and worrying ain't gonna do any of us any good." He rounded the table, bent, and kissed the top of Kit's head. "Don't you stay up too late, either. I've been through enough of these to know that if something changes, I'll spring out of sleep and be on my feet. Always have in the past."

At Kit's nod, he straightened and walked over to the sink. He stood, looking down at Viv's face for a few moments, then lifted his arms awkwardly. "I know you're probably past the age now for . . . Well, it's been real nice having you back at home here and there over the past few days . . ."

Viv set her glass of water down slowly and slipped her arms around Royal's back, giving him a hug.

"You're safe here now," Royal said quietly, tightening his arms around her. "Like you always should've been. I promise."

Though Viv remained stiff in Royal's arms, she pressed her cheek against his shoulder, closed her eyes, and bit her lip. Her arms were slow to leave him as he pulled away.

"You try to get some sleep tonight, too, okay?" Royal motioned toward Kit. "Your sister's been cleaning up the house over the past couple weeks. Y'all's old room was one of the first ones she overhauled, so the two of you can be roommates again for the night."

Viv opened her eyes and met Kit's, the soft, vulnerable

expression on her face clearing and a stoic one taking its place. "Kit and I are past the age for sharing a room, Dad." She tried—and failed—at a smile. "Besides, this whole thing should blow over by morning, and I need to be on my way as soon as the storm lets up enough for me to walk safely back to the Suttons'. There's no telling how much cleanup will be waiting for us at the farm tomorrow morning."

Royal's smile dimmed as he stepped back from her. "I hate for you to run off again so soon, but—" His head drew back, and color flushed his cheeks. "I didn't mean it like that, Viv. I really didn't. I just meant—"

"I know what you meant." Viv waved a hand in the air, grabbed her glass of water, and took a slow sip, as though Royal's mention of her running off didn't sting. But her hand, clenched tightly around the glass, shook, and her knuckles turned white.

Royal hesitated, lingering by Viv's side, then nodded briskly and gestured for Mackey to join him. "Come on, Mackey. Let's get started on your room. By the time we finish and you take a shower, I guarantee you'll be ready to get some sleep, and this storm'll just be a bad dream."

"I want to put the blue sheets on my bed this time," Mackey said as they left the kitchen and walked down the hall. "I don't want the white ones, cuz I used them two weeks in a r—"

A door clicked shut, and their voices faded. Outside, the wind whistled along the rafters, and a distinctive flap of mesh wire beyond the closed front door started up again.

Kit winced. "I wonder if we'll still have a screen on the front porch by the end of this."

Viv drained her glass, then dumped the ice out, the frozen cubes clanking against the sink. "I wonder if Pearl Tide will have any viable crop left by the end of this."

Her voice was tight and held an undercurrent of accusation.

Kit dragged her hands over her face, the cold condensation from her own glass of ice water clinging to her palms and chilling her overheated cheeks. "I've thought about that. More often than not all day."

"He wouldn't have been here if it hadn't been for you." Viv stood with her back to Kit now, staring at the closed blinds covering the small window above the sink and curling her fingers around the edge of the counter. "He wouldn't have wasted hours boarding up this house when he should've been sinking cages and securing equipment back at the farm."

"I know," Kit said. The guilt she'd felt when Beau first arrived earlier that afternoon had only intensified throughout the day.

He should—as Viv had pointed out—have been at the Sutton house, helping Nate, Cal, and Viv secure their crop and protect the future of their business. But even though she'd encouraged Beau to do so multiple times as they'd worked outside Teague Cottage, he'd refused to leave until Viv had arrived.

"He chose to be here," Kit added quietly. "I asked him to go back several times, but he'd made his decision. I could tell it had been difficult for him to leave the farm and come here instead. But he'd made up his mind. He wanted to be here, to help protect the house—and us—and there was no talking him out of it."

"You should've tried harder."

Kit eased back in her chair and slung an arm around the backrest. "What would you have had me do, Viv? Try to force him to leave? Shove him down that dirt road and push him inside the gate? I seriously doubt Beau would allow anyone to force him to do something he didn't want to do. You, of all people, should know that by now."

Viv spun around, her mouth set in a tight line. "And what's that supposed to mean?"

That Beau wouldn't allow anyone—including Kit—to talk him into something he didn't want to do, or reveal anything he believed had been told to him in confidence. That's what she'd meant. Kit's mouth twisted. She'd learned that truth firsthand in the parking lot of Vernon's Raw Oyster Bar a couple of days ago, when she'd asked if Viv had told him she was in love with him. He'd protected his friendship with Viv, along with Viv's private emotions, just as he'd promised he would protect Kit's confidences.

It was commendable, really. Virtuous and honorable. All things she'd imagined Beau to be years ago. But revealing that conversation to Viv now would do nothing to ease her anger. If anything, it would inflame it.

"Nothing," Kit said. "I didn't mean anything by it."

"Yes, you did. You know exactly what you meant."

Kit gestured tiredly with her hand. "Well, why don't you tell me? Because I—"

"You meant that I couldn't force him to care about me the way he cares about you." Her mouth trembled. She pressed her lips together, then, voice tight, asked, "Isn't that what you meant? That Beau will never look at me the way he looks at you? That no matter how loyal or dependable or supportive I've been, I still couldn't turn his head, but you"—she flicked a hand in Kit's direction— "you swam right back in and grab his attention." She snapped her fingers. "Just like that. Like you never left." A sound of frustration escaped her lips. "You trying to tell me that you didn't know?"

No. That wasn't at all what she was trying to say.

Kit leaned one elbow on the table and rubbed her temple. This was exactly what she'd been trying to avoid. "I know," she whispered. "I know he's noticed me, and . . ." She raised her head and met Viv's eyes. "I also know how much he values his friendship with you, and how strong it is."

"And you'd take that away from me?" Viv's eyes welled, and tears seeped out of the corners. "The one person I have who truly cares about me? Who thinks highly of me and doesn't blame me?"

Kit stood slowly, her throat tightening, as a realization struck her. One she could no longer put off voicing out loud. "No. I wouldn't." She shook her head. "I won't." She pressed her hand to her chest, over her heart, hoping to lessen the pain and force herself to say the words. "No matter how Beau feels about me, or how I may or may not feel about him, I'd rather have a shot at rebuilding my relationship with you. Beau isn't the only one who cares about you. Dad does, too. So does Mackey." She swallowed hard, her hands shaking. "And so do I. I love you, Viv. Always have. And I want my sister back. You just name the terms."

Viv bit her lip, tears spilling over her cheeks. "Do you love him, though? Do you love Beau?"

Kit nodded, her own eyes filling with tears. "But I love you more. I know it'll take time. I know I hurt you when I left and that you're still angry with me. But I'm hoping, in time, we can rebuild what we had. That we can be sisters again. Not just sisters—but best friends, too. Like we used to be."

"I don't know if that's possible." Viv wiped her cheeks, then shoved her hands in her pockets, her wounded eyes meeting Kit's. "We're strangers now. Can't you see that? Can't you feel it?"

"I know." Kit pulled in a deep breath, her lungs burning. "But starting again now as strangers is better than where we left off fifteen years ago. Back then, we were both so angry . . . so hurt. We had no place to vent what we felt, except at each other. Things were only getting worse, and if we'd stayed on the same path we were traveling, we both would have been too broken to pick up the pieces when it was over. And we would never have been able to mend things between us. Or start over, even."

"Was that why you left?" Viv asked, her gaze moving past Kit to the front door, outside of which the storm was gaining momentum, the wind shaking the shutters and rain whipping fiercely at the boarded windows. "Because you knew what she would do?"

Voice barely emerging, Kit forced herself to speak. "I was hoping she wouldn't. That she'd prove me wrong and get well, but I think I knew deep down that she wouldn't. You were right. I gave up on her." Her gut sank, and her limbs grew heavy. "I lost hope. I didn't think there was any chance left of her getting better. And I think she knew that. When I told her—"

Her voice broke, and she looked down, twisting her hands together, as she recalled the day she'd told her mother she was leaving.

"When I told her I was going away," Kit continued, "and that I wouldn't be back until she chose to seek treatment, I could see it in her eyes. This dull, lifeless look. Like she'd given up, too. As though it didn't matter if I stayed or went. She just looked . . . resigned." Wet heat streaked down her face, and she wiped her cheeks. "I told her she was hurting all of us—not just herself—and that if she was determined not to fight back for herself, then I couldn't stay and watch her fall apart. Watch all of us fall apart, really. I told her I'd always be there for her if she wanted help. That she could call me anytime and I'd come right away." She shrugged. "I hoped my leaving might help. That if I set boundaries and made it clear what I would and wouldn't tolerate, maybe she'd come around. Maybe she'd at least try to get help. But she never called, and after a couple years, I started thinking that at least my leaving would give me a chance to move on."

Viv remained silent, her gaze fixed to the front door, as the storm raged outside.

A sharp crack echoed, and the ensuing crash signified another severed oak limb.

"I thought if I could heal—if I could stay strong," Kit continued, "then maybe I could be there for you and Dad. And Mackey. That maybe I could help all of you heal, too. That is, if things got worse . . . which they did."

A renewed deluge of rain pounded the roof and pelted the sides of the house. The bulbs in the stained-glass light fixture above the kitchen table flickered.

Viv pushed away from the sink and crossed the room. She stood by the kitchen table for a few moments, then pulled out the chair next to Kit, sat, propped her elbows on the table, and leaned into them.

"When you left, I felt like you abandoned me," Viv whispered. "Like you'd just packed your bags and left me behind. Forgot about m—"

"I never forgot." Kit reached out and covered Viv's hand with hers on the table. "I thought about you every day. I thought about all of you. Missed you. I wanted to come back so badly, but I knew it wouldn't fix anything. I couldn't help but wonder if things would've been different if I'd stayed. That maybe my leaving contributed to her getting worse."

"Staying didn't fix it, either." Viv sucked in a strong breath, her hand shaking beneath Kit's. "And in the end, I left her, too. I should've stuck it out. Should've stayed and seen it through. But every day was worse than the one before it, and after a while, I felt empty. Like there was nothing left for me, much less for her. Do you know what she said to me the day I left?"

Kit shook her head, remaining silent.

"I'd just dragged her home from Lou's Lagoon, high as a kite, middle of the night. She was out of her mind, rambling as usual." Her voice trembled. "She talked about you. About how different you were from her—and from me. She looked me right in the eyes and said she and I were the same. And that's why I understood her. Why I stayed. That she and I were the same." Tears pooled in her eyes. "And it hit me then . . . what was happening. That I'd already lost who I was. For years, I had spent every day worrying about, caring for, and cleaning up after her. Her problems were my problems. Her life was my life. I was getting sucked in further and further every day, and I remember thinking, if I didn't get away from her . . . away from the life she led, I'd never find my way back to who I was. Or who I might've been without her." Her voice hitched. "That scared me to death. I didn't want to live her life. Not anymore. I *couldn't* live her life for her. Would never be able to. No matter how hard I tried."

Kit squeezed her hand. "You did what you had to do to make it through. To survive. We both did."

Viv turned her head; her eyes, red rimmed and full of guilt, met Kit's. "I didn't mean it when I said I hated you."

Kit squeezed her hand harder. "I know."

"But sometimes I hated myself." Her expression crumpled, and tears coursed down her cheeks. "I hated myself as much as I loved her." She squeezed her eyes shut and lowered her head. "I'd get so mad at myself for giving in to her time after time. I couldn't understand why I couldn't find a way to tell her no, to stop bailing her out of everything, and after she . . . after she died, it was almost a relief. I'd spent years afraid that we'd lose her, and then one day it was all over." She lifted her head, her eyes seeking Kit's again, a look of helpless self-recrimination on her face. "There's something wrong with me for feeling that way, isn't there? I shouldn't be relieved that's she gone."

"No," Kit whispered. Heart breaking for her sister, Kit released Viv's hand and slid her arms around her shoulders instead before pulling her close. "There's nothing wrong with you. You've just been afraid and worried and hurt for so long. It's only now that all of it is gone—now that she's gone—you have time to think and look back." She hugged Viv tighter, thinking of the first few months she'd spent away from Teague Cottage and her mother. All the regrets and fears and uncertainties she'd had to wade through just to get up in the morning. "It's hard not to wonder . . ."

"What might've been?" Viv asked, settling her cheek on Kit's shoulder and hugging her back. "How things might have turned out differently if you'd stayed instead of leaving? Or if I hadn't left at all? Would she still have done it?"

Outside, the wind grew fierce, the rafters shook, and the rain intensified, drenching the house in a steady rhythm. The bulbs above their heads flickered again, then went out, leaving the kitchen in darkness. Only the howl of the wind and the drum of rain against the house remained.

"Why did she do it?" Viv asked, her voice catching on a sob. "Why'd she give up? And why wasn't our love and support enough?" She shook her head, her hair brushing Kit's chin. "The why is the hardest part," she continued. "I don't understand why she wouldn't accept our help. I don't understand why she gave up, or why she did it."

Kit's throat closed, and she rocked back and forth slowly in the chair, hugging Viv close as they both cried. "I don't think we'll ever know why. There's just no understanding it."

CHAPTER 12

Strangely enough, it was the silence that woke Kit. She opened her eyes, and her gaze settled on thin strips of sunlight that slipped in through small gaps around the closed front door of Teague Cottage.

She lifted her head from the kitchen table, wincing as muscles in the back of her neck spasmed against the change in position, and found the seat next to her empty. Viv, having fallen asleep by her side last night, had left at some point, leaving Kit to spend the night alone at the table, her cheek pressed to the smooth wood as she slept.

A succession of short taps and bangs, seeming to originate from the front porch, echoed sharply against the quiet emptiness of the kitchen.

Kit pushed back her chair, stood slowly, and stretched her neck from side to side gently, hoping to lessen the knot forming at her nape. She blinked hard and rubbed her eyes, her eyelids feeling puffy and heavy with the weight of the previous night's tears. She walked to the front door and opened it, sucked in a breath between her teeth at the sharp burst of bright sunlight hitting her face.

"Easy there." The taps and bangs stopped as Royal's deep tenor sounded by her side, and his strong hand cupped her elbow, steadying her step. "There are some shingles at your feet, so watch your step."

Kit forced her eyes open and focused on the porch floor. Shingles, leaves, small branches, and dirt littered the front porch. Ragged holes and deep dents scarred the entire length of the screen that had once enclosed the porch, leaving large sections dangling beside the front steps.

"It was worse than we thought it'd be, wasn't it?" Her voice emerged husky and hoarse. She cleared her throat and swallowed hard. "How bad is the damage?"

"Not as bad as it looks." Royal squeezed her upper arm and smiled down at her, the crow's-feet beside his eyes crinkling with his easy smile. "Seems the storm only skimmed us, like they said, though it got close enough to knock on the door." He gestured toward a small radio perched on the steps; a morning news report emerged from it at a low volume. "They say it hit about eight miles out. Close enough that we'd feel it but far enough away to avoid the worst scenario. It weakened a good bit over-night, too, so that was a help. Worst winds they've clocked so far were in the sixties. Downed some trees, damaged some houses, and knocked the power out, but otherwise, we were lucky."

Kit glanced around and noted that several of the large boards she and Beau had nailed up yesterday were stacked neatly on the lawn by the front porch steps. "How long have you been up?"

Royal shrugged. "A couple hours."

"What time is it?"

He tilted his wrist and glanced at his wristwatch. "Close to nine."

"And you did all this since you got up?" She gestured toward the uncovered windows. "Is Viv helping you?"

Royal shook his head. "Haven't seen her this morning.

She wasn't in the house when I got up, and you were sleeping good in the kitchen, so I didn't want to wake you. Figured I'd come on out and work on this 'til you and Mackey got up."

Kit dragged her hand over her face. "Viv and I talked last night."

Royal nodded. "I heard some of it." His chest rose on a deep inhale. "I knew she'd been hurting—that we all were—but I never figured she blamed herself as much as she did." He reached out, his callused hand cupped her chin and tilted her face up to his, and his eyes met hers. "I want you to hear me when I say this—neither one of you is responsible for your mama's illness, and neither one of you could've done anything different to stop what she done. You both tried to help her the best you could. Thing is . . ." He turned his head and eyed the wispy clouds drifting high above the trees, moisture glistening along his lashes. "None of us could've done any more than we did. Sylvie hurt so much . . . She just lost her way." He faced her again, giving a smile tinged with sadness. "I fought accepting it for a long time. But some things just are, and there's nothing any of us can do about it."

Kit cradled his wrist in her hands, dipped her head, and kissed his palm, blinking back her own tears.

"Us talking again," Royal said softly, "it's a new start. A chance for all of us to begin again. To rebuild our family"—he motioned toward the damaged screen and roof and smiled wider—"and our home. It's a new day for all of us."

Mostly. Kit forced a smile and stepped back, her thoughts turning to her declaration to Viv the night before. She hadn't realized she'd made the decision to let Beau go until it had risen to her lips, but she supposed she'd known it was the only way. Regaining Viv's trust would be tenuous at best. It'd be impossible to build a relationship with Beau without hurting Viv, and she couldn't turn her back on her twin again. She wouldn't.

Viv's happiness—and that of the family—came first now. It was, after all, what she'd planned for years. Why she'd returned. And to move forward, she had only one thing left to do. She had to tell Beau.

"Beau stopped by about an hour ago."

Kit looked up at Royal, tried to temper the longing that surged within her as she met Royal's searching gaze. "How was he?"

"Fine." Royal reached out and tucked a strand of hair behind her ear. "He asked for you. I told him you were still sleeping, but that I'd let you know he stopped by."

"Did he mention the farm?" She looked across the front yard toward the dirt road leading to Beau's house. Large oak limbs lay in disarray across the road. "How bad is the damage?"

Royal sighed. "He downplayed it, I think. Said it was less than they expected, but I could tell he was worried. He mentioned that he, Nate, and Cal had already been working pretty hard at cleanup."

"And Viv?" Kit asked quietly.

He shook his head. "Beau didn't mention her."

Kit dragged a hand through her hair, and her eyes smarted with tears as her fingers caught in a tangle. Having slept at the kitchen table all night, she probably looked awful—her hair was in tangled knots, and one side of her jaw ached from pressing against the corner of the table as she'd slept—but it'd be best to face this discussion with Beau while she still had the nerve. She could pick up the pieces later.

"Think I'll head over there and check in on him," she said. "Maybe Viv's there helping with the cleanup."

"If she is, ask her to check in with me, please." Royal grabbed a hammer from the porch floor and turned it over in his hands. "I'd like to see her face. Talk to her for a bit, if she has the time."

Kit lifted to her toes and kissed his cheek. "Of course."

She went back inside the house long enough to wash her face, brush her teeth, and pull her hair back into a pony-tail. Afterward, she left again, easing past Royal on the front porch, carefully opening the damaged screen door, and walking down the front porch steps. By the time her feet hit the front lawn, the taps and cracks of Royal prying boards from windows had resumed.

Kit made her way down the driveway, stepping carefully over several thick oak limbs that had fallen during the storm, their jagged ends pointing toward the sky. She tilted her head back and breathed deeply, filling her lungs with clean, salt-tinged air, the soft breeze cooling her bare face, neck, and arms.

Despite the fierce lashing of rain and wind, the majority of live oak trees lining the dirt road still stood tall, their thick trunks and long branches sprawling in all directions with sturdy strength. Moss draped along limbs rippled in the soft morning breeze, and tree frogs, presumably pleased with the newly formed freshwater puddles, croaked to-gether in a vibrant chorus that echoed through the dense forest.

Golden light cut through the tangle of moss-laden limbs as the sun cleared the tree line, and Kit picked up her pace, her spirits lifting at the renewed beauty of a storm-free morning. But her steps halted at a large obstruction in the center of the road.

A cage—one of Beau's—lay in the road, half-buried in mud and dirt. She crouched down, brushed away a layer of dirt and moss, and peered inside. The mesh bag inside the cage remained in one piece, and what looked like sev-eral dozen oysters were still inside, scattered and chipped, most of them resting in a haphazard pile at one end of the cage.

"Oh, no . . ." Her voice trailed away as she spotted a lone oyster resting on the dirt, the storm having flung it from the cage.

She picked it up, wiped the mud off with the hem of her shirt, and turned it over in her hand. The shell had cracked open, and it was a loss, as would be a lot of Beau and Viv's crop, she imagined.

Kit stood and glanced around. The sight of another damaged cage several feet ahead in the center of the road made her shoulders slump. Beau should—as Viv had pointed out last night—have spent the final precious hours before the storm lowering cages to the bottom of the creek and securing equipment to minimize the damage.

But he'd come to Teague Cottage to help her instead.

Kit bit her lip and ducked her head, continuing up the winding dirt road, still cradling the dead oyster in her palm.

The gate to the Suttons' property was open, and she entered, casting a look around. Several large limbs, similar in size to the fallen branches at Teague Cottage, littered the front lawn, and four more cages lay damaged in the grass.

Rhythmic clinks and clanks rang out across the property, and Kit followed the sound to the backyard and along the deepwater dock. She spotted Beau toward the end of the dock, standing in front of the culling table, with several damaged cages stacked in piles around his feet. His hands, strong and skilled, moved over the oysters strewn across the table, picking out the largest ones, dropping them into buckets at his feet, and placing the smaller ones into mesh bags at the opposite end of the table.

The hybrid bay boat was overturned nearby, one end submerged beneath the waters of the creek and the other lodged between two dock pilings. The Suttons' larger boat was absent, taken out, she supposed, by Nate and Cal, who were probably scouring the creek for cages.

Kit hesitated, her eyes drinking in the tall, lean lines of Beau's muscular figure, her hand tightening around the dead oyster in her palm. "Do you think you'll be able to save any of them?"

Beau's gloved hands stilled over the oysters, and his head lifted her way, his blue eyes seeking hers. He smiled, but it seemed forced. "I'm going to try."

He studied her for a moment, his attention roving over her face and lingering on her mouth before dropping to her closed fist.

She unfurled it, walked over to him, and held out her palm. "A few cages were blown into the road, and I saw several in your front yard. I was hoping the oysters might've made it, but from the looks of them, I think the majority—if not all—are gone."

He tugged his gloves off, then cupped one of his hands around her upturned palm and took the oyster with the other, inspecting it. "Unfortunately, I'm afraid that's all we'll find when we start rounding up the ones that were thrown from the creek." He tossed the oyster into a bigger bucket placed several feet from the culling table and squeezed her hand. "The cottage looked okay this morning. It'll take a few days to clear out the broken limbs and repair the roof, from what Royal showed me, but it didn't look like any severe damage was done."

She smiled and covered his hand with hers. "Because of you. If you hadn't helped us the way you did, we would be in a lot worse shape."

He lifted her hand to his mouth and kissed the inside of her wrist. "It was worth it."

Beau released her, tugged his gloves back on, and returned his attention to the oysters on the table, his big hands resuming their task.

She rubbed the inside of her wrist with her thumb, already missing the warmth of his touch. "What can I do?"

He glanced up briefly, then motioned toward the culling table. "You're welcome to help sort. Toss the market-sized ones that are still viable in this bucket"—he nudged the bucket closest to him with the toe of his boot—"put the babies back in the bags at the opposite end of the table, and throw all the damaged ones over there, in the recycling bucket."

Kit dipped her head in agreement and took up a position on the opposite side of the table. Beau reached into a bag underneath the culling table, withdrew a pair of gloves, and tossed them to her. She put on the gloves, then dug in, sifting through the oysters, tossing several market-sized ones in the bucket nearby, and throwing even more in the recycling bucket behind her.

"Is Viv here?" she asked, keeping her gaze fixed firmly on the task at hand.

His hands stilled briefly, then resumed sorting. "No. I haven't seen her this morning." Shells clanked as he tossed a handful of dead oysters in the recycling bucket. "I figured she got caught by the storm when she didn't come back last night, and your dad told me the two of you stayed up talking most of the evening." His hands paused again. "How'd it go?"

She shrugged. "Pretty good, all things considered. I think we have a shot at making things better between us, if we work at it."

The pile of shells in front of her blurred, and she ducked her head a bit more, blinking rapidly and willing the tears back.

"Do you want to talk about it?" he asked quietly.

She shook her head. "Not right now. But later." Her eyes burned, and it was hard to speak. "You and I need to talk later."

Beau's hands slowed for a few moments, and her skin prickled under his scrutiny, but he continued sifting through the oysters, his hands picking up the pace.

They worked in silence for a while, the sun rising higher and the air growing more humid as one hour passed, then another, until sweat trickled down Kit's back and her arms ached. She stepped back from the now almost empty table and stretched her arms overhead as the low hum of a motor approached.

A large, sporty hybrid bay boat approached, then stopped at the dock. The engine cut off, and Cal, carrying a big cage, stepped onto the dock and headed their way. Nate followed, hopping off the boat and onto the dock, then joined Cal, Kit, and Beau at the culling table.

"How'd it look out there?" Beau asked, sweeping a small pile of oysters into one big palm, then dumping them in the recycling bucket.

"Better than expected," Nate said, wiping his forearm across his glistening brow. "Most of the cages we lowered to the bottom yesterday were safe, though a few were covered with silt from the runoff and a few cages were damaged. But it's the drop in salinity that's worrying me. I'm scared the ones that survived might drown with all the fresh water that's poured into the creek."

Beau frowned, and the creases of worry lining his mouth made Kit's stomach drop. "Did you bring in another load of cages?" he asked.

Cal nodded as he set the large cage he had carried down by the culling table, unlatched it, and withdrew a mesh bag. "The rest are in the boat, ready to be sorted."

"Figured we'd keep sorting," Nate said. "Save what we can now." He glanced at Kit and managed a small smile of greeting. "How'd you and yours make out last night?"

"Good." Kit chanced a glance at Beau, who was studying her expression. "Thanks to Beau."

Nate clapped a hand to Beau's shoulder and laughed. "Yeah. He's a good man, just in case you didn't know it already."

Kit looked down and continued sorting through the last of the oysters on the table. "I know," she said softly. "He's one of the best."

Cal dumped the mesh bag of oysters out onto the culling table, filling the surface with a fresh batch of oysters to sort, and Nate clapped his hands together.

"Sun up the way it is," Nate said, "I'm in need of a tall glass of water. Anyone else care for one?"

They all voiced their agreement, and Nate excused himself to get drinks for everyone. The sun's rays grew sharper, and a bead of sweat burned Kit's eye. She wiped her face with the hem of her T-shirt and fanned it out.

"There's a ton left to sort," Beau said, dragging a large pile of oysters in front of him. "I imagine you're tired. You don't have to stay, you know."

Kit nodded but continued working. "I want to. I'd like to help, as long as that's okay with you?"

Beau reached out and covered her hand with his, coaxing her eyes up to meet his. "Thank you." He glanced at Cal. "You toss a lot in the boat?"

Cal grinned. "Everything that was left. It's full."

Beau released her and patted Cal on the back. "Good job." He smiled, but his pleased look dimmed as he met Kit's eyes again. "We'll keep working 'til we knock the rest of 'em out. Then maybe you and I can have that talk?"

Kit's hands slowed over the oysters as an urge to prolong her time with Beau surged through her. "Okay," she said quietly. "After this, we'll talk."

Several hours later, the sun had dropped low on the horizon, splashing bright shades of lavender, pink, yellow, and blue across the sky that draped Hope Creek's banks and reflecting off the water, transforming the creek into ripples of colorful silk.

Beau stripped off his gloves and dragged his hand through his damp hair, his body slicked with sweat.

Kit seemed to have fared about the same.

He glanced across the now finally—thank the Lord!— empty culling table and studied her face as she peeled off her gloves and stretched her arms over her head. Her eyes were closed, and dark circles of fatigue had formed beneath her eyelashes. She sported a light sunburn on both cheeks, and her neck was flushed with heat.

"Burning up?" he asked.

Her eyes opened and met his, and her face flushed an even deeper shade of pink as he examined her expression. "Yeah. I didn't realize we'd been at this for so long."

Beau glanced behind him, where Nate and Cal carried the last buckets of market-sized oysters that they'd been able to salvage to the storage shed. Their steps were slow, and Cal's shoulders drooped, as though a weighted barbell had settled over them.

Beau managed a small smile. "I doubt any of us will have trouble sleeping tonight."

He rolled his shoulders, the ache between his shoulder blades the most pronounced of all his newfound pains, then returned his attention to Kit. She stared down at her hands, her teeth worrying her bottom lip.

"Something on your mind?" he asked, though he thought he knew the answer.

She'd spent most of the day working alongside him in

silence, glancing up only once every half hour or so to take a swift glance at the driveway before ducking her head to sort oysters again. No doubt she'd been looking for some sign of her sister. Viv hadn't shown all day. But that wasn't all that had been on Kit's mind. Something was bothering her today—something much beyond Viv's absence or the previous night's storm and resulting damage.

A heavy breath escaped her, and she looked up, a wary look in her dark eyes. "I think we need to have that talk, if now's a good time?"

He motioned toward the sky, the beauty of the sunset doing little to still the nervous apprehension coursing through him. "There are a few cages that need to be put back on the creek. Feel like riding out with me? We can talk on the way."

She nodded and walked around the culling table, releasing her ponytail and smoothing out her hair around her shoulders. Her fingers caught in a tangle, and she winced.

"Come on." Smiling, he reached out and took her hand in his, leading her in the direction of the storage shed. "There's a restroom connected to the shed. We can clean up there before we leave, and I'll let Nate and Cal know where we're going."

It took several minutes for them both to clean themselves up in the restroom—Beau stole an extra minute or two to dunk his head beneath the faucet in the sink and rinse his hair with cool water. After telling Nate and Cal he'd handle setting the rest of the cages back in the water, he and Kit boarded Nate's sporty hybrid and cast off, then cruised out onto the creek and glided along the smooth water as the colorful hues of the sunset spilled over and around them.

The humid air had cooled slightly, and a soft breeze swept over the boat, ruffling Beau's hair against his forehead and slipping through Kit's long brown strands. He smiled as he glanced at her, admiring the gentle expression on her face.

Warm hues of the sunset tinged her face and neck in soft shades of pink and lavender, and her hair, wet when she left the restroom earlier, had dried nicely in the breeze, rippling gently over her shoulders and back.

"Hard to believe a storm just tore through here, isn't it?" he called out over the hum of the boat's engine.

She looked at him, her soft mouth parting and a hesitant smile lifting her lips briefly. "Yes, it is." She turned away from him again, her gaze returning to the creek curving in front of them. "But it did."

They continued on, and Beau sped up, the sun dipping a bit lower with each passing minute, until they reached the long lines of floating cages. He stopped the boat by an empty stretch of line, grabbed the first of four cages that rested in the bottom of the boat, and started tethering it to the line. Kit pitched in, and after a few minutes, the task had been completed and the sun had set, taking its burst of color along with it.

A chorus of crickets, tree frogs, and toads took over, throbbing in a soothing rhythm along the banks of the creek, as the moon—not quite full anymore—rose high in the sky and the stars began to shine.

"Did you ever find anything as beautiful as this in Highlands?" Beau asked softly, sitting beside Kit on the large deck at the bow of the boat.

She bit her lip, eyes still trained on the sky above her, and managed a small smile. "No. It was gorgeous, for sure, but nothing will ever compare to this." She glanced over at him, then looked away, avoiding his eyes. "That's one reason I've decided to stay."

His hands moved by his sides, and he curled them around the gunwale to keep from reaching for her, to keep from pulling her close and holding her tight. Her words were exactly what he wanted to hear, but there was something underlying them—a hint of sadness or regret—that made him pause.

"I just . . ." Her throat moved on a hard swallow, and her expression softened in the glow of the starlight. "I don't understand how I could love this place so much again. How I could find happiness again in a place where my mother was so sad."

He allowed himself to touch her then, to curl his hand around her knee and squeeze gently. "She wasn't sad all the time," he said softly. "You told me yourself on the shrimp boat that you have good memories. That there were times she was happy. That is true, isn't it?"

She nodded silently.

"When Evelyn died," he said, "I didn't think I'd ever smile again, much less be happy. But then, when I thought about where to go . . . where to start over, this was the first and only place I could imagine finding happiness again." He turned to her, smoothed his finger along her cheek. "It wasn't Hope Creek so much that called to me. It was you. The memory of you and your family. How close you and your family were at one time. How happy you were sashaying up that dock of yours, carrying those oysters and shrimp."

She laughed. He'd never heard a more beautiful sound.

"I never sashayed," she said.

"Oh, yeah, you did." He smiled. "And I loved it. I loved how happy you were. How happy all of you were."

Her laughter died, and her smile dimmed. "But then I left. I left my mother when she needed me most. I left Viv, too."

"Because you needed to. Leaving was what you need to do at the time." A breeze swept over them, lifting a strand of her hair over her cheek. He smoothed it back and tilted her face up to his. "But now you're here. You came back, and whatever the problems are, you're working through them as best you can because you still love each other. Viv will come around. There's no chance she won't. Because your family's love is—and always has been—the greatest treasure on this island. It's part of what brought me back. What led me to bring Cal here and hope for the same. You can't give up on that."

She studied his face and leaned closer, her gaze dipping to his mouth, but then she turned away again and returned her attention to the sky. "It really is beautiful."

Beau stood, retrieved a soft blanket from a storage bin beneath the bench seat, and returned, holding it up. "Hop up," he said. "There's a better way to appreciate it."

She hesitated, glancing from him to the blanket, then back, but slowly stood and watched as he spread the blanket out over the large deck, lay down, and held out his hand.

"Here." He patted the space beside him with his free hand. "I'll show you. Free admission to the heavens, right here."

Kit smiled. "You think you're smooth, huh? I'm pretty sure I've heard that line somewhere before . . ."

Beau laughed. "Nah. Just a front-row seat to the best view of the stars." He slid his finger in a cross over his chest. "You have my word."

Her smile widened, and a mischievous light glimmered in her eye, but she took his hand and allowed him to lead her to the space beside him on the blanket. He cupped the back of her head as she lay down beside him, and looked up at the night sky.

"Over there," he said, pointing to a swath of hazy light to the southeast of them that stretched in an uneven line through a scattering of bright stars that surrounded it. "Do you see it?"

"The Milky Way," she said, smiling. "And there . . ." She pointed toward the tree line, at sporadic specks of light flashing among the branches. "Fireflies too. I haven't seen those in years."

"Now," he said softly, "what'd I tell you?"

"Free admission to the heavens," she whispered, staring up at the bright stars and the glowing moon.

"And was I right?" he teased, slipping his hand over hers by his side and weaving their fingers together. Her palm was warm and soft, and he eased closer, resting his thigh against hers.

A soft sigh of pleasure escaped her, and she moved her head, resting her cheek against his shoulder. "You were. I can't imagine anything better."

"Can't you?" he asked quietly.

She moved against him, rolling over on her side, and rested her small palm on the center of his chest, right over his heart. Her hand flexed against him, pressing firmly, as she rose to one elbow and leaned over him, her long hair falling over one of her shoulders and brushing his neck.

"Yes," she whispered, her gaze lowering to his mouth. But shadows lingered in her eyes, a wealth of sadness mingling with the desire in her gaze.

"Kit?" He lifted his hand, smoothed it beneath the fall of her hair, and slid it around the back of her neck. "What is it? What do you need to say?"

Her mouth parted, and she moved to speak, her lips trembling, but no sound emerged.

He waited, drifting his thumb gently along her smooth nape, meeting her eyes, urging her to speak.

"I . . ." Her eyes lowered, and her gaze fixed on his chest. "I love you. But . . ."

His heart thumped painfully, and the rush of pleasure he'd felt at her initial words faded as tears filled her eyes. "But what?"

She closed her eyes, tears slipping from her lashes. "It's not the right time."

He pulled in a breath, a shudder running through him. "What do you mean?"

"I mean . . ." She opened her eyes and met his again, pain in the dark depths. "I can't rebuild a relationship with Viv and pursue one with you at the same time. It would be too complicated, and it . . . it would hurt her too much." Her chin trembled. "I've hurt her enough as it is. She and I need time to get to know each other again as we are now. We need time to trust each other again."

He smiled tightly. "And I would get in the way of that?"

She stared down at him, her fingertips drifting over his mouth, her thumb lingering on his lower lip. "I think it'd be difficult to navigate for both of us. And it's not just Viv I'm thinking of. There's Cal, as well." Her breath caught, and she turned her head, her gaze seeking out the soft glow of fireflies in the trees. "I've lost my mother in the worst way. A way I imagine was almost as hard as the way Cal lost Evelyn." She faced him again, her hand on his chest curling into his shirt. "I care about Cal, and I don't want to risk hurting him in any way. Even if it were unintentional. I need to heal my own family before I try to be a part of yours. As much as I wish things were different, now just isn't the right time for us."

He wanted to be angry. Wanted to argue and rage at the unfairness of it all, at the fact that he was losing her. But the sincerity in her eyes and the emotion in her voice when she spoke of Cal were enough to reassure him there might still be a chance for them . . . one day.

Beau cradled her face in his hands, his eyes seeking hers,

as she looked down at him. "I'll wait," he whispered. "Until it's the right time. As long as it takes."

Pain moved through her expression. "I'm sorry, Beau. I—"

"No." He shook his head and wiped away a tear from her cheek, his own breath catching. "There's nothing to apologize for. You're protecting your sister and my son." Despite the deep ache inside him, his smile returned. "And you love me, just as I love you." He tugged her closer, his lips brushing hers. "That alone is enough to carry me through forever."

A soft cry escaped her, and her hand released his T-shirt and slid up his chest. Both of her soft palms cupped the back of his head as she lowered her mouth to his and parted his lips with hers.

He closed his eyes and slid his arms around her, his palms gliding over her back and hips; his legs tangled with hers as he held her tightly against him. She settled perfectly against him, her soft curves filling his hard planes, and he lifted his hands to her hair, wound the silky strands around his fingers as she pressed closer, her smooth cheek rubbing against his rough jaw. He breathed her in, savoring her kiss, her sweet scent, and the intoxicating taste of her on his tongue, wishing he could make the moment last forever.

She lifted her mouth from his and dragged in a raspy breath, her heart hammering against his chest, her skin heating beneath his touch. An almost desperate plea entered her voice when she asked, "Can we stay here a little while longer? Can we just have this . . . for a few more minutes?"

Her cheeks were flushed, the stubble lining his jaw having left its mark, and her lips had deepened to a shade of rose. He kissed her again slowly, the feel of her soft mouth parting against his tongue making his body tighten.

He pulled away with a ragged groan and tucked her head beneath his chin. With her cheek resting on his chest, her soft breaths swept over his thin T-shirt above the strong throb of his heart.

"Yeah," he said softly, cradling her closer and kissing the top of her head. "We'll stay as long as you want."

They lay, wrapped in each other's arms, for another hour, as the sky darkened to midnight velvet and the moon grew brighter. The night chorus of crickets, toads, and tree frogs grew stronger, pulsing around them; and their bodies, pressed tightly together, grew warmer as the night air grew cooler. Waves lapped against the boat, rocking it gently beneath them with the push and pull of the tide.

Beau closed his eyes and focused on the feel of Kit against him: the soft, warm weight of her splayed across his chest, abs, and thighs. He smoothed his hands over her back and shoulders, memorizing the shape and feel of her beneath his palms. Listened to her soft breaths and the rapid beat of her heart.

Soon Kit stirred against him. The quiet words she uttered next were as painful as he'd imagined they'd be.

"I need to go back," she whispered.

Beau tightened his hand around her, the reluctance in her tone reflecting his own urgent need. But he gentled his grip, nudged his thumb beneath her chin, and brought her gaze back to his.

"I'll wait," he repeated, his heart aching. "Forever if that's what it takes."

CHAPTER 13

Teague Cottage was dark, save for the dimly lit porch light, by the time Kit walked home from the Suttons' house. The large oak limbs that last night's storm had broken had been cleared from the driveway and stacked into a tall pile on the lawn, and all the boards had been removed from the windows. She ascended the front steps, glancing at the tattered remains of the screen enclosing the porch and the freshly swept porch floor, and entered the house quietly.

The kitchen was empty, and no one was in the living room, but that was to be expected, Kit supposed, as it was after ten o'clock. Royal and Mackey had probably spent most of the day clearing the limbs from the driveway, removing boards from the windows, cleaning the porch, and lowering the boats back onto the creek. And all the while, she'd been with Beau.

Kit rubbed her forehead, fighting the urge to turn around and return to him. Instead, she trudged down the hallway to her room, then closed the door behind her after she entered.

"I was wondering when you'd make it back." A soft click sounded, and low light from a lamp on the nightstand spilled across the room. Viv, reclining in one of the two beds, sat up and eyed Kit's face. "I take it you went to Beau's?"

Kit hesitated and examined her sister's expression. Her eyes were puffy, as though she'd been crying, but the anger that had resided in her eyes before they'd spoken last night had diminished, leaving mostly sadness behind.

"Yes," Kit said. She reached up and ran her hand over the back of her neck, kneading tight muscles. "I thought you'd be there, but when you weren't, I stayed and helped clean up the storm damage."

"Was it bad?" Viv asked.

Kit nodded. "Bad enough." She thought of the increasing look of trepidation on Beau's face each time they had sorted through the contents of a mesh bag and found a significant portion of the oysters in most of the cages damaged. "Beau and Nate figure y'all lost at least a third of the crop last night, and they expect to lose more from shock or the drop in salinity in the water over the next few months."

Viv grimaced and rubbed her hands over her face. "That's a heavy blow to our new plans. I doubt anyone will be willing to invest in our expansion now."

"Not necessarily." Kit spread her hands, searching for a silver lining of some sort. "I think local restaurants—especially ones like Vernon's Raw Oyster Bar—have grown accustomed to relying on your crop. I doubt they'd want to see it disappear. They'll understand, and I imagine they'll be patient enough to wait until you get things going again, without taking their business elsewhere."

A humorless laugh burst from Viv's lips. "They won't have much of a choice," she said. "There aren't but a handful of outfits down here doing the same thing we're doing, and I bet they'll be clawing their way out from under damage, too. It'll be at least late next summer before our youngest crop—if it survives—will be ready to divvy out."

"It could've been worse," Kit said quietly. "Most of the equipment looked in good shape, and a good portion of market-sized oysters were still viable. We sorted enough out for Beau and Nate to deliver at least two more shipments this week."

Viv issued a tight smile. "Every bit will help, I guess."

They both grew quiet, and Kit, exhausted and desperate for a change of subject, walked to the dresser and withdrew a pair of soft shorts and a T-shirt.

She changed her shirt, asking as she pulled the clean one on, "Where'd you go today?"

"To the beach," Viv said. "I go there sometimes to walk and think. There's a dune that's kind of out of the way, and no one usually ventures out there. It's a good place for some solitude. I came back a few hours ago and helped Dad and Mackey clean up outside."

Finished changing, Kit crossed the room, turned back the sheet, slid into bed, and sighed as her aching muscles relaxed. "The place looks a lot better, except for the screen. I don't think Dad will be able to mend it this time, considering the damage."

Viv laughed softly. "That old thing's made it through a lot over the years. Probably time to replace it." Her laughter faded. "It's past overdue for a change around here, anyway."

Kit smiled. "This is a nice change." She rolled over, easing onto her side, and tucked one hand beneath her cheek. "You do realize that if you sleep here tonight, this will be the first night in over fifteen years that we've shared this room?"

Viv rolled over, too, and tucked her hand under her pillow, returning Kit's smile with one of her own. "That's the plan."

"I thought you said we were too old to share a room," Kit teased.

Viv's smile slipped. "Maybe. But I wanted to sleep at home tonight. Is it okay with you if I stay?"

"Of course." Kit met her eyes and smiled encouragingly, her heart warming at the prospect. "Besides, seeing as how you didn't dump all your junk on my bed again, I'm taking that as an invitation for me to stay, too."

Viv laughed again. "I was mad when I did that."

"Yeah, I could tell." She laughed with Viv. "And you must've been mad for a long time, because that was a pretty big pile of junk. Took me hours to sort through it all."

"I was mad," Viv said softly. "I've been angry about a lot of things for a long time."

They grew quiet again, the night chorus of croaks and chirps drifting in through the open window.

"Are you staying?" Viv asked. "For more than tonight?"

"Yes. For good, if you'll have me?"

"That'd be nice." Viv narrowed her eyes and studied Kit's face, her lips curving. "But then again, I'm not too keen on giving up my closet space."

Kit smiled. "I promise not to take up more than my fair share."

"Well, then, I think I can handle that." Viv turned the lamp off and rolled over again, returning to her back, crossed her arms behind her head, and stared at the ceiling.

Kit stayed on her side, roving her gaze over Viv's silhouette beneath the moonlight streaming in the window. A bittersweet ache filled her heart as memories of late-night bedroom talks during their teenage years flooded her mind, and she held on to the nostalgic feeling as long as she could, her eyes growing heavy.

"Kit?"

"Hmm?"

"What was it like?"

Sleep tugged strongly at her body, and her thoughts were hazy. Kit opened her eyes, struggled to focus on Viv's silhouette again. "What was what like?"

"Highlands," Viv whispered.

Kit gave in, allowing her eyes to slip closed again, and smiled. "Beautiful. There are hiking trails everywhere, and you can climb as high as you want. So high you can see for miles. The air's clean and crisp up there. Smells like pine. And in the fall . . ." Her mind drifted over years of memories, moments she'd enjoyed the most. "There are so many colors in the fall. The only blue there is in the sky—everything else is so warm and rich . . . trees so tall they touch heaven. Leaves so bright and intense, they look like they're on fire. No matter how cold it got, I took one look at that color, and I was still warm on the inside. It was more than just a change in location—it was a change in perspective—and it made all the difference."

A breeze whispered through the open window and blended with Viv's quiet breaths.

"Did you miss being here?" Viv asked.

"Yes," Kit whispered. "Very much. But I knew I had to leave, had to find a way to move on. And at the time . . . in the state I was in, being there was what I needed." Her chest tightened as she recalled Beau's touch and consoling tone only an hour earlier, and she wondered how much time would stand between them now. "The good memories of you, Dad, and Mackey—even Mama—they kept me strong. They were enough."

Two hours' worth of pounding hammers, a series of sharp yanks, and one expletive from Royal was all it took for Kit, Viv, and Royal to remove the wood battens holding the screen in place on Teague Cottage's front porch the next afternoon.

"Now the screen!" Mackey, serving as supervisor for the project, stood in the middle of the front lawn, tilted his head to the side, and pointed at the right side of the porch. "That side first. It's the ugliest."

Kit smiled. "I don't know, Mackey." She climbed down the ladder, set her hammer on the front steps, and joined Mackey. Rubbing her chin, she surveyed the damaged screen. "I'm thinking the left side is the ugliest."

"Nope." Viv rose from her crouched position by the front porch railing, walked down the steps, and bumped Mackey's arm with hers. "Y'all are both wrong. It's the center that's the most grotesque." She motioned toward a gaping hole, courtesy of debris from the storm two nights ago. "That right there needs to come down ASAP."

Kit leaned around Mackey, met Viv's eyes, and grinned. For the first time in ages, she, Viv, and Mackey stood side by side, taking good-natured jabs and laughing, and it felt great. It felt like . . . family.

After her late-night conversation with Viv yesterday, Kit had slept hard and well and had woken up this morning refreshed and, surprisingly enough, hopeful.

Viv had still been sleeping in the bed next to hers, and Kit had lain in her own bed for another half hour, as the sun slowly rose outside, its rays trickling through the open window, along with a warm breeze, and simply savored the moment. Afterward, she'd left the room quietly, showered and dressed and cooked breakfast. It hadn't taken long for the enticing aroma of bacon and eggs to coax Royal and Mackey to the kitchen table, and Viv had joined them moments after. They'd all sat and eaten together.

It seemed such a small event—a family having breakfast together—but the easy conversation and sincere smiles they shared across the table had been rare in the past and had been absent altogether for years. They lingered for over an hour, Royal, Kit, and Viv enjoying a second, then third cup of coffee. Mackey, delighting in their presence, ate four helpings of eggs and told more jokes than Kit was able to count. And when Royal suggested he tackle the damaged screen on the front porch—remove it even—they all readily offered to assist, eager for more time together.

"You two stop your yapping," Royal said, laughing. "I put Mackey in charge, and that means he calls the shots. So what you say, Mackey? Which section you want us to take down first?"

Mackey thought it over, narrowing his eyes as he studied the screen and glancing from Kit to Viv and back again. Then a wide smile broke out across his face. "All of it," he said, nodding. "Take down the whole thing."

An hour later, Kit, Viv, and Royal had followed Mackey's directive to the letter, and the entire screen, along with the screen door, had been removed from the front porch. The four of them stood on the front lawn and admired their handiwork, their gazes moving over the newly opened space, taking in the cleaner lines of the porch beneath the bright glow of the late afternoon sun.

"I think it'll do," Kit said, smiling.

"Better than that," Royal added. "It's a fresh start." He looked at Viv, then Kit, warmth entering his expression. "A chance to start over and mold this old house into whatever we want it to be." He headed toward the front porch steps. "Let's break out the rockers and give it a look-see."

The view from the unscreened front porch did look brand new. Kit leaned back in one of the weathered wicker chairs they'd retrieved from inside the house, and shielded her eyes with one hand as she scanned her surroundings.

"Whatcha think?" Royal asked, sitting in a rocking chair next her.

"I think it's a great change," she said. "It really opens up the view. Makes it look more spacious."

And welcoming, she thought, smiling. With the screen gone, she was afforded an unimpeded view of the live oaks lining the dirt road, their sprawling branches reaching in various directions beneath the blue sky and bright sun, and the freshly manicured front lawn. The new mailbox Beau had installed stood nice and neat beside the driveway.

"Makes it feel different, too," Mackey said. He sat on the top porch step, tipped his head back, and closed his eyes. A grin appeared as he soaked up the warm sun. "We done good, didn't we?" he asked.

"Yeah," Kit said. "But we can do better." She glanced at Viv, who sat on the step beside Mackey, then looked at Royal. "I guess you know Viv and Beau's oyster farm took a big hit during the storm?"

Royal nodded. "I figured as much. I imagine even the wild oyster beds were damaged."

"But the good news," Kit said quietly, "is that the farm Viv and Beau have built can regrow a new, healthy crop, given time and a sound investment from the right folks."

Royal eased back in the rocker and stretched his legs out, still surveying the new view.

"Viv and Beau were right when they spoke of the decreasing population of wild oysters that night at the community center," Kit said. "The wild crop is diminishing, and I think it was affecting your business even before Beau and Nate started Pearl Tide?"

Royal sighed. "Yeah. There's truth in that." He smiled at Viv. "And I don't blame you or Beau—or even Nate, hard as that is to admit—for trying another approach. Truth is, shrimping hasn't been the same in years, either, and I was proud of you for finding another way."

Viv, blinking rapidly, looked down. A small smile appeared on her face.

"But I've spent my whole life on the water. Can't imagine living it another way, and I don't want to give up the way we've always done it. There's value in tradition. Always has been," he said, chin trembling. "It was already hard to scrape by, but now . . . it's almost impossible to make a living off clusters when you're competing against those singles that sell for three times as much—even more in the summer months."

"But the thing is," Kit continued, "why compete when you don't have to?"

Royal glanced at her and frowned. "What do you mean?"

"I mean, there's a third option. One that might preserve your business and pave the way for Viv and Beau's to thrive, too." Kit hoped that she could at least do this one thing for Viv, her dad . . . and Beau. Something that would give them all a fighting chance at rebuilding their dreams. "Call your partners, Viv." She grinned. "Tell the Suttons that the Teagues have issued an invitation for them to join us for supper here at Teague Cottage right after dark."

Beau stood at the end of the driveway leading to Teague Cottage, eyeing the brightly lit front porch and pondering whether or not his son had stretched the truth.

"You sure you heard right?" Beau asked, glancing at Cal, who stood beside him.

Cal smirked. "Yeah, for, like, the fifteenth time, Dad."

Beau bit back a grin. "What's that?" He gestured toward Cal's mouth. "Sarcasm?"

Nate scoffed. "Typical teenager." Standing on the other side of Beau, he propped his hands on his hips and narrowed his eyes at Cal. "You sure it was Royal you spoke to and not just Viv?"

Cal rolled his eyes. "Kit's the one who called and invited us over, but Mr. Teague got on the phone, too, and said to tell y'all not to be late, because you'd ruin his spread."

Nate made a face—an odd mixture of curiosity and disgust. "What spread was he talking about?"

"Food, I guess." Cal waved his hand in the air, dismissing further questions, and strode up the driveway toward the front porch. "I told y'all a thousand times, he and Viv invited us over for supper. Now, are y'all coming or not? All I did today was work—didn't even stop for lunch— and I'm starving."

Beau sprang into a jog, moving briskly up the driveway, then slowed Cal's steps with his hand on his shoulder. "Hold up, there. Why don't you let me go first?" He rolled his shoulders as he climbed the front porch steps and smiled. "Just in case Royal woke up in a bad mood today."

He was joking . . . kind of. Beau walked onto the front porch, leaned to the side, and peered between the white lace curtains fluttering in the breeze against the screen of the open window. Lights were on inside, and there was movement—tall silhouettes moved to and fro, from one room to another, then back. The tantalizing aroma of fried shrimp wafted outside, making Beau's stomach rumble impolitely.

"Just knock on the door, Dad."

Beau cut his eyes over his shoulder at Cal. "Give me a minute, okay?"

He turned back to the door, dragged a hand through his hair, and flicked a small clump of mud off the hem of his T-shirt. It was difficult to spiff up too much. He'd spent the better part of the day on the water, flipping over cages, inspecting mesh bags for damage, and securing new lines.

And his shirt and jeans showed it. It'd been hot, grueling work, and more times than not, he'd caught his mind drifting away from his work to thoughts of Kit.

He'd found it difficult to concentrate on much of anything after Kit had told him she loved him. His mind—and heart—had spilled over with the memory of how good she'd felt in his arms, her soft, warm weight pressing against him, and it'd been even harder to forget that he'd agreed not to pursue her for the time being.

The polite smile he'd summoned to his lips fell. He understood and even agreed with what Kit had decided, but that didn't make it any less painful to follow through . . . or, more to the point, to back off. And then, the very day after Kit had left him, Viv had called and, according to Cal, had summoned them all over with Royal's blessing.

He ran his hand through his hair again, smoothing it down, an excited shiver of hope that Kit had changed her mind running through him. And maybe she had. Maybe she—

The door swung open, and Beau stepped back, his eyes widening, at the sight of Royal in the open doorway.

Royal frowned. "You plan on standing out here on my porch forever, son?" His lips twitched. "Or you actually gonna come in?"

Beau smiled despite the heat rising in his cheeks. "I'd like to come in, sir, if the invitation still stands?"

Royal grinned. "That it does." He thrust out a hand. "I'm glad to have you and hope you brung your appetite."

Beau hesitated, then shook his hand. Royal's firm but friendly grip put his mind at ease. "It's nice of you to have us over, Royal. We've had a long day on the water, and if the food tastes as good as it smells, we're anxious to dig in."

"Well, that's good," Royal said. "Cuz we got a ton of fixings." He stepped back and gestured for Beau to precede him, then smiled at Cal and Nate. "Y'all come on in and get comfortable."

At first, it didn't seem as though that would be possible. The small kitchen was full. Every inch of the countertops was covered with large plates of fried shrimp, clusters of steamed oysters, baked potatoes, buttered corn, collard greens seasoned with fatback, and jugs of sweet tea, and the wooden table in the center of the linoleum floor seemed gargantuan for the small space.

"Dad dug out the hidden leaves, dusted them off, and extended the table just for y'all," Viv said, striding around the table toward Beau. "We've been looking forward to having you over."

Beau smiled, noting the sincerity in her grin and her relaxed expression. The dark circles under her eyes, which had grown increasingly prominent over the past few weeks, had lightened, her cheeks were a bit more freckled, as though she'd been out in the sun for an extended time, and she looked well rested.

"I noticed the front yard and porch have been overhauled." He tipped his chin at her. "I'm guessing that was your handiwork?"

"Yep." Viv grinned. "Mine and Dad's and"—she gestured over her shoulder—"Mackey's and Kit's."

Beau glanced at the other side of the kitchen, and his chest warmed at the sight of Kit. She stood in front of an opened drawer by the sink, gathering utensils and helping Mackey count out how many glasses of ice to prepare.

He tore his attention away from her and refocused on Viv. "It looks beautiful."

"That mailbox you put out there turned out to be a nice touch," Royal said, striding past Beau into the kitchen. "We're mighty proud of it—especially Kit."

As her name was mentioned, Kit turned around, and

those beautiful eyes of hers met Beau's. "It does look nice," she said, smiling briefly at him before glancing over at Viv. "Beau was thinking of Viv when he installed it. Said he hoped it would be an improvement she'd welcome."

Viv studied Kit's expression silently, then glanced at Beau. "Whatever your reasons, it is appreciated."

There was no resentment or residual anger in Viv's voice—simply gratitude.

Beau smiled. "I was happy to do it."

"Well," Royal said, clamping a hand on Beau's shoulder, "now that we've thanked you for it properly, let's all grab a seat, bless the food, and dig in. I think you've got a teenager chomping at the bit to eat."

It took several minutes for everyone to maneuver around the table, choose a seat, and get settled, and a few more minutes for Mackey to fill glasses with ice, pour sweet tea in each, and place one at each setting, but before long, all seven of them were seated comfortably—and closely—around the kitchen table. Royal, seated at the head of the table, said the blessing, and everyone dug in.

The clanks of forks against plates, the clinks of ice in glasses, and low murmurs of chatter filled the small kitchen as everyone ate. Cal, exhausted and ravenous after the long day of work, devoured his shrimp, oysters, and potato, went back for seconds, and made room for a third helping of shrimp.

"Slow down, son," Nate said, laughing. "You're gonna eat Royal out of house and home."

Cal grinned around the last bite of shrimp and rubbed his full belly. "That was delicious, Mr. Royal. Thank you."

"You're welcome, Cal." Royal wiped his mouth with his napkin, placed the napkin beside his empty plate, and eased back in his chair. "Reckon now that most of us have staved off the night's hunger, you're probably curious as to why we asked y'all over."

Beau nudged his empty plate aside and leaned his elbows on the table. "I'll admit I was surprised when Cal said you wanted to see us again so soon."

"I was the one who asked that you come," Kit said.

Beau glanced at the other end of the table, where Kit sat beside Viv. Her hair was pulled back again, exposing her smooth cheeks and the graceful curve of her neck. She leaned forward and folded one hand on top of the other on the table. Her gaze lowered to his mouth before she turned away and focused on Nate, at Beau's side.

"I spoke with Dad about the damage you incurred during the storm," Kit said. "And Viv filled me in on some details regarding what you'd need to recover and produce a plentiful crop next summer. I'm thinking it's going to take a lot of time, energy, and effort, with very little payoff in the immediate future."

Nate nodded hesitantly and glanced at Royal. "We've suffered a blow, that's for sure. But we've also had contingency plans in place, in the event that we might encounter troubles like this storm. We came out better than we'd anticipated."

"I agree." Kit looked down at the table, her fingers twisting together. "I don't mean to . . . Well, I don't know how to put this, so I'll just say it like it is." She looked up and her eyes met Beau's again as she said gently, "I still don't agree with you."

Beau frowned and searched her expression. "What is it you don't agree with?"

"Consistency."

"Consistency?" Beau shook his head. "I don't—"

"The night you spoke at the community center," she prompted. "When you said that Pearl Tide Oyster Company would deliver oysters of consistent quality on a predictable basis to customers." She grimaced. "I think it's pretty evident after the recent storm, that the weather, at least, isn't predictable, and that this factor, as well as others we may not have considered, will prevent Pearl Tide Oyster Company from always producing consistent quality on a predictable basis, don't you?"

Beau sighed and sat back in his chair. He glanced at Nate, who shrugged slightly. "I'll concede that you have a point, but when I said that, I was referring to the overall production of the farm. I'm aware there'll be times like the recent storm that will impede the quality and availability of our product."

Kit's cheeks flushed. "I'm sorry. I didn't mean to criticize you or—"

Beau held up a hand. "No," he said softly. "I understand where you're coming from."

She relaxed, her hands stilling on the table. "The only reason I brought it up is to pave the way for a proposition."

Nate's head swiveled from Kit to Viv, then Royal. "What kind of proposition?"

Royal lifted his hands, palms out. "Ain't coming from me. I'm hearing this the same time you are."

"What I'm suggesting," Kit said, "is a merger." She glanced at Viv and Beau. "Or, if you'd rather think of it another way, you could consider it as an expansion of the Teague and Sutton partnership."

Royal tilted his head to the side and narrowed his eyes at Kit. "You mean, a partnership between Teague's Seafood and Pearl Tide Oyster Company?"

"Yes," Kit said. "If the storm showed us anything, it's that there will always be some unpredictability to oyster farming, but the same is true for harvesting them wild.

And I truly believe, Dad"—she looked at Royal—"that what Beau and Viv are doing is benefiting Hope Creek in a way the wild oyster population desperately needs. There's a lot of room out there . . . more than we remember sometimes. And if Pearl Tide Oyster Company expands, they'll need extra hands on deck. When the wild oyster season is over, that's the perfect time for us to step in and help with the expanded crop, and when the farm runs into setbacks, like the storm we had recently, your shrimping runs and— if it's in season—wild oyster harvests will help offset losses for all of us." She smiled. "Don't you see? It's the perfect marriage between our traditional shrimping and oyster harvesting methods and Beau's innovative mariculture."

Beau stilled as her eyes darted his way, her cheeks blushing a brighter red.

"I mean . . ." She shook her head. "I didn't mean marriage. I meant . . . partnership." She glanced at Viv and bit her lip. "A renewed, expanded partnership between the Teagues and the Suttons, under the leadership of Viv and Beau."

Viv returned Kit's stare, her brow furrowing, then looked at Beau. "What do you think, Beau?"

He stretched his arm over the back of his chair and studied Kit's face, the hopeful gleam in her eyes and her eagerness to make both Royal's and his businesses a success sending a bittersweet ache through him. "I think it's a great idea." He glanced at Nate and Royal. "But the final decision will be up to the two of you, I think. Any feud our families had over Hope Creek started with y'all, so it'd be fitting if y'all decided to end it."

Nate pursed his lips and tossed a sidelong glance at Royal. "Whatcha say, Royal? I wouldn't be opposed to strengthening both of our business outlooks, and I think that water's deep enough to hold both of us, don't you?"

Beau searched Royal's expression. The slow smile stretching across the older man's face widened his own.

"I'd say that creek's deep enough to hold us all." Royal stood and thrust his hand out. "Shake on it?"

Nate stood, as well, and smiled as he shook Royal's hand. "We're in business."

CHAPTER 14

Beau turned over the oyster cage in his hands and ran his fingers across two bent wires along the bottom.

"That one busted, too?" Nate asked, tossing the cage he held onto a large pile of others stacked at the end of the Suttons' dock.

" 'Fraid so." Beau eyed the cage one more time, then threw it onto the pile with Nate's. "Did you and Cal find any more in the woods, or"—he nodded toward six cages Nate had stacked on the culling table—"were these the last ones?"

"There are a few more missing, and we've looked everywhere else, so they've got to be out in the woods." He tipped his head back and squinted against the sharp rays of the afternoon sun while studying the high treetops lining the dirt road at the end of the driveway. "Those things have to be somewhere out there. I'm thinking, what with all the wind we had, they're probably perched up in one or two of those live oak branches." He grimaced. "It's not exactly high on my list of exciting things to do, but if we want the insurance company to replace them, we've got to prove we had 'em in the first place."

"You want me to check it out after I—"

"Nah." Nate waved his hand in the air, then dragged another oyster cage across the culling table and began inspecting it for damage. "I'll help you with this batch, and when Cal and Viv make it back from the creek, he and I'll hoof it out there for a while, see if we can't locate 'em."

Beau nodded and set a cage on the culling table in front of him. His hands cramped as he turned the cage over, and he paused briefly, flexing his fingers and massaging his palms.

It was no wonder his body was balking on him. For the better part of the past week, he'd spent most of each day outside: boating on the creek to the floating farm, hauling in cages, tumbling and sorting oysters, then checking equipment, counting cages, and searching the grounds for misplaced or damaged cages. The last couple of hours of daylight he'd spent doing what he was doing now—inspecting cages, keeping the ones he thought were good candidates for successful repair, and tossing the ones that were too damaged into the growing pile at the end of the dock.

He hadn't been too concerned when he and Nate had started the post-storm cleanup a week ago—the cages they'd found at first had suffered only minor damage and were few in number. Only as they'd moved through one line after another of floating cages, tumbling and sorting, it had quickly become apparent there were more missing than they'd initially guessed, and the more damaged cages they found, the more the losses racked up.

"Don't frown so hard," Nate said, elbowing him. "A week ago, this would've had me scratching my head and popping antacid, but considering the fact that we've brought new partners on board to cushion the fall, we're going to be in pretty decent shape by the time all of this shakes out."

Beau smiled, but he couldn't quite summon the same excited energy he'd first felt when Royal and Nate had struck
a bargain and agreed to merge Teague's Seafood and Pearl
Tide Oyster Company. The reason was simple: Kit.

"You talked to her recently?"

Beau started, his head jerking up and his eyes meeting
Nate's, and he wondered if he'd spoken his thoughts out
loud. Though, if that were the case, he wouldn't be surprised. He'd had a hard time focusing on anything lately
without thinking of her . . . or rather, the lack of having
her around.

"Don't look so surprised." Nate turned the cage he was
inspecting on its side and ran his gloved palm along the
loose metal wires. "It's easy to see you miss her. Even Viv
remarked on it a couple days ago."

Beau winced. That wasn't good. The whole point of him
and Kit keeping their distance from each other was to
avoid causing Viv distress over a romantic relationship between them.

He drew in a deep breath and tossed the cage he'd finished inspecting into the damaged pile. "What'd she say?"

"Oh, nothing out of the way—just that you seemed
quiet lately. Didn't look real enthused about the farm, like
you used to, and she asked if I might know what was
bothering you."

Beau stiffened. "And what'd you say?"

Nate shrugged. "Nothing much. Just told her I thought
you were a bit down, is all." He glanced at Beau and
raised an eyebrow. "You have seemed down lately, and
I've had a pretty good guess that it has something to do
with not hanging around Kit as much as you were for a
while there." He frowned. "Did something happen with
you two? For a while, it seemed like y'all were getting on

well." He laughed. "Maybe even a little too well for my liking at the time. You were smack-dab in the middle of those Teagues, which"—he lifted a hand—"turned out to be a pretty good thing, considering we ended up with a new set of partners and investors. But I've noticed only Mackey and Viv have come around to work on the farm this week. And every time I ask about Kit, Mackey says she's on the shrimp boat with Royal. I understand her wanting to spend time with her dad, but I thought she might have wanted to take advantage of working the farm a bit, too, seeing as how the two of you had become close." He shrugged. "Or maybe I was wrong about that."

Beau dragged another damaged cage toward him. "You weren't wrong. Kit and I were close," he said. "But there were other things to consider."

Nate narrowed his eyes. "Other *people* to consider, you mean, right?"

Beau blew out a heavy breath and shook his head. "What is it with you and Royal? Kit and I aren't teenagers, and whatever's going on between us is our busines—"

"Is family business, because the two of you are part of the family now," Nate said firmly. "Maybe not blood family, but it takes all of us working together to make this venture work, and we're all invested, so we're all curious." He grinned. "But, okay, I won't ask any more questions if you'd rather I not."

"I'd rather you not," Beau stated firmly.

Nate grinned wider. "That's all you had to say."

A motor hummed and water sloshed, signaling a boat's arrival.

"Ah, there they are now," Nate said, tugging his gloves off and gesturing toward the hybrid bay boat slowly approaching the dock. "Lord, looks like they've got more cages on the boat." He patted Beau's arm. "Guess we best prepare for being out here longer than we thought. Those cages in the woods might have to wait 'til tomorrow."

Nate headed down the dock to the boat, and Beau followed, tugging his gloves on tighter.

Cal hopped off the boat first and smiled as his feet hit the dock. "Most of the cages were fine, but we found a few more that looked pretty beat up." He spun back around, bent over the boat, and hauled out one of several cages stacked on the aft deck. "You maybe can fix this one, Dad."

Beau walked over as Cal lifted up the cage, and took it from him. He turned it over a time or two, peering at the metal wires. "I think you're right. I can probably bend these back in and tighten it up. How many others did you bring back like it?"

"Four, I think." Cal glanced in the boat, his brow furrowing. "But there are about five that don't look too good."

"It could've been worse," Viv said as she cut the boat's engine, grabbed a couple of cages, and hopped onto the dock, too. "From what I can tell, we've finished going through all the floating cages, and the majority are in great shape. The only ones left to tend to are the ones in the boat now and the ones we can't account for."

"And Cal and I are going to start looking for those as soon as Beau and I finish inspecting these cages and taking pictures of the damaged ones." Nate pointed at the pile of damaged cages at the end of the dock. "Insurance rep said she had to have pictures or video of all the damaged ones. I figured it's best we give her both, so that all our bases are covered. The better payoff we receive, the faster we'll be able to drop a new crop in the creek."

"You mind if I give you a hand instead of Nate?" Viv asked, eyeing Beau. "I'd like to discuss something with you, and that way he and Cal can get a head start on locating those missing cages."

Beau took the cages from her and hefted them, along with the one he'd taken from Cal, on one shoulder, trying not to show his concern. He may have been in his own world of missing Kit, but it hadn't escaped his notice that Viv had grown quiet lately, as well. "Sure," he said quietly. "That'd be fine."

Cal, sweaty from working hours on the water under the hot sun, took his cap off and ran a hand through his damp hair. "Can I grab a soda before we start, Pop? I'm dying of thirst."

"Yep." Nate draped his arm over Cal's shoulders and hugged him as they headed up the dock and walked toward the house. "We'll rest a few minutes in the kitchen before we traipse out there. Then we can start over by the . . ."

Beau watched Nate and Cal amble away, then smiled. "Cal's really taken to the water lately, hasn't he?"

"Sure has." Viv smiled, her gaze following Cal and Nate, too, as they entered the house. "And he wouldn't have wanted to come in just now, other than the fact that he was thirsty and ready to tackle the next job." Her attention returned to Beau, and warm approval shone in her eyes. "You've done it, Beau. You've got him to love Hope Creek as much as you do. He's really happy here."

"Yeah," Beau said. "But you had something to do with that, too. Showing him the ropes and teaching him the trade. You helped him feel at home here."

Viv studied his face, her smile dimming. "That's kind of what I wanted to talk to you about." She motioned toward the cages stacked on his shoulder. "You want to put those down while I grab the rest? We can inspect them while we talk. Knock two birds out with one stone?"

Beau nodded. "Sounds like a plan."

Five minutes later, they were settled at the culling table and had established a steady rhythm of inspecting and sorting cages.

"So what is it you want to talk about?" Beau asked, glancing at Viv as he flipped a cage over and tested the bent wires on the other side.

"You and Kit." Her hands stilled on the cage in front of her, and she eyed him from the opposite side of the culling table. "You miss her, don't you?"

Beau slid his gloved hand slowly along the frame of the cage he was inspecting, deciding honesty was best. "Yeah."

"A lot?" She tapped her fingers against the cage she held. "It's okay to be straightforward with me. I promise this isn't what you think it is."

Beau sighed, his hands stilling on the cage in front of him. "Yes, I miss her, Viv. A lot."

She held his gaze and managed a small smile, but shadows still lingered in her eyes. "I figured as much. And who wouldn't? Even I think my sister's pretty fantastic . . . well, once I stopped being mad at her."

Beau grinned, a soft breath of surprised relief leaving him. "Then why'd you ask?"

"Because I needed to hear you say it." Her voice faltered. "That and one other thing, too."

Beau placed both hands flat on the cage and faced her, giving her his full attention. "And what's that?"

"Well, I've made a decision, see? And I want to be sure that I'm right before I follow through with it." She hesitated, a sheepish expression crossing her face. "It means I have to pry a little, but I promise you it's for a good reason."

"Pry away."

She bit her lip. "Do you love her?"

He noted the slight tremble in her hands and the guarded eagerness in her expression and considered dodging the question or refusing to answer altogether. But the thing was, he'd never lied to Viv. And he missed talking to her in an open and honest way, without fear of repercussion.

"Yes," he said quietly, the excited exhilaration he felt at acknowledging it out loud at war with the guilt surging through him at hurting Viv. "I love her."

Viv nodded, her smile returning. "Thank you for telling me. I needed to hear that." She blushed and waved a hand in the air. "Not that I expect you to believe that after the way I behaved the last time we had a similar conversation, but it's the truth." She tucked a few loose strands of hair behind her ear and ducked her head, the mannerism—one of very few—similar to Kit's. "It's easy for me to say that now, because I know that I don't love you the way you love Kit. Or, if I'm guessing right"—she shrugged—"how Kit loves you."

Beau remained quiet, a knot of tension deep inside him slowly unwinding.

"I don't mean to offend you," Viv said quickly. "It's just that we've always been honest with each other, and I don't want to change that. I, uh, really need it right now."

Beau reached out, covered her hand with his. "Go on."

She looked down at his hand and smiled. "Kit and I used to sit on our dock years ago, and you'd go striding by." She peeked up at him and grinned. "You were just a boy, but I'll admit you looked like a full-grown man to us. Like a . . . dream, really. And that's what you were to me. A handsome, safe, seemingly well-off gentleman who would serve as the safest of safe harbors." Her smile slipped. "I wasn't in love with *you*—just the idea of you. Of all you represented. The safety and security and escape

I never had. That's why I came here that night two years ago." She glanced at the creek, listened to the soft waves lapping at the dock. "I came to this place—to you—looking for those things. And I made the mistake of imagining that you were the ticket to those things."

She turned her hand over in his and squeezed. "And don't get me wrong, your friendship was the lifesaver I needed at the time, and I still do. Your friendship is the most valuable one I've ever had. Besides Kit's, that is . . . which is why I've made the decision I have."

Beau frowned. "And what decision is that?"

"I'm leaving." She raised her brows, excitement and fear mingling in her eyes. "It's what I've always wanted to do. To get away, to see another part of the world for a while, to find my own space in it. I just never thought I could while my mom was around," she said, her voice shaking. She cleared her throat and shook her head. "But now things are different, and . . . maybe one day I'll find my way back here. But for now, I need to get away and start over. I need to do what Kit did."

Beau's frown faded, and he looked away, his throat tightening.

"Are you angry with me?" Viv whispered.

"No." He faced her then, taking both of her hands in his. "Not at all. I'll miss you, though. And Kit . . ." He shook his head, his chest aching at the thought of her reaction. "Your leaving is going to break her heart. She came back for you."

"I know," Viv said quietly. "And I understand why she did what she did now, but if I've learned anything from my mother, it's that you can't live for someone else. You can live only your own life. That's what Kit was doing when she left fifteen years ago, and it's what I need to do now. Not just for me, but for Kit, too." She tugged her hands free from his, cupped the back of his head and, rising on her toes, kissed his cheek. "And for you. Both of you are the most important people in my life, and it's past time for you to have a chance to be happy again. Y'all can move on together, and by the time I get back, I'll be a better person to know."

Beau smiled, his eyes burning, as he walked around the table and hugged her. "You're one of the best people I've ever known already, Viv. I'm lucky to have you as a friend."

She smiled back, her expression brightening. "And I hope I'll be even luckier to have you as a brother one day."

Kit scooped a large heap of ice into a plastic bag filled with freshly caught brown shrimp, knotted the top closed, and lifted it high. "Here's the last of it. Are we delivering to Vernon today or tomorrow?"

Royal, standing beside her in front of the deveining and packing table in the Teague Cottage fish house, took the bag and hefted it up a time or two, testing its weight. "Perfect five pounder, and tomorrow'll be soon enough for delivery."

He walked over to the freezer on the back wall, opened the lid, and dropped the bag of shrimp in with several dozen others they'd packed that afternoon.

Kit shrugged her shoulders, stretching the tight muscles between her shoulder blades, and moved her neck from side to side. She smiled, the slight ache in her biceps and calves and the lingering tingle on her windswept skin conjuring to her mind the hours she'd spent on the water with Royal earlier that morning.

It had become a morning ritual over the past week—waking up at six in the morning, dressing, and joining Royal on the front porch to enjoy a cup of coffee and watch the sun rise. The new screen-free porch had become Royal's favorite spot, and it had even overtaken Kit's preference for the "thinking tree" spot she'd enjoyed so much over the years. Now the hour around sunrise, spent kicking back in the wicker chair, sipping hot, strong coffee, enveloped in the scent of Royal's morning cigar, had become Kit's favorite time of day.

Not just for the coffee and contemplation, but for the company, as well. Royal, growing more at ease and optimistic every day, relished having a full house again, and his drive for shrimping had returned full force, along with his love for the water. Even on days when the fishing was slow, Royal would navigate the boat along Hope Creek, find a calm, clear spot to view the horizon, and cut the engine, allowing the vessel to bob in the waves while he sat and enjoyed a smoke or just closed his eyes for a few minutes, a slow smile crossing his face as he soaked up the sun.

These were the kind of days Kit remembered—and loved—the most from her childhood, and it was wonderful to see Royal more like himself again.

"You got enough energy left to help me and Mackey finish painting the guest room?" Kit teased.

A look of mock affront crossed Royal's face. "You trying to say I'm too old to tackle another labor-intensive task today?"

Kit laughed. "Nope. Just asking if you're interested in making the effort this late in the day."

He glanced at his wristwatch and grinned. "It ain't late, girl. It's only five o'clock. Still two or three hours of daylight left, and it's supposed to be mild out tonight, so it's a good time to leave the window open for the walls to dry after we finish."

"It'll involve moving a dresser, too," Kit warned.

Royal laughed. "So be it. This ol' back of mine's got enough gumption left in it to move a dresser."

And it did. Mackey was already hard at work by the time they walked to the house and made their way into Sylvie's old bedroom. He had painted half the walls of the room light blue and stood by one of the remaining unpainted walls with a paintbrush in his hand, dripping blue paint on the hardwood floor.

"Oh, Mackey." Kit grabbed several sets of old newspapers Royal had placed in the room for Mackey earlier that morning and started spreading them out over the damaged areas. "You need to make sure you've got the papers spread out before you start painting again, okay?"

Mackey frowned. "Oh. But the blue looks good, doesn't it?" he asked. "Even on the floor?"

Kit winced. "Well, the walls are beautiful, and the floor . . . well, the floor—"

"Looks fantastic, too," Royal said, walking across the room and hugging Mackey. "It's about time this room had some life in it again, and the colors you chose are perfect, son."

Mackey beamed.

Smiling, Kit blinked back a sheen of tears as she glanced around the room. Mackey had done a great job overhauling the room. Over the past week, he'd stripped the bed and spot cleaned the mattress, swept the floor, packed up and removed (with Royal's help) all of Sylvie's clothes and jewelry, and dusted down the furniture. He'd also taken down the curtains, washed them and rehung them, after cleaning the windows.

Sylvie's favorite view of Hope Creek had never been so clear or beautiful. A bittersweet ache welled inside Kit. Her mother would've loved it, and she'd have been proud of Mackey's hard work.

After removing the screen from the front porch, Royal had decided it was time to renovate other areas, as well, and Sylvie's old room had been at the top of the list. The old rule of not entering the bedroom had been abolished, and Royal, opening the door wide one night, had referred to it as the guest room—or, as he'd put it, Kit's new room, seeing as how she'd announced her intention to stay. And the new partnership with the Suttons had further fueled his excitement to redesign some of the space in Teague Cottage.

Royal was ready for change, and Kit, surreptitiously wiping away a tear, was glad to see him happy.

"I can't do that one yet, because of the dresser," Mackey said, pointing his paintbrush at an unpainted wall.

Kit ducked to avoid the drops of paint that were flung across the room. "Well, that's why we're here. If we hurry up, we'll have the room painted by the time Viv comes back from the farm. That'd be a nice surprise." She walked over to the dresser, braced her hands on one corner, and lifted her chin at Royal. "Come on, Dad. Time to get that back of yours warmed up."

After they moved the dresser to the center of the room, it took a little over an hour to finish painting the room. Kit leaned into one side of the dresser and gave it a final push, helping Royal position it a few inches from the wall Mackey had just finished painting.

"Now," she said, heaving out a breath and smiling. "I think you can safely say you've finished decorating this room, Mackey."

Mackey, drying his hands with a towel, looked around, his eyes wide. "It looks good, don't it?"

"Better than good," Kit said. "It's gorgeous."

Royal murmured a sound of agreement, then flopped on the freshly made bed. "Y'all kick back and admire it for a minute."

Laughing, Mackey jogged across the room and hopped on the bed, then laid his head on Royal's chest. "It's gorgeous, ain't it, Dad?"

Royal kissed the top of his head and smiled. "You done perfect, son." He stretched his free arm out and turned his palm up. "I got another shoulder free," he said. "Don't care how old you are. You're always welcome to it."

Heart turning over, Kit walked over to the bed and lay down, too, and rested her head on Royal's shoulder. They lay there silently for a few minutes, gazing at the blue-painted walls and watching the long lace curtains flutter in the breeze flowing through the open window.

"Your mama loved this room," Royal said softly. "She'd have been proud of what you've done, Mackey."

Kit lifted her head and glanced to her left, then smiled wider as Mackey giggled with pride and nuzzled his cheek closer to Royal's chest.

"Y'all got room for one more?"

Kit looked to her right, where Viv stood in the doorway, a hesitant smile on her face as she studied them lying on the bed.

"There ain't no question about that," Royal said. "You're part of the family." He patted Mackey's shoulder. "Roll a little to your left, son. Your sister needs her space."

An excited squeal left Mackey at the prospect of all of them piled in the bed—something they hadn't done in years. Kit had been nine the last time she recalled them doing so.

"There's too many of us," Mackey said, laughing. "You think it'll break?"

"Nah," Royal said, smiling wide, as he scooted over a couple of inches. "This old bed's strong. It'll hold us all."

Viv smiled as they all shifted over; then she gingerly lay down beside Kit. She stared at the ceiling for a minute and laughed. "Whose idea was this? I feel like a five-year-old."

Royal slipped his arm out from under Kit's head, reached out, and playfully mussed Viv's hair. "Y'all will always be five years old in my book. Or at least, you'll always be my little girls—no matter how old you are." He turned his head, and his dark eyes moved beyond Kit's face to focus on Viv's expression. "No matter *where* you are. I hope you know that."

Viv grew quiet, her arm tensing against Kit's.

"Viv?" Kit slipped her hand in her sister's. "What's going on?"

Viv was quiet for a moment, then said, "I thought about what you said. You know, the night you talked about Highlands?"

Kit nodded, her breath catching.

"I want to go," Viv said quietly.

Mackey shot upright, his chin trembling. "Go where?"

Royal smoothed his hand over Mackey's hair. "Viv needs some time on her own, I think."

Viv pressed her lips together, a wet sheen forming over her eyes. "You knew I was thinking of going?"

Royal nodded, a sad smile appearing on his face. "I guessed as much. You've had the same look on your face that you had when you left for the Suttons. The same yearning in your eyes."

Kit bit her lip and studied Viv's face. "You want to go to Highlands?"

Viv nodded.

"For how long?" Kit asked. "A couple weeks or—"

"No." Viv shook her head. "I want to start over there— or someplace like it—like you did. I need a change in scenery." She shrugged. "A change in perspective. A chance to start over. And I guess that'll take as long as it takes. I know this isn't ideal. I know we've partnered up with the Suttons, and that I had grand plans with Beau, but that didn't exactly work out the way I planned."

Kit squeezed her hand tight. "Viv, I—"

"No." Viv smiled. "It's the way it should be. You'll have a chance to start over now, too. A chance to do so here, in a place you love." She raised her head and smiled at Royal and Mackey, then met Kit's eyes again. "With people you love. And I'll have the same opportunity." Her voice softened when she added, "Don't you remember how you felt when you left, Kit? Don't you remember how much you needed to go?"

Kit closed her eyes and nodded. "I understand if this is what you want—what you need—but . . ."

"Please let me do this, Kit," she said softly. "Let me do this for me. For you and Beau. And for Dad and Mackey." She grew quiet again, then said, "Beau asked me once what Mama would've wanted for us."

"She would've wanted you girls to be happy," Royal said, blinking back tears. "That's all she ever wanted. No matter what her problems were or how low she ever became, she always looked up to you girls. Loved you girls. She wouldn't have wanted you to live a life of regret. She would've wanted you to move on and be happy, and if that means I have to lose you for a little while—like I lost Kit—it'd be worth it to have you back whole and happy."

Viv smiled. "I think this would be a chance for me to be happy." She held her hand out and wiggled her fingers. "Is that okay with you, Mackey? If I take some time on my own? Do you think you could take care of things here for me while I'm gone? Maybe keep this room spiffy for when I come back?"

Mackey remained silent for a moment, then reached out, slipped his hand in Viv's, and squeezed. "Yeah," he said, managing a smile. "I can do that."

Kit studied Viv's face again. "I hope you know how much I'll miss you—how much we'll all miss you. I hope you'll find your way back to us soon. There's still another six months left on my apartment lease. You're welcome to use it if you'd like until you find a place of your own."

Viv threw her arms around Kit's neck and hugged her tight. After a moment she whispered, "Well, if you're feeling generous and decide to give me that car of yours, I think I'd make my way back here faster. Every place on this island that's worth going to is within walking distance." She laughed, her breath tickling Kit's ear. "You don't need it here, anyway, do you?"

Kit smiled and buried her face in Viv's hair. "No," she whispered. "I don't plan on going anywhere. I'm already home."

CHAPTER 15

Kit grabbed the handle of an overly stuffed suitcase, hefted it off the dock and into Royal's hybrid bay boat, then glanced over her shoulder and huffed out a breath. "How much more you got, Viv? If we load too much more, the boat might sink before we make it to shore."

Viv, who had walked up the Teague dock with small overnight bags in both hands, laughed as she joined Kit by the boat. "This is the last of it." Her steps faltered. "Except for—"

"Already got it," Beau said, striding up behind Viv with another stuffed suitcase.

"And you forgot your to-go bag." Royal hustled up behind Beau, holding a clear plastic bag packed with two sandwiches, crackers, and other snacks. "You can't drive all the way into Charleston this late without something to put in your stomach before bed."

Viv tossed her bags in the boat and, grinning, took the bag from Royal. "Thanks, Dad. But I'm pretty sure there's a restaurant at the hotel, and I can always grab something out of the vending machine if I get desperate."

Royal frowned. "Those hotel restaurants ain't got nothing but pretty, overpriced food that has no taste. And can't nobody live off the junk that sits in a vending machine for weeks." He pointed at a sandwich wrapped in foil. "That right there is tuna, and I wrapped it up real good so it'll stay cold for a while. There's crackers . . . I know you like peanut butter . . . And if you get up in the middle of the night and have a hankering, you just dig on down in there and you'll find—"

"Everything I need," Viv said, then began to laugh. Her laughter trailed off as she looked up at Royal. She bit her lip. "You've done so much for me. I don't just have everything I need. I have everything I want, too." She lifted to her toes, threw her arms around Royal, and hugged him tight, burying her face in his shoulder. "I'm gonna miss you, Dad."

Royal's chin trembled, and he ducked his head, hugging her closer. "Well . . . I'm sure gonna miss you."

Kit looked away and focused on the waves rippling along the creek as she surreptitiously wiped a tear from her cheek. Three days ago, Viv had followed through with her decision to leave Hope Creek by selecting a date of departure and starting the arduous task of packing her belongings. Kit had helped, and they'd focused on necessities at first, but the longer they had worked, the more evident it had become that Viv planned on staying in Highlands for far longer than a brief visit.

The more they'd packed, the more Viv had suggested they pack, and by last night, almost all of Viv's belongings were stowed away in carefully secured bags. All that was left was to ferry Kit's car back to the parking lot by the Hope Creek Water Taxi dock, which Kit had taken care of yesterday.

Kit wiped away another tear and started slightly when Beau's hand squeezed her shoulder.

He looked down at her, concern in his eyes. "You okay?" he asked softly.

She swallowed past the lump that had lodged in her throat and tried for a smile. "Yeah," she whispered. "The moment just snuck up on me sooner than I expected, I guess."

She'd been prepared—she really had. Last night had been difficult. She and Viv had stayed up late, spending their last night together in their old bedroom. They'd opened the window and snuggled down in their own beds, talking quietly as the warm early summer breeze swept in, stirring the air. Kit had tried to keep the conversation going as long as possible, struggling to keep her eyes open and hold on to the sweet nostalgia she felt with Viv by her side, but eventually, despite her best efforts, sleep had claimed them both, and the alarm had woken them both early this morning to begin the final preparations for Viv's departure.

"You said you'd come back no later than Christmas, right?"

Kit glanced over her shoulder just as Mackey edged his way into the middle of Viv and Royal's embrace to claim his own hug.

"You said Christmas, huh, Viv?" Mackey repeated, his voice muffled, as he pressed his cheek to Viv's neck. "You're coming back no later than Christmas."

"Yeah, bud." Viv's voice trembled, and she wrapped her arms tight around Mackey, her eyes meeting Kit's over his head. "I promise that I'll be back for Christmas, if not before. No matter what happens between now and then, I promise to stay at least a week when I arrive, okay? How does that sound?"

Mackey murmured his approval.

"That sounds wonderful," Kit said, smiling at Viv.

Viv squeezed her eyes shut, tears glistening on her lashes in the late afternoon sun, gave Mackey one more hard squeeze, then gently extricated herself from his arms and kissed his cheek. "I have to go, kid. I'll be late checking into the hotel, if I don't."

Royal cleared his throat. "Come on, Mackey. We've got some oysters to roast up. Nate and Cal are coming by soon, remember?"

Mackey's expression lit up. "Oh, yeah. And can I have the first oyster this time?"

Royal slung an arm over Mackey's shoulders and led him back up the dock. "Sure you can."

Mackey peered up at Royal and grinned. "And can I roast my own oyster? You said I could. Last night you promised, remember?"

Royal smiled. "Yeah, I remember."

Viv sighed as they ambled up the dock and into the backyard of Teague Cottage. "I'm glad to see he's taking it better today."

Kit's mouth curved. "Which one? They were both having a hard time with your leaving for a while."

It was true, and Kit still couldn't figure out whether Royal or Mackey had struggled the most to hold back tears over breakfast this morning. But as the day had worn on, the excitement on Viv's face as she spoke of her plans for the first few days in Highlands had perked them both up, and her happiness had seemed to set their minds—and hearts—at ease.

"Do you think they'll be okay soon?" Viv asked, the first real hint of regret in her voice.

"They already are." Kit walked over and squeezed her shoulders. "Dad and Mackey are happy for you—just as I am. And you're gonna be late to your hotel room if we don't get on that boat and hightail it down the creek."

"Yep." Beau hopped onto the boat, sat in the driver's seat, and wiggled the boat keys. "And Royal doesn't just hand his keys over to anyone." He grinned and cranked the engine; his eyebrows lifted when it purred. "I feel important."

Viv laughed. "You ought to. But you'd better watch how you drive this thing. You break it, and Dad'll break you." She boarded the boat. "And it won't matter how much in love you are with his daughter—you'll still suffer the consequences."

Kit's cheeks heated as she followed Viv onto the boat, but a thrill of pleasure spiraled through her as she met Beau's warm gaze.

She'd been apprehensive at first when Viv had confided in her that she knew Beau had fallen in love with Kit, just as Kit had with him. What was even more surprising was that she'd openly encouraged him and Kit to pursue a relationship with each other. There had been no animosity or resentment in her tone—just sincerity.

And that one sacrifice had been enough to lift Kit's hopes that one day, she and Viv might find their way back to one another again as best friends as well as sisters. No matter how long they had to be apart, as long as the separation led to Viv's happiness and a chance at strengthening their relationship down the road, it'd be worth it.

"I'll be careful," Beau said, smiling, as he turned his attention back to the creek. "You'll think it's Royal himself at the helm."

Beau carefully maneuvered the hybrid bay boat away from the dock and steered it along Hope Creek, picking up speed as they went. Nate and Cal stood at the end of the Suttons' deepwater dock, waving as they passed.

"Bye, Viv!" Cal shouted. "Call me once in a while."

Viv sprang up from her seat beside Kit and waved back. "I will," she called back. "You take care of that baby crop for me. I expect to see a ton of deep cups the next time I swing through here."

"We'll do you one better," Nate called. "I'll challenge your dad to another roast-off to celebrate your return."

"I'll be looking forward to it!" Viv continued waving until the boat rounded a bend and tall cordgrass, lowering in the late afternoon breeze, blocked her view.

Kit slipped her hand over Viv's as she sat back down beside her on the bench. "You can always come back anytime," she said over the whip of wind and the purr of the boat's motor. "No matter where you are or what time of year—you just make your way back to the dock, and we'll pick you up and bring you home."

Viv drew in a deep breath and nodded, her gaze drifting out toward the horizon, as the boat reached the mouth of Hope Creek and crossed into a larger river, weaving its way along wide curves toward the shore.

They both grew silent, holding hands and admiring the view.

Viv glanced back and rested her chin on Kit's shoulder, whispering near her ear, "Mama would've wanted us to be happy."

Kit looped her arm through Viv's and smiled. "Yes."

Viv's eyes, filled with relief, roved over the boat's wake. "She knew we loved her," she said softly. She faced Kit again and leaned against her side. "Both of us."

Kit closed her eyes as the swift breeze ruffled her hair, the strands tickling her cheeks, and the heavy weight on her heart lifted. She breathed deep, filling her lungs with clean, salt-laden air, and smiled as the waves lapped at the boat.

Sylvie was at peace now, and they could all finally move on.

"We're here." Beau slowed the boat, and the whip of the wind died down as they drew close to the Hope Creek Water Taxi dock. He glanced over his shoulder at Viv. "Soon as we tie up, I'll unload your bags, and you'll be good to go."

The boat stopped by the taxi pickup, and Beau stepped onto the dock to tie up.

"Well, if it ain't the Teague girl again. You leaving?"

Kit stood and, shielding her eyes from the sun with her hand, focused on the small figure lounging at the opposite end of the dock. *Lou Ann Cragg.* She smiled.

"No," Kit said, grabbing a plastic bag and stepping onto the dock. "I'm right where I want to be."

Lou Ann frowned, her hand stopping halfway to her mouth, a lit cigarette dangling between her fingers. "Then what's all them bags for?"

Viv followed Kit onto the dock, hefting a bag over her shoulder. "They're for me. I'm the one who's leaving." Her lip twitched. "Not that it's any of your business."

"Oh, put your back down, girl." Lou Ann lifted the cigarette and took a drag, narrowing her eyes at Viv as she studied her from head to toe. "You look different." She thumped her cigarette lightly, knocking the built-up ash off the tip. "All gussied up . . . Where you headed?"

Viv raised an eyebrow. "Jeans and a T-shirt is hardly gussied up, Lou Ann. And I'm heading to Highlands."

Kit grinned. Even Viv's voice had lifted with excited anticipation.

"Oh . . ." Lou Ann looked Viv over one more time, then nodded with a satisfied smile. "Good for you." She lifted her hip, withdrew a cigarette pack from her back pocket, and held it out toward Viv. "You want one for the road? To celebrate?"

Viv stared at the cigarette pack for a moment, then shook her head. "No, thanks. I'm starting fresh, and quitting those is at the top of my list." She hefted the bag she carried into a more secure grip and smiled at Kit. "I want to be present for everything—feel everything—from here on out."

Kit lifted her chin, a newfound sense of pride streaming

through her at the healthy glow on Viv's face. She turned on her heel and walked across the dock to Lou Ann. "Here," she said. "These are for you."

Lou Ann reached out and took the plastic bag with one hand, then inspected it closely. "Oysters?" She cut her eyes toward Beau, who was lifting the bags from the boat one by one and placing them on the dock. "These them deep cups of his?"

Kit grinned. "Of *ours*. You're looking at a new partner of Pearl Tide Oyster Company. The Teagues and Suttons are joining forces, you see." She softened her tone, when she added, "And you were very kind to me when I first arrived a few weeks ago. I wanted to return the favor." She gestured toward the bag of oysters. "Careful of the bottom. There are holes for any ice that melts to drip out of. I figure they'll stay cold 'til you make it home and get settled for the night. A few of those steamed would go great with a cold beer."

Lou Ann lifted the bag in her hand, testing its weight, then smiled wide. "Dang sure will. Thank you for this."

"You're welcome." Kit nodded, then walked back over to Viv and withdrew a set of keys from her pocket. "And these are for you."

Viv's eyes widened. "For the car, right?"

"For the car." Kit laughed, then threw her arms around Viv and hugged her tight, whispering, "And Teague Cottage. You have a house key to let yourself in whenever you come home."

Viv hugged her back so tight, Kit could scarcely draw breath. "I love you, Kit," she whispered.

Kit blinked hard, wet heat tickling her cheeks. "I love you, too."

A half hour later, Kit stood beside Beau at the helm of Royal's hybrid bay boat, the salt breeze whipping through her hair and her eyes focused on the bursts of color along the horizon as the sun slowly set.

"It's so beautiful," Kit said after drawing in a deep lungful of fresh sea air. "I'd forgotten how gorgeous and peaceful it really is down here."

Beau palmed the steering wheel with one hand, maneuvering the boat around a sharp curve lined with dense cordgrass. "Did you miss it at all while you were in Highlands?"

Kit nodded. "A lot." She thought it over for a moment, then said, "But I missed the people I loved more. I missed being home, and I missed . . . the way home used to feel."

The boat emerged from the curve, and Beau directed it toward the mouth of Hope Creek. "And does it feel like home now?"

"Yes," she said, tilting her head back and looking up at him. "It feels more like home than ever."

He smiled and moved to speak but hesitated, a hint of regret in his eyes. "You miss her already, don't you?"

"Viv?"

He nodded.

"Yeah." A humorless laugh left her. "I missed her before she even left. But . . . as strange as it sounds, we're much closer now even apart than we were when I first came home. And if time away is what she needs to heal, then it'll be worth it in the end." She returned her attention to the sunset; the bright pink, purple, and gold hues streaking across the sky and reflecting off the water warmed her on the inside. "Viv and I are both on our way to being happy again, and that's what our mom would've wanted."

Beau blew out a heavy breath and tugged her tight to his side. "That's good, because I have no intention of ever letting you go. And you'll be too busy to miss Viv too much, because I've got a lot planned for us."

Kit laughed. "Oh, really?"

"You can bet on it." After slowing the boat, he dipped his head and brushed his lips across hers. His blue eyes, full of affection, lingered on her lips before he focused on the creek again. "I'm thinking a few more Sutton family and Teague family get-togethers are in order. And a few trips on the water with Cal would be a great chance for you and him to get to know each other better. After that, I'm thinking we're way overdue for another night of stargazing in the moonlight." He grinned, his blond hair ruffling in the breeze. "And this time, I think we'll plan ahead a bit better. Maybe bring a few warm blankets, a lantern, and a lot more time."

"Really?" Warm tingles spread over Kit's skin, urging her to brush her lips along Beau's strong neck and jaw. As she did, the salty taste of his skin mingled on her tongue with the fragrant island air, filling her senses and her heart. "I can't think of anything I'd rather do than spend an entire night in your arms."

"It'll be longer than that," Beau said softly, slowing the boat to a crawl and wrapping both arms around her. "There's nothing I'd rather do than spend a lifetime with you. In case you haven't noticed, I'm desperately in love with you."

Kit grinned as his lips met hers, and whispered against his smile, "I love you, too."

Epilogue

"Mama, Daisy won't give me any stones!"

Kit, who'd been eyeing the empty waters of Hope Creek in the distance, glanced over her shoulder and smiled at the five-year-old brunette frowning a few feet away on the edge of the dock. Her daughter Ashley stood beside another little girl, who was an exact replica of Ashley, and pointed accusingly at her twin.

"I asked her to give me at least one," Ashley said. "And she won't give me any."

Kit stifled a grin. It was a routine occurrence—her twin daughters fussing over one thing or another—and though it grew tiresome at times, she'd always been pleased to see them continue to stick by each other, no matter how many arguments they had. Actually, everything about Ashley and Daisy had been a blessing.

Six years ago, after one year of stolen kisses, frequent trips on the water with Cal, and more sensuous nights spent under the stars with Beau than she'd thought possible, Kit had been overjoyed when Beau proposed. He'd chosen to do so on one of those very nights they'd spent together under the stars, the full moon glowing brightly and the soft summer night breeze cooling their sweat-slicked skin, after a few particularly pleasurable hours in each other's arms.

That night had been perfect, as had the months that followed. They'd chosen to marry quietly on the island, with Cal serving as Beau's best man and Viv making a return visit from Highlands to stand as maid of honor. The most surprising—and delightful—discovery had been made three months after the honeymoon. Kit had been nervous about becoming a mom, and she and Beau hadn't spoken in depth about having children, though they'd tossed the idea around a bit. At the time, their focus had been on Cal, who had broken out of his shell and was thriving on Hope Creek Island.

Still, they'd both been overjoyed at the news of the pregnancy and even more excited at the prospect of twins. When Beau had set eyes on Ashley and Daisy moments after their birth, he'd fallen for them then and there. From that moment on, the twins had Beau wrapped around their little fingers . . . and the same had been true for Cal, Mackey, Royal, and Nate.

"Did you ask Daisy for a stone nicely?" Kit asked, squatting down beside Ashley and tucking a strand of hair behind her ear.

Ashley thought this over for a moment, then made a face. "I could ask her nicer, I guess."

Kit grinned. "Then please do so."

Nodding with intent, Ashley rejoined Daisy by the edge of the dock and asked for a stone again in low tones, tacking on a *please* at the end. Daisy hesitated, narrowing her eyes at her sister.

"Daisy . . . ," Kit said, injecting a warning in her tone.

"But I wanted to practice skipping them," Daisy said. "So I can show Aunt Viv when she gets here."

The mention of Viv's name was enough to coax Kit's attention back to the creek and make her hands wring with anxious excitement. Afternoon sunlight danced over the creek's waters, but there was still no sign of Beau's hybrid bay boat with Viv in tow.

It'd been almost eight months since she and Beau had last seen Viv. For the past seven years, Viv had remained in Highlands, visiting frequently, but preferring her independence away from Hope Creek. With each return visit, Viv had looked more and more healthy, vibrant, and energetic. The cool, clean air of the mountains suited Viv, and her happiness was enough to appease Kit and Royal . . . though they both found themselves longing for her presence again.

And today's visit was extra special.

"Here you go, ladies." Cal's deep voice sounded from the other end of the dock before he walked over to Ashley and Daisy, his hands full of small stones. "What do you say we give these a try? There's enough here for you both to have plenty of practice by the time Dad gets back with Aunt Viv."

Kit glanced at Cal and smiled. At twenty-two, he had grown into a mature, confident man and had recently graduated from the College of Charleston with a degree in marine biology. He was eager to begin his work on Hope Creek, seeking to protect local wildlife. Today the whole family was celebrating his hard work and well-deserved accomplishment by having a friendly, old-fashioned Sutton and Teague oyster roast-off, which would be supplied with the most recent summer crop from the thriving Pearl Tide Oyster Company.

"Thank you, Cal," Kit said. "It doesn't take long for them to get riled up."

Daisy scowled. "Ain't nobody getting riled up."

Cal laughed. "I think someone's been spending too much time with Royal."

"Whatcha mean?" Royal called as he strode across the

backyard. He joined Cal on the dock and grinned. "Ain't no such thing as spending too much time with me, is there, cutie?"

Daisy squealed. "Nope. Help me do the skips, Papa."

Laughing, Royal squatted down beside Daisy and demonstrated how to skip a stone across the soft ripples of the creek. "See your sister yet?" Royal asked over his shoulder.

Kit faced the creek again and narrowed her eyes on the mouth of the river in the distance. "No, not yet. But they should be here any minute now." She glanced at her wristwatch. "Viv said she'd be here by six, and it's almost that now."

"Don't worry," Cal said. "Dad'll be here soon enough. I'm going to go help Pop set up the pots."

"You ain't gonna join me this go-round, Cal?" Royal asked, his lips twitching. "I'm telling you that good old-fashioned sheet metal and burlap sack steams them oysters up better than any pot and strainer Nate could stir up."

Cal laughed. "I'll think about it. You might just change my mind one of these days."

Kit shook her head, grinning. The partnership between the Teagues' and the Suttons' businesses was strong, but the familial bond that had formed—especially after Ashley's and Daisy's birth—was even stronger.

"Oh, there they are!" Kit waved her arms in excitement as she glimpsed Beau's hybrid bay boat enter the mouth of Hope Creek and head toward the Teagues' dock. The sun, hovering low on the horizon, silhouetted Beau's strong frame at the helm, and Kit could just make out two other figures in the boat. "Dad, is Viv bringing a guest?"

Royal's hands stilled on his knees, he glanced at the creek, and his eyes narrowed on the approaching boat. "Not that I know of. At least, she didn't mention it."

"Well, from the looks of it, I think we're going to have an extra person at dinner."

Royal shrugged. "No worries. She can share the guest room with Viv. Or if she doesn't mind sleeping on one of the smaller beds, she can use yours and Viv's old room."

Kit bit her lip, stifling a smile. "I don't think Viv brought a friend, Dad." She eyed the figures more closely as the boat drew nearer, the muscular shape of a man, who was embracing Viv as she pointed out various sites along the creek, coming into view. "Nope. I think she might've brought a boyfriend."

Royal frowned. "She never mentioned a boyfriend."

Kit held up a hand. "Now, Dad. Viv's over forty— you've got no say in this. So please remember your manners and give the guy the benefit of the doubt, okay?"

Royal grumbled but agreed to comply, then turned back to Daisy and offered her another stone-skipping lesson.

It was funny, really, the way Royal continued to think of her and Viv as little girls, but having two daughters of her own, she could very well see Beau behaving the same way with Ashley and Daisy.

The low hum of an engine approached, and Beau waved from the helm.

Kit waved back, then walked over to meet him as he docked the boat and cut the engine. "I missed you."

He grinned, his handsome features tan from hours on the water. "That fast?"

She laughed and blew a kiss to him. "Always."

And it was true. Every day her love for Beau grew stronger, and she could feel it was the same for him.

"Hey, sis." Viv, bright eyed and beaming with suppressed excitement, eased around Beau, hopped off the boat, and threw her arms around Kit. "Mmm. There's not a hug in the world as good as one from your sister."

Kit laughed and squeezed her back. "I'm so glad you're here. It's been so long since your last visit that I began to think we wouldn't see you again until Christmas."

"Oh, no." She stepped back and took Kit's hand in hers. "I'm thinking about sticking around awhile. Permanently, in fact."

Kit examined her face, looking for a hint of teasing. "Are you serious? You're moving back?"

"I'm giving it serious thought." She leaned close and whispered, "And I didn't come alone, either."

Kit craned her neck and peeked over Viv's shoulder at the six-foot-tall man exchanging pleasantries with Beau. "I see you've brought company." She grinned. "Rather handsome company, in fact."

Smiling, Viv whispered, "He's perfect. You're going to love him—and so will Dad, as soon as he gets to know him."

"There's my girl," Royal bellowed, standing and walking over to Viv.

She sprang into his arms and hugged him tightly. "Oh, I've missed you, Dad." She pulled back a little and raised an eyebrow. "You got the wood fire going and the sheet metal in position? Kit told me y'all planned on celebrating Cal's graduation with a roast-off."

"A roast-off we're gonna win," Royal said, pumping a fist in the air. He paused, glancing at the man stepping off the boat with Beau. "Who you brung with you?"

"A good friend"—Viv motioned the man over—"and then some." She waited until Will joined them, then said, "Dad, meet Will Jackson."

"Nice to meet you, sir." Will, a clean-cut, respectable-looking man, held out his hand.

Royal grudgingly shook it. "Well, I expect we'll get to know each other better over a beer and some oysters." He gestured toward the backyard, where Cal was helping Mackey build a fire for the roast and Nate was lining up pots and strainers for steaming. "Head on up there, and tell Cal I sent you. The rest of us are right behind you."

Will thanked him, and Beau led him toward the back-yard, pausing to brush a kiss across Kit's cheek.

Viv stopped to hug the twins and playfully tugged one of Daisy's braids. "This one's shooting up there," she said, smiling. She bent and kissed Ashley's cheek. "And this one's not far behind. I tell you what, you two are beauts!" She laughed. "But then again, you'd have to be, seeing as how you're related to me and your mama."

The girls laughed, and Daisy bounced in place. "Watch me skip this stone, Aunt Viv." She reared back, tilted her hand, and flung the stone in her hand, and it skipped across the water.

Ashley squealed. "That was perfect! Wasn't it perfect, Papa?"

"Sure was." Royal handed the girls one more stone each. "One more throw and then we need to head on up to the yard. We got oysters to roast."

Kit pressed her fingertips to her mouth as Royal squat-ted between the girls again, then helped guide their hands as they skipped more stones.

"Feels familiar, doesn't it?" Viv whispered, slipping an arm around Kit's waist.

Kit blinked back bittersweet tears, recalling all the times Royal had taught her one task or another on the shrimp-ing boat or guided her during their wild oyster harvests on the creek. "Yeah. Very much so."

They stood there arm in arm for a few more minutes, the salt breeze blowing through their hair and the setting sun warm on their backs, watching Royal teach the girls how to skip stones, treasuring every moment and looking forward to so many more. Then they headed toward the house, their hearts filling up with bittersweet warmth as Royal, who trailed behind them with the girls, answered their questions in low, contented tones.

"It's called Hope Creek, ain't it, Papa?" Daisy asked.

"That it is," Royal said.

"I bet there's tons of fish in it." Ashley's skipping steps echoed along the dock. "How deep does the creek go, Papa?"

Royal, a smile in his voice, said, "Oh, Hope runs deep. Deeper than the lowest you could ever go."

Please read on for an excerpt from CALDER GRIT by Janet Dailey!

During the summer of 1909, a battle rages in Blue Moon, Montana, between immigrant homesteaders and cattlemen determined to keep the range free. In a fierce struggle that echoes the challenges of today, history is made.

As the countryside explodes in violence, the Calder patriarch has the power to stop the destruction, though some believe Benteen Calder is only stoking the flames for his own gain. One man courageously straddles the divide . . .

That man is Blake Dollarhide, the ambitious young owner of Blue Moon's lumber mill. When Blake's spoiled half-brother takes advantage of the innocent daughter of a homesteading family, Blake steps in as Hanna Anderson's bridegroom to restore her honor and give her unborn child his name. But Blake doesn't count on the storm of feelings he develops for sweet Hanna. When the war between the factions rages anew, everyone wonders if Blake will stand by the close-knit community he serves, or the wife he took in name only . . .

A marriage of love is more than Hanna ever dreamed of. For her family, surviving the rugged trip west, claiming a parcel of land and planting their first crops on the vast prairie are the only things that matter. Which is why the unexpected passion she feels for her husband is all the more poignant. But even as she longs to trust the strong bond growing between her and Blake, Hanna knows it will take courage and grit to overcome the differences between them. And even greater strength of will to put down roots in this wild new country.

The epic tale of the settling of the American West comes to vivid life in this inspiring saga of love, hope, and endurance.

CHAPTER 1

Blue Moon, Montana
July 4, 1909

Hanna stood next to her stern-faced father, one foot tapping out the beat of the polka. Couples whirled around the rough plank floor to the music of the old-time accordion band. She would've given anything to join them. But Big Lars Anderson had already turned down three cowboys who'd asked to partner with his daughter. Hanna would've said yes to any of them, just to get out there and dance. But Big Lars had made his position clear. Those rough-mannered men from the ranches, even the polite ones, weren't fit company for an innocent girl.

As if being guarded like a prisoner wasn't bad enough, her mother had forced her to dress like a twelve-year-old, in a white pinafore, with her long, wheaten hair in two thick braids. But even the girlish costume couldn't hide the breasts that strained the bodice of her gingham dress. She was almost seventeen years old, with a woman's body and a woman's mind. When would her parents stop treating her like a child?

As the music flowed through her limbs, Hanna gazed at

the deepening sky, where the sun was just setting behind the rugged Montana mountains, turning the clouds to ribbons of flame. It was so beautiful. How could she complain after such a glorious day—a celebration of America's freedom in her family's new home?

As she breathed in the fresh, free air, her memory drifted back to the tiny apartment in the New York slum, where she'd helped her mother tend the babies that just kept coming. Her father had worked on the docks, barely making enough to keep food on the table. When her older brother, Alvar, had turned fourteen, he'd gone to work there, too. In the desperation of those years, the American dream that had brought her parents from Sweden had been all but lost.

But then the news had traveled like wildfire through the tenements. Thanks to the passage of the new Homestead Act, there was free land out west. All they had to do was get there on the train, build a cabin, farm the land for five years, and it would be theirs, free and clear.

Now the dream had come true. Hanna's family and their neighbors had claimed their parcels of rich Montana grassland. The fields had been plowed; the wheat was planted and growing. On the anniversary of America's independence, it was time for friends and neighbors to celebrate an Independence Day of their own.

The festivities had begun earlier that afternoon with picnicking, races, games, and now a dance, with fireworks to end the day. It was the homesteaders, like Hanna's family, who'd planned the event; but the whole town, as well as the folks from the big cattle ranches, had been invited. That included the woman-hungry bachelor cowboys who'd shown up hoping to dance with the daughters of the farm families.

So far, the cowboys hadn't had much success. The immigrant fathers had guarded their girls like treasures. They wouldn't trust rough-mannered ranch hands anywhere near their precious girls.

But the girls, even the shy ones, were very much aware of the men.

"That cowboy is looking at you." Hanna nudged her friend Lillian, who stood on her left. Lillian, an auburn-haired beauty, was only a little older than Hanna, but she was already married, which made all the difference in the way she was treated.

The cowboy in question stood on the far side of the dance floor. He was taller than the others, with black hair and a hard, rugged look about him. Hanna knew who he was—Webb Calder, son of the most powerful ranch family in the region. And yes, he was definitely looking at Lillian.

"Does he know you?" Hanna asked.

Lillian shrugged and glanced away, but not before Hanna had noticed the color that flooded her cheeks. She was married to Stefan Reisner, a humorless man even older than Hanna's father. Lillian wasn't the sort to play flirting games with men. But it was plain to see that Webb Calder had made an impression on her.

As if to distract Hanna, Lillian gave a subtle nod in a different direction. "Now *that* cowboy, the one in the blue shirt and leather vest. He was just looking at *you*."

Hanna followed the direction of her friend's gaze. Something fluttered in the pit of her stomach as she spotted the rangy man standing at the break between the wagons that surrounded the dance floor. He was hatless, his hair dark brown and thick with a slight curl to it. His features were strong and solid, and there was pride in the way he carried himself—like a man who had nothing to prove.

But even though he might've been looking at Hanna

earlier, he wasn't looking at her now. His gaze scanned the dance floor and the watchers who stood around the edge. He started forward. Then, as if he'd been called away, he suddenly turned and left.

Blake Dollarhide swore as he made his way among the buggies and wagons toward the open street. The Carmody brothers, who worked at his sawmill, had been warned about picking fights with the homesteaders. But with a few drinks under their belts, the two Irishmen tended to get belligerent. If they were making trouble now, Blake would have little choice except to fire them. But before that could be done, he'd probably have to stop a fight.

With the dance on, Blake had hoped to get a waltz or two with pretty, blond Ruth Stanton, whose father was foreman of the vast Calder spread, the Triple C Ranch. It was no secret that Ruth had her eye on Webb Calder, who would inherit the whole passel from his father, Chase Benteen Calder, one day. But there was no law against Blake's enjoying a dance with her. He might even be lucky enough to turn her head.

Taking anything away from Webb Calder would be a pleasure.

Ruth had been free for the moment. Blake had been about to cross the floor and ask her to dance when he'd heard shouts from the direction of the street. A quick glance around the dance floor had confirmed that the brothers weren't there. Dollars to donuts, the no-accounts had started a brawl.

Blake broke into a run as he spotted the trouble. The two Carmody brothers, small men, but tough and pugnacious, were baiting a lanky homesteader who'd probably left his friends to find a privy. The confrontation was drawing an ugly crowd.

"Pack your wagon and go back to where you came from, you filthy honyocker." Tom Carmody feinted a punch at the man's face. "We don't need you drylanders here, plowin' up the grass to plant your damned wheat, spoilin' land what's meant for cattle. Things was fine afore the likes of you showed up. Worse'n a plague of grasshoppers, that's what you are."

"Please." The man held up his hands. "I don't want trouble. Just let me go back to my family."

"You can go back—after we show you what we do to squatters like you." Tom's brother, Finn, brandished a hefty stick of kindling. Readying a strike, he aimed at the homesteader's head.

"That's enough!" Blake's iron grip stopped Finn's arm in midswing. A quick twist, and the stick fell to the ground. Finn staggered backward, clutching his wrist.

"I warned you two about this," Blake said. "I'm sorry to lose two workers, but I can't have you stirring up this kind of trouble. Any gear you left at the mill will be outside the gate."

"Aw, they was just funnin', Blake." Hobie Evans, who worked for the Snake M Ranch, was the chief instigator against the homesteaders. He'd probably goaded the Carmody brothers into targeting the lone farmer, hoping others would join in and give the poor man a beating to serve as example.

"Don't push me, Hobie. This is a peaceful celebration. Let's keep it that way." Blake glanced around to make sure the farmer was gone and his tormentors had backed off. "Before I had to come out here, I was planning to dance with a pretty lady. For your sake, you'd better hope she's still available."

Blake strode back, past the wagons that ringed the dance floor, intent on seeking out Ruth. But in his absence, something had changed. Webb Calder was on the dance floor with the pretty, auburn-haired wife of one of the farmers. Ruth was on the sidelines, looking stricken.

Blake nudged the cowboy standing next to him. "What's going on?" he muttered.

"Webb got Doyle Petit to talk the drylanders into lettin' us dance with their women. My guess is, soon as this dance is over we can start askin' 'em." The young cowboy grinned. "I got my little gal all picked out—the one in white, with the yellow braids. She's right next to that big farmer—he's her pa. See her?"

"I see her." Blake gave the girl a casual glance. She appeared to be a child, almost, in her white pinafore, with her hair in schoolgirl braids. But then he took a longer look and the bottom seemed to drop out of his heart. He swore under his breath. She wasn't a child at all, but a stunning young woman with an angel's face and a body that even the girlish pinafore couldn't hide.

"Ain't she somethin'?" The cowboy asked. "What do you think?"

"I think you'd better be damned fast on your feet," Blake said. "Otherwise, somebody else might get to her first."

Somebody like me.

As the music faded, Webb Calder escorted the pretty redhead back to her husband. A few words were exchanged. Then Webb turned back to the waiting cowboys. "All right, boys. You can invite the young ladies to dance. But remember your manners. Any Triple C boys not on their best behavior will answer to me."

There was a beat of hesitation. Then the eager cowhands broke ranks and walked across the floor to ask the fathers' permission to dance with their daughters. Blake had decided to hang back and let the lovestruck cowboy enjoy a dance with his dream girl. But when he looked across the floor, he saw that someone else had already claimed her.

Seen from behind, the girl's escort was almost as tall as Blake, but a trifle broader in the chest and shoulders. He was dressed in city-bought clothes, his chestnut hair neatly trimmed to curl above the collar of his linen shirt.

Blake mouthed a curse. As usual, his half brother, Mason, had seized the advantage and run away with it.

Whirling blissfully around the dance floor, Hanna gazed up at the man who held her in his arms. The smile on his handsome face deepened the dimple in his cheek. His green eyes reflected glints of sunset.

"You looked like an angel, standing there in your white dress," he said. "Do angels have names?"

"My name's Hanna Anderson, and believe me, I'm not an angel," she said. "Just ask my parents."

He chuckled. "But you're an angel to me because you just saved me from a very boring evening. So that's what I'll call you—my angel."

Hanna had never heard such flattering talk. Who was this charming stranger? Certainly not a cowboy. He was too well dressed and too well spoken for that. "I'm Mason Dollarhide," he said, answering her unspoken question. "I run the Hollister ranch south of town. It may not be the biggest spread in Montana, but it sure is the prettiest. Almost as pretty as you."

"Now you're playing games with me," Hanna said. She wasn't a fool. But after what seemed like a lifetime of scrubbing, tending, washing, mending, working in the fields like a man, and never being made to feel attractive or desirable in any way, she let his words wash over her like the sound of sweet music.

Missing a step, she stumbled slightly. His hand, at the small of her back, tightened, drawing her so close that she could feel the light pressure of his body against hers. Heat flashed through her like summer lightning, making her feel vaguely naughty. Did he feel it, too?

"I would never play games with a precious girl like you." His voice had thickened. "I'd wager you've never even been kissed. Have you?"

"That's none of your business," Hanna said, although she hadn't been kissed, except by a neighbor boy when she was ten.

He chuckled. "Feisty little thing, aren't you?"

"I just don't like people forming ideas before they know me, that's all," Hanna said

The music was drawing to a close, but his hand—smooth, with no calluses—didn't release hers. "I'd like to get to know you better, Hanna," he said. "Why don't we walk a little, where we don't have to raise our voices over the music?"

Hanna glanced back over her shoulder. Her father was talking to Lillian's husband. Lillian was nowhere in sight. Neither was the rugged cowboy who'd danced with her. Hanna felt the gentle pressure of the stranger's hand against her back, guiding her off the floor. She didn't resist. Nobody would miss her if she stepped out for a few harmless minutes.

They made their way among the wagons. He stopped her next to an elegant-looking buggy that was parked outside the circle. "This is my buggy," he said. "Get in. I'll take you for a ride."

He offered a hand to help her up, but she stopped him. "No. I can't go for a ride with you."

"But why? It's a beautiful evening. And I've got the slickest team of horses in the county."

"You don't know my father. He'd punish me, and he'd probably find a way to damage you, too. He's a good man, but you don't want to cross him. Let's just stand here and talk."

"All right." He nodded, leaning against the buggy. "So, is your mother here, too?"

"No, she took the wagon home early with my brothers and sisters. I wanted to stay for the dance, so my father remained with me. We were planning to ride home with a neighbor."

"I could offer you both a ride. Maybe if he got to know me, he'd let me see you again. I'm not one of those cowhands that might take advantage of a sweet girl like you. I've got my own ranch—at least it'll be mine when my mother passes away."

"Don't bother asking. My father would never accept." Hanna was beginning to feel uneasy. What if her father were to catch her out here, alone with a man? "I'd better go back before he comes looking for me."

She turned to go. Mason blocked her path. "Wait." His hand cupped her jaw, tilting her face upward. "Lord Almighty," he murmured. "Angel, I feel like I just stepped into heaven. You're the most beautiful thing I've ever seen."

Hanna's heart broke into a gallop as he bent closer. His lips were almost touching hers when an angry voice shattered the spell.

"Damn it, Mason, let that girl go. Her father's fit to be tied. If he finds her out here with you, he'll skin you alive!"

Hanna turned. The tall cowboy she'd noticed earlier,

the one with the blue shirt and leather vest, stood a few feet away from them. "Get inside and find your father, miss," he said. "You can claim you went to the privy. If he asks, I'll tell him I saw you coming from that direction. Meanwhile, I need to have words with my brother, here."

Hanna gasped, shocked that a man would mention bodily functions to her. But at least he'd come up with a good excuse for her father. Hot faced, she fled back toward the dance floor, weaving her way among the buggies and wagons. That was when a cry went up from somewhere out of sight.

"*Fire!*"

Turning, Hanna saw a distant column of smoke rising against the twilight sky. The prairie was burning.